EVERYONE

MUST

PAY

Also by Colin Hurrell

One Passenger Too Many

EVERYONE
MUST
PAY

COLIN HURRELL

For Sandra and Steve

my wife and son who endlessly supported, and encouraged,
the writing of this book

PART ONE

1965

1

To twelve-year-old Paul Pearce, the living rooms of the terraced houses of 1960s Britain all had a remarkably similar appearance. Certainly, the house owned by his parents was very comparable with the one in which he now sat, some thirty miles from home, belonging to his aunt and uncle. He was sat on the floor beside a standard fireplace that was surrounded with small, heat-resistant tiles. Being the latter half of summer, the fire was not lit, and had not been for some months. However, the coal scuttle, together with the set of brushes and tongs, still stood on the plinth, flanking this centrepiece of the room.

The Murphy push-button operated, black and white television occupied the corner between the fireplace and the main bay window. It was tuned to a broadcast of *Sunday Night At The London Palladium* and it cast its glow around the gradually-darkening room. The programme selection was specifically for the amusement of Paul and his younger sister, Rebecca, while the four adults in the room preferred to continually talk amongst themselves. Had the two children not been there, the television would not have even been turned on, as no-one else had any interest in what was being shown. Their preference was to just talk, exchange opinions and catch up with latest events in both their own lives and what they knew of the world outside. Their conversation was relatively loud and, despite being sat less than a yard from the screen, Paul found that he still could not hear many of the young Jimmy Tarbuck's punchlines.

Three of the four adults were contemplating whether the Americans would indeed be able to land a spaceship on the moon within the next few years and the relative chances of the Russians beating them to it. The fourth, Paul's aunt, was noticeably as silent as she often tended to be during such discussions.

'Well, it seems to me that neither of them has much chance of ever getting there,' Paul's father was saying. 'Not in this decade, as Kennedy challenged, nor any other. It's one thing flying a little high above the Earth but getting to another planet is something else entirely.'

'Technically, the moon isn't a planet,' his brother-in-law, and Paul's uncle, corrected. 'The Americans seem pretty confident about it though. As for the Russians, they don't seem to have done much at all since that Yuri Gagarin went up. All the news we hear about it is certainly only about the American advancements, with nothing of the Soviet programme.' He took a long, final draw from his cigarette before stubbing it out in the ashtray that was already full, and precariously balanced, on the arm of his chair.

'Maybe they're just keeping quiet because they've already done it and they don't see it as a big deal,' injected Paul's mother. 'They probably have something like *Fireball XL5* sat on a runway and ready to go at a moment's notice should anyone fancy a quick visit to the moon.' Above the elongated introduction of the headline act in London, Paul immediately understood his mother's reference to one of his favourite TV programmes. He was about to grasp the rare invitation for him to say something, anything, and finally contribute to the conversation, when Uncle Ray continued the serious vein and the opportunity was lost.

For as long as he could remember, this kind of scenario had been a fixture of Paul's life, every fourth Sunday. A family get-together dutifully attended by all his immediate family just so that his mother could see her brother. It was certainly one which neither he, nor his siblings, had any real participation in. Paul was unable to understand the reasons for it being such a regular event. He was certain that, as soon as he eventually moved out of the family home, he would have as little as possible to do with his own annoying younger sister. He definitely would not subject any of his own children, should he have any in the future, to such visits if they did not want to go. Even if there were any such occasions which could not be avoided, at least he would not insist on them wearing smart shirts with stiff collars. The one that he had been forced to adorn had been irritating his neck since leaving home that afternoon.

Paul's sister was two years younger than him and still attending junior school whilst he had advanced, because of his age, to the local secondary. They simply seemed to have nothing in common other than their parents and living under the same roof. They could never seem to find anything to talk to each other about and, he felt, never had. She was sitting on the floor next to him, making those false, forced laughing sounds that he found so annoying, whilst she attempted to give the impression that she understood Tarbuck's humour.

Paul's parents were sat together on the two-seater blue-grey settee with his aunt and uncle sat on the matching single chairs either side. Paul liked his Uncle Ray as he seemed to take a genuine interest in so many aspects of Paul's life. That is, apart from those times when he was deeply engrossed in conversation with his mother and father, as he was now. Unfortunately, the affection that Paul felt for his uncle did not extend to his quiet aunt. There was just something about the way that his uncle's second wife, Auntie Bea, acted and reacted to everyone that meant he just could not bring himself to think of her as real family.

Perhaps it was her frequent silences when in a family gathering that exuded such a negative impression. Uncle Ray had only recently married her, a pretty woman some twenty years his junior at twenty-one, after the untimely death of Auntie Jean. In her defence, Auntie Bea had suddenly been thrust into a ready-made extended family circle, having only just escaped her own unhappy one. The experience had simply not lived up to her innocent expectations, or so Paul had once heard his mother say. It would undoubtedly have been a difficult adjustment for the woman. The situation unavoidably meant that she was only three years older than the stepson, Paul's cousin Thomas, that she had immediately acquired as part of the transaction.

At that moment, Thomas was upstairs with Paul's half-sister, Brenda, his father's daughter with his own first wife. They would be listening to some record or other on Thomas's Dansette portable player. Although he could not hear it above the sound of the television and the general talking, Paul knew that this was likely to be the record that his older sibling had bought earlier that week and had insisted on bringing along. Over the preceding few months, the pair of teenagers had developed a preference for disappearing upstairs to play *Juke Box Jury* during such family gatherings, rather than indulging in any of the conversations driven by those of the older generation. This month's LP record under scrutiny was yet another by that set of long-haired layabouts, as Paul's father constantly referred to them, that called themselves The Beatles.

Without a word, Auntie Bea suddenly got up from her chair and collected the glasses from where they had been left, since the shared evening meal, on the dining table in the other downstairs room. Once in the kitchen, she rinsed each one under a running tap before refilling them with second servings of the drinks that had accompanied their meals. A small amount of red wine generously expanded with lemonade for the adults, in the same proportions as might be used when diluting a drink of squash, and a simple lemonade for both Paul and his Tarbuck-appreciating sister. As for the older children, Thomas and Brenda, she could not be bothered negotiating the steep stairs whilst holding full glasses. Those two would just have to tear themselves away from the Beatles music, that she would have rather been listening to herself, and make their own if they wanted any more.

With three separate journeys from the kitchen to the living room, carrying two glasses each time, she gave everyone downstairs their allocated refreshments before slowly returning to her own seat. She had been glad of the momentary distraction from the talk of space travel and the drivel that was coming from the one-eyed monster in the corner of the room. However, her excuse for a short absence had passed. Now she was condemned to sit out the rest of the long evening, smiling at all the appropriate times and occasionally expressing an opinion, or observation, but only when the conversations dictated that she had to.

Eventually, the evening discussions of varying subjects drew to their natural conclusions and talk drifted, as usual, to the children needing an early night as it was a school day the next day. With the teenage reviewers from upstairs having now finished their deliberations over the merits, or otherwise, of the latest offering from The Fab Four, all eight members of the extended family congregated to bid a farewell to each other.

'What did you think of the LP?' Auntie Bea casually asked Thomas and Brenda.

'It's a good one,' replied Thomas on behalf of both of them, handing Brenda back her record that he had carried back downstairs for her as if she had not been capable herself. He also tilted the cover so that everyone could see the picture that it sported. 'I think I'll get a copy myself. What have you lot been doing?'

'Working out what is probably wrong with the space programme,' said Bea, somewhat unenthusiastically, 'on top of watching the Palladium show.'

'The fifth Beatle,' exclaimed Thomas excitedly, clearly referring to Jimmy Tarbuck whilst also pointing to the picture on the album sleeve now being held by Brenda. Always the extrovert, he then made the most of his chance to be the centre of attention and launched into a passable impersonation of the television show's host from Liverpool. As he told a joke, he moved from one side of the room to the other, using it as his makeshift stage, much to everyone's amusement, especially Paul's. His physical actions were identical to those that Tarbuck often adopted, including occasionally nodding his head so that his own hair bounced in the same manner as the upcoming television star. Although his hair was notably lighter than Tarbuck's, Thomas had a similar youthful appearance and his hair was also combed forward to a fringe, helping the illusion. Moreover, he was able to convincingly emulate the comic's voice and timing.

Paul had always admired his cousin's confidence, not only when entertaining the family, which he did often, but also to comfortably adopt another persona. Paul looked up to him in many respects. He really liked him and aspired to having a similar outgoing personality in the future.

Thomas bowed gratefully in response to the resultant collective applause from his family before collecting all the visitors' coats from the hallway. For the next few minutes came the, largely unnecessary, ritual of arrangements, agreements, and confirmations regarding the next time that they intended to meet. Such deliberations happened every time that they parted and were always as predictable as the final conclusions. They would always end up agreeing to meet at the same time of day, four Sundays hence, alternating between their respective houses for hosting duties. As it turned out, the proposed date for the following month coincided with Paul's thirteenth birthday, so an extra special evening was alluded to for once.

However, what Paul did not know at the time, what none of them could have known, was that this particular family evening would be the last occasion of its kind.

2

With Uncle Ray, Auntie Bea and Cousin Thomas standing on the doorstep to wave them off, Paul and the rest of his immediate family walked to their red Austin 1100 that was parked across the street. It had been specifically positioned so that it faced the direction that they would be heading. That way, there would be no need to awkwardly turn it in the narrow road in front of such a critical audience. Being a four-door car, rather than their previous cramped two-door Ford Anglia, the children were able to quickly get into the back seat. Occupying their usual positions, Brenda sat on the left, Paul on the right, behind his father in the driving seat, with Paul's younger sister, Rebecca, sat between them. Paul's mother, unable to drive, like so many others of her gender in the 1960s, sat in the passenger seat, beside her husband.

Suddenly, Bea remembered that she had not performed her usual ritual of giving her youngest niece and her nephew a little extra pocket money. It was something that she habitually did whenever she saw them, thinking it to be an appropriate, and expected, gesture from an aunt. She called across the road to them and waved her arm to beckon the children back to the house for a moment. So, with the car's engine already running, Paul and Rebecca got out again to return to the front door. Both sported quizzical looks and were pretending that they had no idea of the reason that they may be being summoned back, although neither had any doubt.

'For your piggy banks,' said Bea, handing each of them a shilling from the purse that she had quickly retrieved from the small table just inside the door.

'Thank you, Auntie Bea,' said Paul and Rebecca, politely and in unison, before returning to the Austin and climbing into the back seat once more.

With a final wave from all five, through opened car windows, to the trio that were already at their own home, their car pulled away down the street at the start of the short journey home. From the experience of countless previous occasions, they all expected that it would take them no more than an hour.

'Ray is crazy if he thinks we're going to see a man on the moon in our lifetime,' said Paul's father to his wife. 'I know he's your brother and everything, but how can he be so stupid when you're so level-headed.'

'He's not stupid, he's just got his opinion,' she answered. 'Besides, I don't think it's that crazy to imagine. *Fireball XL5* goes much further than that already, doesn't it Paul?' she said whilst turning her head round to wink at her son.

Paul smiled back. 'That's right, Mum. Steve Zodiac could get to the moon and back before lunchtime.' Steve Zodiac, as all those in the car knew, was the fictional pilot of the futuristic reusable space craft, *Fireball XL5*, invented by TV producer Gerry Anderson and featured in his marionette-based children's programme that bore the same name. Paul had never cared much for the similar, subsequent series,

Stingray, about undersea adventures. He still preferred the inspiring images of outer-space and this was still some months before Gerry Anderson's even-greater success with *Thunderbirds*.

'I give up. Everyone in this family, except me, must be crazy,' the driver said, unexpectedly negotiating a left turn to take them towards Hartview town centre. They would normally bypass this town by taking the alternative, faster road, so Paul was immediately puzzled by the unexpected change to their usual journey. 'I think it's up here Becky,' his father announced.

Rebecca was suddenly alert, sitting up in her assigned centre seat so that she could see between her parents and through the windscreen. Within a minute she saw what she had been eagerly waiting all of the evening to see and the car slowed, coming to a full stop opposite the toy shop.

'Let me out Paul,' she said to her confused brother. Paul begrudgingly got out of the car to let his younger sister slide across the back seat and get out herself. She ran to the window of the closed toy shop with her father, now also out of the car, close behind.

Paul looked at the pair of them, bewildered, but climbed back into his seat and closed the car door. 'What's going on Mum?'

'Your Dad promised that she could have another troll doll.'

Paul sighed and looked over to where his sister had her nose pressed against the window of the shop whilst she pointed excitedly into the dark interior. It was presumably at yet another variation of her favourite toy, indicating her

13

preference to her father. They were talking, but not loud enough for Paul to hear what was being said. Not that he was at all interested in his sister's latest fad. Paul simply assumed that she had once again been able to wind their father around her little finger enough for him to agree to buy her something else to sit on her already-overcrowded bedroom windowsill. His father would presumably now be returning here at a time when the shop was open, with cash in his wallet, ready to delight his youngest child when he got home. It would most likely be while they were both at school, as he knew that Hartview was on the route that his father drove every weekday on his way to, and from, work.

After a few more minutes of them both nose-pressing and staring into the dark shop, and yet more pointing and quiet discussion, the two of them returned to the parked car with wide smiles, annoying Paul even more. Paul got fully out of the car once again to allow Rebecca to slide into the middle before getting back in himself. He had already decided that he was not going to slide across to the middle seat himself just so that the process became easier for her. Besides, that would have meant that she got the more comfortable position for the rest of the drive home.

With a silent smile and a nod exchanged between the adults in the front seats, the car was pulled away from the kerb and driven on down the quiet road. It was not much further to Hartview's High Street and, as they turned onto this road with its parade of silent shops, Paul closed his eyes for a moment in partial submission to the tiredness that was starting to envelope him. The car accelerated down the deserted street with its two-story buildings on either side, shops below and storerooms above, towards the four-way junction ahead.

The buildings continued up to, and beyond, the junction, obscuring any view of the perpendicular roads. Paul, opening his eyes again, could see, over his father's shoulder, that the traffic lights were green anyway. Closing his eyes for a few seconds more, he only opened them again as the car was crossing the solid white line of the intersection.

He saw an amber light flash through his vision and then he heard his mother scream like he had never heard her do so before. From her front seat, she had seen the lorry rapidly approaching from the right only at the very last moment. The Austin's brakes were applied suddenly and harshly, but much too late, and Paul bowed forwards as they were. A fraction of a second later, the advancing lorry slammed into the front half of the car. Both offside wheels lifted clear of the tarmac. With no seatbelts being used inside, all the car's occupants were helplessly thrown upward with the initial force.

As the car rolled and smashed onto its left side, Paul's mother and his older sister, originally being sat in the front and rear, respectively, were showered in glass from the shattering door windows. Both their heads made direct contact with the surface of the road which was still moving underneath them through the resultant opening. The sudden sideways momentum continued, despite the rapid slowing of the lorry which was now pushing the crippled Austin diagonally across the crossroads. Paul was already uncontrollably flying through the air when the rear of the car hit the far traffic light pole. The pole bent under the strain, and the car continued further to the corner of the building on the opposite side of the junction. The front half of the roof, mostly the portion above the driver's seat, rapidly buckled inwards towards Paul's father. It hit his head, but not because he was being thrown towards it. It had simply collapsed deep enough into the head space. The steering wheel had fractured under the unusual strain of the weight and momentum of his rising body, and he had become impaled on the resulting shard, thus holding him in position.

Paul, and to a lesser extent also Rebecca, had no such restraint and Paul's head hit the unforgiving metal, hard. The grotesque, twisted, lorry and car combination had come to rest against the corner building, and steam started billowing from the split radiator of the lorry.

3

Paul woke in a hospital bed, immediately aware of the pains in his head before he started wondering where he was, and why. He could not recall the precise events of the crash, but he instinctively knew that he must have been involved in a serious incident. This was not his bed at home, and he could smell the familiar antiseptic aroma of a hospital, caused by the extensive use of Betadine.

He tried to move, moaning when the pain seemed to surge in his head, and he realised the bruising to his body. His vision was blurred but he could make out the approach of a woman, dressed in blue, who had heard his stirrings from nearby. She lightly touched his forehead, but somehow it did not feel like a hand against his skin. He was unaware of the bandage that encircled his head.

'How are you feeling love?' she asked. It was an unfamiliar female voice. Where was his mother?

'Rough,' was all he could think to initially reply. Then, as the panic started to rise, 'I can't see properly. What happened? Where's my Mum and Dad?'

'All in good time,' she said calmly and gently. 'You've been through a very bad experience. Lie back and rest some more and I'll call the doctor to you.' The nurse walked swiftly away to inform her colleagues and superiors that their latest patient had regained consciousness.

When the doctor finally arrived to check Paul's condition, he was similarly evasive about precisely what had happened to cause him to be where he was. Paul was starting to panic about not being able to focus his eyes and the whereabouts of his family. Why weren't they here with him?

The doctor tried to assure him that the problems with his vision had been fully expected and that he would be able to see properly within a few weeks. As for Paul's family, though, the doctor would not be drawn into any discussion about it.

It was two days later, after continually asking but getting no proper responses from anyone, that Paul finally learned the truth about the consequences of the accident. He awoke from a sleep to recognise his uncle's voice speaking to someone at the foot of the bed. His vision was still blurred, but he could see Ray's outline, and also that of his aunt. He could see that she was sporting her unmistakable beehive blond hair, even though it felt like he was looking through glass smeared with Vaseline. There was also someone else, who seemed to be wearing a suit, and a woman dressed in police uniform. He could tell from the shape and colouring of her hat.

The man in the suit informed Paul, as empathetically as he could, that the road accident he had been involved in had been very serious. Both his parents had been killed almost instantly but, he lied, would not have felt any pain at the time. There was nothing that could have been done for them, as both had passed away before either the police or ambulance had arrived. They had been on the scene within a matter of minutes, being a town centre. His older sister, Brenda, had also died, although, in her case, it had been on the way to hospital in the ambulance. Her injuries had been so severe that they simply could not save her.

Paul's blood understandably ran cold and his eyes filled with tears as each piece of devastating news was revealed to him. He sobbed uncontrollably, as his aunt and uncle tried their best to console him, each holding on to a hand.

The last thing that the man in the suit could tell him was that Rebecca had, like him, survived the crash and was at that moment in another ward of the same hospital with her minor injuries, recovering well. It was Paul who had been kept in that specialist ward because of the head injuries he had sustained. Through his grief over the news of his parents and older sister, though, he heard little of those details. Only that Rebecca had also, thankfully, survived.

It took many hours for him to stop crying that day and he often continuously cried during the days that followed, laid in that hospital bed. Over the ensuing weeks, as the doctor had promised it would, his eyesight gradually repaired itself and the world returned to sharp focus for him. His dark thoughts also developed their own focus. No matter how long it took, no matter what it might have to involve, he swore that he would dedicate his life to ensuring that he would have vengeance on all those responsible for the events of that fateful night. The events in Hartview that had caused him to become an orphan.

PART TWO

1977

4

Frank Bird jumped down from the space between the rear of the tractor unit and the high box-type semi-trailer that he had just coupled to it. Having attached the trailer's airlines and electrical cables to the unit's colour-coded connection points, he now only needed to raise the trailer's front landing legs and he would be ready to hit the road in his maximum-size articulated lorry. Reaching under the left side of the trailer without the need to look beforehand, he expertly located the large handle, avoiding the risk of smearing his hair with the accumulated road dirt from its underside. Too many times he had seen young drivers ruining the look of their carefully coiffured locks by unnecessarily ducking low, but rarely low enough, to seek out the exact position of the stowed handle before reaching for it. At just two years short of his milestone fortieth birthday, he did not particularly care much about his physical appearance anymore, but he drew the line at oily black streaks through his ginger hair.

As he rotated the handle anti-clockwise, he idly watched the telescopic legs raise from the tarmac until the front of the trailer was entirely supported by the tractor unit via the central, horizontal plate that was commonly known as the fifth wheel. Once satisfied that the clearance from the ground was adequate, he twisted the handle against the hinge on its shaft and restored it to the hook underneath the trailer.

Before climbing back into his cab, though, Frank stepped back to look up at the side of the trailer, towering above him and proclaiming his company name. Using the camera that he had brought from home specifically for the purpose, and that had been hanging from his neck, he took three photographs from varying angles. He tried his best to frame the entire articulated vehicle in each one, taking account of any unfortunate reflections of sunlight. He knew that, by the time the photographs had been developed at the local chemist, there would be no second chance of capturing the iconic image if it turned out that he had got the exposure wrong.

As he packed the camera back into its carry-case, he looked again at the large vehicle, effectively trying to indelibly burn the sight directly into his memory, and sighed. There was a familiar voice from behind him.

'The end of an era?' said Robin, the mechanic, in his strong North-Eastern accent. It was an accent rarely heard in the small Lancashire town of Clayborough, close to the major motorways of the county. He was predictably dressed in grease-stained overalls and was holding a large, used oil filter in his grime-covered hands, glistening in parts with warm engine oil. He had just extracted it from one of the other tractor units that he had been servicing in the garage behind him when he had noticed Frank standing on the forecourt, staring affectionately at his weighty responsibility.

'Something like that,' replied Frank. 'Just a little bit of paint and then five years of my life gets consigned to history.'

'Not quite, Frank. At least, it won't be forgotten history. You still get to drive the same lorry, delivering and picking up from the same places. Still seeing the same customers that you managed to sign up in the first place.'

'I suppose so,' said Frank, shrugging his shoulders. 'I even managed to be considered for haulier of the month once. Did I ever tell you?'

'Aye, you did,' replied Robin, feeling that he now had been told all about Frank's dubious nomination several times.

The tractor unit had already been recently resprayed in the colours, and with the name, of the new owners of the haulage business. It was now green, with Crossbow Transport Limited boldly painted on each door and also above the vast windscreen. In each case, the initial letter was enhanced to represent a bow which was firing an arrow along a stretch of cartoon road, depicted to the left of the official company logo. The separate trailer that Frank had just prepared for the road was the last one of the small fleet still displaying the name of his former company, and it was destined to have all of that finally obliterated at the nearby paint facility that day. The new owners were a national company and had simply bought all the assets of the smaller operation as part of their continual expansion plans, increasing their number of vehicles and effectively acquiring yet another regional distribution hub in the process.

Throughout the brief conversation, Frank Bird's eyes had never strayed from the large, bold red letters emblazoned on the side of the white trailer. Wazzo Haulage Limited, his company name originally inspired by an anglicised pronunciation of oiseau, the French word for a bird. History now.

'Better take her on her final journey then,' he said to the

mechanic as he started walking back towards the cab.

'It's hardly as dramatic as that Frank. We'll get her back and, when we do, she'll just have been reborn into the new world order.'

Frank chose to ignore what he perceived as an insensitive response and did not look back or answer, thinking it best not to divulge even more of his true feelings about losing control of his fleet. To him, it was a very significant day. As he climbed up into the cab and adjusted his seat ready for the short drive to the respray, he had to admit to himself that he also felt a sense of relief that he no longer had to worry about things like the excess fuel costs for such non-earning trips.

Robin turned and walked back towards the garage, hearing Frank's powerful diesel engine burst into life behind him followed by the familiar hiss of air as the handbrake was released. As the sound of the departing lorry decreased and became drowned out by the nearby ambient traffic noise, he walked back inside through the large, open, retractable doors. An entrance large enough for an articulated lorry to drive through and into the interior of the garage, be that for servicing or overnight storage.

He returned his attention to the tractor unit that was expectantly awaiting a replacement oil filter.

5

It took less than an hour for Frank to deliver and uncouple the empty trailer to its paint-oriented fate and return, in just the tractor unit, to the lorry depot with its incorporated garage. The garage that he had previously owned. Road haulage had been his life and passion ever since he had been discharged from the army, after being taught to drive military lorries as part of his three years of service for his country. Having taken full advantage of the opportunity to drive one of the largest vehicles on the roads before his twenty-first birthday, the age that the civilians had to wait for, he had immediately loved the experience. He had known from his very first day behind the wheel that it was what he would want to do once back on civvy street.

He had always adored the freedom of the open road, in control of such heavy freight, and with the ability to work all day with no boss constantly looking over his shoulder. He did not even object to the frequent traffic queues such as those that formed on the country's motorways at exceptionally busy times of the day or week, or possibly caused by an accident blocking a carriageway ahead. On such occasions, he simply turned the radio-cassette louder, enjoyed the music and waited patiently for the congestion to ease. He was being paid the same to sit stationary, or chugging slowly along, as he would be driving on an empty road. It was all part of the job as far as he was concerned. Such delays on the road would always mean a later hour to return to the depot each time. However, even on smooth-running days, without any obstacles, he would never leave to go home until the full day's working hours had passed. He could always find something to fill the remainder of the day, such as using the high-pressure washer to clean the unit, or trailer, or both.

Five years before, it had occurred to him that the company he had been working for at the time were charging their clients a lot of money for their freight transport. He seemed to only be receiving a small fraction of those payments in his weekly wage packet in return. He had made a few rough calculations and had decided that he would use his experience, and some of the contacts that he had acquired over the years, to guarantee himself a much larger income from the industry he was in. So, with the help of an equally naive bank manager, he had resigned from his job, bought his own articulated lorry and the garage premises, and formed the limited company which had borne the derivative of his name.

For the first few years the business had done reasonably well and, with drivers employed for each, he had expanded his sole operation to a small fleet of four additional tractor units and semi-trailers. The drivers that he had hired were mostly young, commercially inexperienced army-trained drivers, just as he had once been himself, in need of a chance of breaking into the industry. Three of them were still under twenty-five, with the other not much older. He had always felt it would be easier for him to mould such new drivers to his preferred working methods, without encountering contradictions and conflict. He had also felt much more empathy to their particular backgrounds. Unfortunately, such youth also demanded that much higher vehicle insurance premiums be paid.

Moreover, he had not properly anticipated the amount, or nature, of the work involved in running a business and he had found himself spending progressively more time handling VAT invoices, frequent company returns, pacifying clients over the phone, and producing paperwork for the Inland Revenue about himself and his workforce. He had always wanted to be just out on the road, behind the wheel, but most days had found himself consigned to a desk in a grubby office in the corner of the garage instead.

He had painfully discovered a lot of the reasons why the customers had paid so much more than a driver's wages for the haulage of their freight, exposing major shortcomings in his original calculations. Having purposefully undercut the local competition to initially gain the contracts, he realised, too late, the true cost of insuring, taxing and maintaining large vehicles to the required roadworthy standards. Then there were the additional drains on the purse from premises costs, business and employer insurances, the vehicle insurances, his staff and the need for a large contingency fund for unexpected eventualities. Replacing a burst tyre could easily cost more than a driver's monthly wage.

Eventually, the bank had recalled their loans and, after months of not even being able to pay himself a wage, he'd had to concede defeat. Fortunately, rather than the company becoming unavoidably insolvent and adding himself, and the others, to the unemployment register, a month ago the national company had stepped in and offered to buy the complete set-up. All assets and staff, including himself, would be retained and all debts settled, for a nominal sum. Frank had not made the personal mint that he had dreamed of just five years before, but at least he had retained the job that he loved. As for the new owners, the acquisition would give them the extra lorries and premises from which to operate in the region, more-easily servicing Lancashire and Yorkshire and the slopes of the Pennines between. Although he could, and often had, driven goods to any corner of the country, the focus of his business had always been across the North of England.

So, he was now just a driver again, working on the same level as those four other drivers that he had himself originally employed. Thankfully, he had always prided himself that he had never fostered a divided atmosphere of boss and staff in his workplace and so, now, he could fit right in as one of the boys. More importantly, he could now finally receive a regular wage again and not concern himself with any worries associated with running the business.

Three months before, one of his last tangible actions as company director had been to employ Robin as a mechanic for the modest fleet. Robin's employment history in the business, as it had appeared on his CV, had been very impressive. His written references from the similarly sized haulage company based in his native Newcastle, although Frank had never heard of them before, were faultless. Unfortunately for Frank, though, this attempted cost-cutting exercise of incorporating all future vehicle maintenance within his own business had been another testament to his lack of business acumen. It would have been better, at least financially, to simply continue to sub-contract such work instead. Specialised tools had to be acquired and a dedicated servicing area assigned and fitted within the garage which had previously been just the tractor and trailer overnight storage area. Then there were Robin's wages to add to the expenditures.

It was this last failed attempt to help make the business profitable that had been the final nail in the coffin for Wazzo Haulage Limited. A name that, after the upcoming respray, would never again be seen on Britain's roads. All the other trailers and lorries already boasted their incorporation into the wider family. Now Frank, having parked and secured his own rebranded tractor unit outside, found himself walking into the garage under the new sign that had recently replaced the one that had been inspired by his own surname. This one declared the name of the new owning company, Crossbow Transport, complete with the depicted arrow and road. Beneath that, in smaller lettering, and as if to taunt him and emphasise his failed attempt at cornering his local market, Northern Regional Office.

6

Larry Mason was sat in the grubby annex office of the garage, on Frank's former office chair, behind Frank's former desk, with Frank's former phone held to his ear. He was saying nothing, only listening to the handset. As Frank appeared in the open doorway, he was silently beckoned to enter by the 35-year-old new manager of the Northern Region.

Frank had little respect for this man who had first appeared, and taken over his domain, on the same date that the rapid takeover had been officially completed. Larry had been promoted, and relocated, to the role within the hierarchy of the expanding organisation and had wasted no time in seizing the reins. Contrary to the established working environment, and the way that Frank had always run things, Larry had immediately asserted his authority by insisting on a new set of working procedures, in accordance with the established practices of the parent company. He had also made it crystal clear that any failure to comply would be rewarded with a P45 certificate soon afterwards.

One such practice, that particularly annoyed Frank, was the insistence that all drivers and office staff should wear a green company-issued blazer, whenever they were on duty, and especially when interacting with customers. The psychology behind it apparently justified it, ensuring that it made Crossbow employees appear smarter and more professional than the competition. To Frank, it just stank of insistence on wearing something resembling a school uniform, especially with the Crossbow Transport logo on the breast pocket.

As far as Frank was concerned, the man was a paper-pusher who had probably spent his entire working life behind a desk. He may have been good with phone calls and paperwork, but not with what Frank would regard as real work. He probably only knew the theoretical aspects of road haulage, learned out of a book, if that. Frank doubted whether the man even had an HGV driving licence himself. He had certainly never even seen him climb up into a cab to so much as move a unit around the forecourt. Neither had he witnessed Larry lower himself to hitch up a trailer ready for a late-arriving driver to be able to go straight out on his assigned job as soon as he appeared, as Frank had done countless times himself. It may have just been that Larry felt such manual tasks to be beneath him, even though he was fully capable. Frank still strongly suspected that he had not earned his position by working his way up from the roots of the industry. That annoyed him.

The reality was that Larry knew full well how to drive a lorry, and he had done it for many years when he was younger. It was just that he had eventually decided that a life always on the road had not been for him. Staying in the industry, he had managed to attain jobs in the offices, planning and controlling the logistics rather than executing them.

'What can I do for you Frank?' Larry asked, hanging up the phone, having grown tired of waiting for the Inland

Revenue to answer his call. His question about Robin's taxable payments would have to wait for a time when he was in a more patient mood.

'I've just taken that last trailer down to Clancey's for its new paint job. Chas says it should be finished Thursday or Friday.'

'I'll give him a call later and tell him that we want it back by the end of Wednesday, at the latest, or we'll be demanding a discount to compensate for the lost road hours.'

This was exactly the kind of attitude that Frank found so unnerving. Charles Clancey was an old friend of his and he could not imagine such an ultimatum ever being exchanged between the two of them, in either direction, in the past. However, Larry was there to prove himself, both to his new workforce and to the national company.

'So, am I still taking the 'refer' to move that load of meat?' Frank asked next.

Frank had only bought the refrigerated trailer and added it to his fleet twelve months before, specifically to gain a contract with the local abattoir to transport their excess meat output. It had turned out to represent yet another of his financial miscalculations. The abattoir had made it clear from the outset of the deal that they would only require his services for a maximum of one day a week. Mondays. This would coincide with when there was more meat ready to be carried than they could accommodate in their own vehicles. So, on all other days, this extra trailer invariably stood idle on the garage forecourt while the drivers were out towing their regular trailers, depreciating at a faster rate than the meagre income that it occasionally generated. Frank might have potentially been able to find, and sign up, another customer requiring a chilled environment for the transportation of their goods, but having less drivers than there were trailers available would always mean a strain on the cashflow.

'Yes, here's the paperwork,' answered Larry.

Frank took the proffered carbon-copy delivery note on which was written the full details of the required pick-up and its destination. Already intimately knowing both the customers involved, Frank just blindly signed his name in the boxes above the two vacant spaces that were intended for the signatures of the dispatcher and the receiver of the goods later in the day.

There had been some earlier doubt about whether the usual meat delivery would be required that week and so, just in case of any last-minute change of priorities, Larry had kept hold of the delivery notes relating to it. Frank would have preferred to have been in possession of all his day's required forms since the start of the day, like it had been when he was in charge. That way, he would have been able to drive back from Clancey's Vehicle Sprayers, straight onto the forecourt, couple up the refrigerated trailer and quickly be on his way again, without having to stop and waste time interacting with his new dictator.

Having attached his second trailer of the day to his unit and added the number plate corresponding to that of his tractor unit to the rear, Frank drove it out of the forecourt and turned left onto the main road outside. He thought that he should easily, road conditions being favourable, be able to be back with his unit and emptied trailer, well within his remaining six hours of allowed working time for the day.

After all, he only had to fill the trailer with the supermarket-destined meat at the abattoir, then drive the relatively short distance to the supermarket's distribution warehouse and get it unloaded again. From there, he knew that the meat would soon be repackaged and taken on its onward journeys using their own, smaller refrigerated vans, but that was none of his concern. He just had to be back at his garage before his maximum daily combined amount of working time had passed. That was another one of Larry's new procedures that he found difficult to strictly adhere to, or agree with, despite it being based on a long-standing legal requirement of road hauliers.

As he drove the first leg of his second assignment, Frank reflected on some of those fateful decisions that he had made over the previous five years and that had ultimately signalled the failure of his fledgling company, leading him to this point. Ever since the first bank statements, he had realised that his first, and most basic, error had been to under-value the true ongoing costs of running such a concern. That had directly led to him often under-quoting his customers in misguided attempts to win contracts away from his competitors, to the extent that they simply could not be profitable. He had expanded the business with more lorries and drivers and had thankfully circumvented a lot of that initial deficit with more contracts, better calculated, but he had then made further mistakes. For one thing, there was that crazy idea of being able to make a profit from the little custom that the abattoir gave him, using the trailer that he was coincidentally pulling.

Also, there was the miscalculation of employing Robin to service and maintain the lorries. Apart from proving to not be cost-effective in itself, that had also shown up yet more lack of his foresight. Whenever the time came for a tractor unit to be serviced, he had always given the associated driver a day off, with full pay. With Larry, and the big company, now running things, there was a much more efficient approach, from a business point of view. When a unit could not be out on the road, such as today with Robin servicing one of the lorries, the driver was still expected to go out on the road with another driver, riding shotgun. This would not only speed up any loading and unloading, it would also ensure that the main driver would never have to unexpectedly park up somewhere overnight if he found that he was in danger of exceeding his permitted hours. If the working day had lasted too long, his workmate could simply take over any remaining driving, ensuring that the vehicle was returned to the garage and be available for the following day.

Frank had to grudgingly admit that Larry already seemed to be successfully repairing some of the financial chaos and inefficient working practices that he had inherited from him. It was probably better for all concerned that his five-year journey had circled back on itself and he was now a salaried driver again.

7

When Frank finally did arrive back at base, having uneventfully completed the run, six hours and five minutes later, he was quite surprised to see Larry standing at the garage entrance holding what appeared to be a stopwatch. Frank wondered if the man had a separate stopwatch for each driver or if it was just him that was being particularly monitored. He pretended not to notice Larry summoning him with his wild arm movements. Instead, he just parked the unit so that the refrigerated trailer was positioned in its allocated spot and killed the engine. Rather than getting out straight away, he sat and filled in his hand-written daily log, declaring just five hours and fifty-five minutes for the meat run. Larry suddenly appeared at his door and opened it.

'A word in the office please Frank,' the manager said.

Frank climbed down from the high cab and followed his boss to the privacy of his former domain, knowing exactly what was coming. Once there, with the door closed, Larry made himself clear.

'You're over your hours again Frank.'

'Only five minutes Larry. I've just now left it off the log anyway, so it's not a problem.'

'You know what I said on day one Frank. No exceeding the hours. If you ever run out of time, you're either supposed to pull over and sleep in the cab until the next day or call out another driver to take over for the rest of the run.'

'I'm not going to call out one of the boys to drive it for a poxy five minutes, and I'm certainly not going to spend the night in it just down the road. They've had their own jobs to do and are probably out of time themselves anyway.'

'It's the rules, Frank. Not only mine, but the company's rules, and also the law. Follow them or you might as well find somewhere else to work. I can assure you that it wouldn't be any different with another company, though. At the moment you think you can report a little short on your paper entry, and you'd probably have been okay back in the days when you had this as a small operation. But this company have always been very strict about it, demanding that it's accurate. Besides, we will be changing to using tachographs for the logging very soon. It'll be compulsory to use them instead of paper in a couple of years anyway. The speedo will automatically record all of your driving time and there'll be no hiding place then if the authorities suddenly do a spot check on your working hours. I've noticed that you've pushed over the line a couple of times since I took over. I know today it's only five minutes, but you must get out of the habit before it slips to ten minutes another day, and then maybe half an hour on another. Take this one as an off-the-record warning, Frank, but please don't do it again and make things have to get heavy.'

'Understood,' said Frank like a scolded schoolboy. Then, whilst turning to leave, 'I'll just drop the trailer where it is and be off home then.'

The refrigerated trailer always had to be left overnight on

the forecourt, outside, as there was only enough space for the other five trailers, together with their tractor units, to be stored inside the garage. Ever since the left side had been rededicated for use as Robin's maintenance area, complete with work benches and an array of tools, there simply was not enough room for everything. It had been an easy choice to make, though. The other trailers sometimes contained valuable goods that had been pre-loaded during an evening so that they were ready for immediate distribution the following day. The refrigerated version, designed to mainly transport perishable food, was always empty by the end of each day.

'Leave it and go home now Frank. Do it in the morning. Your hours for the day are up.'

Frank left the office and walked across the garage floor towards the large doors, still open, at the far end. As he walked, he removed his green blazer and held it over his shoulder, hanging from his bent index finger. He could see his Ford Escort, parked where he had left it at the start of the day, at the edge of the paved area outside. His was only one of three cars still there in the staff parking area, with the other two belonging to Robin and Larry. All the other drivers had already returned from their own daily duties and had left, confirmed by the garage space being filled by their tractor units and trailers. He passed the servicing point where Robin was finishing up, rubbing Swarfega Hand Cleaner into, and over, his hands.

'Hi Frank. You okay? You look a bit battered.'

'I just had a run-in with the Great Bustard,' said Frank, purposely disrespectfully referring to their mutual superior by his unofficial, and unknown to him, nickname.

'Trying to crack the whip again is he?' said Robin. 'He's probably trying to beat you into submission and make sure you don't keep feeling like this place is still yours.'

'I certainly feel beaten.'

'By the way, I've got an apprentice joining me next week. Larry came up with the idea and said he wanted me to start training someone up ready for when the place starts expanding with more lorries. He's got big plans for the region, maybe taking over another small outfit as well. So, I interviewed someone for it this morning. He seemed like a good guy.'

'I hope you've told him what he's letting himself in for. I'd better be off, anyway. I'll see you in the morning if you're here before I leave. I've got an early start. That is, so long as The Great Bustard doesn't mess around with the schedule again.' With that, Frank walked on towards his car.

There was a time, not so long ago, when any such hiring and firing decisions would be Frank's, and Frank's alone. Now, in this new world, he found that he did not need to be consulted, nor even asked for any opinion on the matter. Four units was hardly enough to keep Robin busy and yet they bizarrely wanted someone extra. Still, it was no longer his problem and, at least, he still had a job and could still drive a lorry.

For now, anyway.

8

At 8:30 the following Monday morning, James was preparing to leave his rented room for his first day at his new job. He was joining one of the most well-known road haulage companies in the UK as an apprentice mechanic, located at their new regional centre just a few miles from where he was living on the outskirts of Clayborough. He had readily accepted the job, which had been immediately offered at the conclusion of his short interview the previous week, and now he was feeling some trepidation at the thought of what now may lie ahead for him. To try to numb his increasing tension headache, he swallowed two paracetamol tablets from a newly-opened box.

He briefly looked around the rented furnished room which had served as his home for nearly the past three months, whilst he had waited patiently for this employment opportunity, and realised that it still contained very few of his own personal possessions. There was simply an old family photo beside the single bed, his cassette-radio, his toiletries and razor, and two stacks of his clothes on the floor. He had never seen any point to hiding his clothes away in a wardrobe or drawers. One pile contained his clean clothes whilst the other was destined for the local launderette at some future time. His one concession to using the provided furniture for its intended purpose was the current position of his waterproof coat, his wide-collared warm lumber jacket, and his fashionable velvet jacket. They were all hanging in the wardrobe, and now visible through its open door.

Everything that he owned in that room would easily fit into the holdall that was on top of the wardrobe, complete with its layer of twelve weeks' worth of dust. That holdall had contained everything he had relocated with, apart from what he had been wearing at the time, when he had first knocked at that house. That had been just fifteen minutes after first seeing the hand-written advertising postcard in the nearby newsagent's window. He and the owner of the house, and thus now his landlord, had instantly hit it off and so, with a week's cash rent paid in advance, he had found himself a comfortable bed to sleep in for that, and every subsequent, night. He had travelled minimally light, in his rusty Ford Capri, but what he did have with him had always been sufficient for his modest needs.

He combed his long, brown hair into his preferred style, with its centre parting, unchanging since he had adopted it as a teenager at the start of the decade. He had already checked that it was not raining and so he pulled on the lumber jacket whilst glancing around the room for any possible forgotten items. After concluding that nothing was likely to be hidden amongst the crumpled bed covers, he patted his pockets to ensure that he had his keys and money with him, at least, and then headed out of the room and down the stairs. As he opened the front door, he called back over his shoulder towards the sound of sizzling bacon that he could hear from the kitchen.

'I'm off to work now. I don't know what time I'll be back.'

'Good luck James,' came the quick reply from his unseen landlord in the rear room. 'This first day is just the start.'

Having the company of James in his house, renting his spare room, had been a godsend for this retired tradesman so soon after the grief of his wife dying. Like a surrogate father, he truly hoped that his new friend would make a success of his new job, especially after months of apparently doing so very little with his life. Ever since James had arrived, it had seemed to him that James had spent the majority of his days just sitting in his room with his radio on. Most evenings James did tend to come downstairs to chat and watch television with him, though. James always paid his rent on time, without fuss and, despite the untidiness of the spare room, was often good fun to have around.

James pulled the Capri onto the forecourt of his imminent employer five minutes before the appointed 9am. He saw the Geordie who had interviewed him the previous Monday, standing in the garage entranceway and apparently awaiting his arrival. He instantly recognised him from the distance thanks to his mop of thick, curly fair hair and matching beard. He saw a row of parked cars completely occupying the nearest edge of the concrete forecourt, presumably belonging to those who worked here. With no available, similar space to either end of the row, apart from a muddy puddle adjacent to the tarmac, James drove to the opposite side of the forecourt and parked his car, unobtrusively in the corner.

As he walked towards the garage, the Geordie approached him until they met in the centre of the open forecourt.

'Hello again James. Welcome to the funny farm,' said Robin with a smile as they warmly shook hands.

'Great to be here, and thank you again for this opportunity,' said James, purposely not referring to Robin by name. When he had attended his interview, James had first been greeted by the site's manager, Larry Mason, and had sat for a while in his office. Larry had given him a brief history of the company and had asked a few general background questions about him before leading him out to meet the man who would potentially be his mentor. It had been left to him to conduct the in-depth part of the interview.

At the time, James had thought he had introduced himself as either Robin or Reuben. He could not be sure which. As a result, he had specifically avoided any need to use it during the ensuing discussion. He had not wanted to ask for a confirming repetition straight away as that might have been construed as a level of criticism of the man's strong regional accent. He now realised that, the longer that time went on without him knowing it, the more potentially embarrassing it could be when the time would eventually come for him to need to refer to him, or about him, by name.

'First thing for you to know is where to park,' said Robin, indicating where James had chosen to leave his Capri. 'That, I'm afraid, is where the refrigerated trailer lives for six days a week. It's used for a meat run on Mondays, usually taken out by Frank, and he'll not be pleased to find you in his way when he gets back tonight.'

'Oh, sorry,' said James, not sure what else he could say.

Robin turned to face the other side of the forecourt and waved his arm towards the row of parked cars. 'That's where we can all park, out of the way of the lorries turning and stuff. Up until today there was just about room for everyone but, now that you're on board, we'll have to say that the mud patch is for the last one to arrive. Today, my friend, that's you. I'll see you inside.'

With that, Robin walked toward the garage, leaving James to reposition his car as best he could in the large, muddy puddle. When he had finished, and with a soaked shoe resulting from getting out of his car again, he walked into the garage as well and found Robin waiting for him at his workbench. He was clearing small tools from a second stool so that they could both sit together and talk some more.

'As you can see, all the drivers are out at the moment,' began Robin as James sat on the indicated, vacant seat. 'You should be able to meet them all later before you go home, so long as they're back in time. They all had early starts today, which is quite common'.

James noticed that the entire garage was empty except for one, freshly-painted semi-trailer. Robin saw him looking at it and explained. 'That's Frank's usual trailer but, as I said, he's using his tractor with the meat wagon today. Not one of his wiser purchases.'

James looked at him quizzically.

'Frank used to own this place,' explained Robin, raising his hands and eyes upwards and around. 'Up until last month this was all Wazzo Haulage Limited. Frank's personal little empire. He'll not thank you for reminding him of that, though. Let's just say he wasn't the sharpest tool in the box when it came to running a business and he ended up selling out to the big boys. That's where Larry came from, putting

Frank's nose out of joint to say the least.'

'He stayed working here afterwards, though?'

'Aye. He apparently didn't do very well out of the deal and didn't really have the choice, as much as he would have loved to tell Larry where to stick it. I've only been here just over three months myself. I met Frank in a pub one evening, when he still thought he was going places with this set-up. I persuaded him that he might like to consider taking on an on-site mechanic for the servicing and everything. I'd just moved here to Clayborough, from Newcastle, where I'd been doing maintenance on lorries, and a bit of occasional driving. I needed something to pay the bills so I thought I might as well try it on. Anyway, he went for the idea and took me on two days later.'

'Handy,' said James.

'Up until recently, there's been very little for me to do, to be honest. Keeping just five tractor units on the road, doing something to each one every four or five weeks, didn't exactly fill every day. I've probably now got the shiniest set of spanners in the North and the garage doors won't need oiling for a while. Anyway, our new big cheese, Larry, came in and straight away had the idea of making his new garage the main servicing site for the whole of the company. The big national company, that is. So, that's just short of five hundred lorries, although not all of them would ever come this way. Those that can be routed near to here, though, are starting to call in for various work to be done on them if their schedule allows. It's complicated to organise and keep on top of, but Larry has persuaded his bosses to let him give it a try. I went from sitting on my hands most days to checking and fixing lorries calling in here at random times throughout every day. They all need to get back out on the road again as quickly as possible because a stationary lorry earns no money, of course, as well as wasting a driver's allowed working hours.'

'Why not just work on them overnight, wherever they come from, like when the driver is in bed?'

'I asked that too. It turns out that the big company have always just concentrated on having their lorries out on the road. They'd just never bothered with setting themselves up with the tools and a mechanic or two of their own. They'd always just used nearby garages instead. Since those garages mainly just work during the day, drivers would be just as idle waiting there instead. After the takeover of Wazzo Haulage, the company suddenly realised that I existed and that they'd got me as part of the deal. I also had the spare time and all the tools and equipment already, so they agreed to experimenting with using me for the main fleet. I have a feeling that, if it actually works out, they'll just shift all these tools to their main depot down South and then do it from there, with me having been given the big elbow.'

'Or they could ask if you'd want to move down there,' said James, trying to make his new colleague feel more optimistic about the prospect.

'I suppose they might,' said Robin. 'Not that I'd want to be moving again any time soon. Anyway, once the idea took off, it suddenly went manic for me here. So, I asked Larry, about a fortnight ago, if I could have some help. That's why you're now here. That, and making my cups of tea, of course.'

With that, Robin led James to the makeshift kitchen, indicated the kettle and pile of grimy mugs and told him how he preferred his tea to be made. He liked it on the hour, every hour, with the next one coincidentally being the one that was scheduled for 9am.

The pair of them were back at the workbench and drinking their first cups of the day when Larry opened his nearby office door, from the inside where he had been for the past thirty minutes, and emerged into the expanse of the garage. Over his clothes, James was now wearing a brand new set of mechanic's overalls, which had been handed to him on his return from the kitchen.

'Sorry I wasn't out here to welcome you myself James,' he said, noticing that James had indeed arrived for work as expected and offering the young apprentice his hand. 'A bit of a crisis already to start the week with, I'm afraid. I've been stuck on the phone with head office for the past half-hour but it's all sorted now. Is Robin filling you in and showing you the ropes?'

'Yes thanks, and I already know where the kettle is,' he said, nodding towards his half-full mug on the bench as he stood up and completed the customary handshake with the man with the pencil moustache.

'Excellent,' said Larry, although a bit unsure how he felt about such immediate familiarity from his latest member of staff. Then, mainly to Robin, 'I need to zip up to Clancey's right now to talk about the latest paint job they did on Frank's trailer. You two okay to hold the fort here for an hour or two?'

'Sure, no problem,' replied Robin.

As Larry walked away, towards his new Audi parked

outside, Robin quietly carried on talking to James. 'Clancey's, my arse,' he said. 'He's off to meet his bit on the side while her husband is at work and won't be back until after lunch. Happens at least twice a week, disappearing with some lame excuse or other. He must think I'm as stupid as I look.'

James smiled and nodded knowingly, pleased to be the recipient of such workplace gossip which presumably indicated that he had already been accepted into the fold by his mentor.

'Right, we've got a PMI due in around ten o'clock and then, about eleven-thirty, we should be getting one for a full service coming through the doors,' said Robin, clapping his hands together.

'PMI?' asked James.

'Preventative Maintenance Inspection,' clarified Robin. 'All units have to be thoroughly checked over for roadworthiness every six weeks or so, so you'll be seeing a lot of those. Doesn't take very long, and the drivers just tend to disappear to the café round the corner for a sandwich or something whilst I'm doing it. Trouble is, up until today that left me on my own to turn lights on and off, rocking the steering and pressing brakes, all whilst struggling to check all is okay from the outside.'

'And after today?'

'After today I just have to drink my tea and look at the lights while you do all the work.'

James knew precisely what he meant. After his own few years' experience of car maintenance, he was hopefully now to be shown the heavy vehicle versions, just as he had applied for. Understandably, being the junior, his role would undoubtedly often include sitting in cabs, rocking steering wheels and pressing pedals on command. Robin, who'd had enough faith in him to offer him the job on the spot last week, would be visually checking the consequence of each movement and, for now at least, would be the one signing off that all was mechanically sound with each unit.

9

Robin and James were still talking and halfway through their second tea of the day, shortly after 10am, when they heard the powerful diesel engine of a tractor unit pulling onto the forecourt outside. Robin leapt up and marshalled the anonymous driver of the unfamiliar unit, painted in the familiar company colours, through the huge, open garage doors and into the undercover garage area. The driver climbed down from the cab and exchanged pleasantries with Robin before departing for the advised sandwich bar, leaving James and Robin to complete the mandatory brief inspection on his vehicle.

James was motioned to temporarily take the man's place in the driver's seat and, after a brief tutorial from Robin, activated all the lights, brakes, and various controls. Robin, from somewhere below him, called for each required individual check from his printed list and placed a tick when he was satisfied with the effects of each. After checking the lights and moving components, Robin proceeded to check the authenticity of the static areas, greasing bearings as he went. James was out of the cab and at his side whilst he talked through his actions, thoughts and findings.

Well within the hour they had checked that everything was satisfactory and had decided that no extra work needed performing on this particular unit. Robin signed off all the paperwork so that the driver could then continue his run, having taken just a short diversion from his usual M6 route and officially used the pause as his required minimum thirty minute break.

Fifteen minutes later, the expected second lorry appeared for its service. As before, Robin summoned and directed the lorry into the garage to a position above the open inspection pit and the driver was advised where he might find some food and distraction while he waited. This, as Robin explained to James, was to be a full 30,000-mile service involving full checks and an engine oil replacement. James was given the task of draining and refilling the oil, including fitting a new oil filter, as it would, in Robin's words, just be a bigger version of what he had long been used to doing with cars in his previous job.

James rapidly adjusted to the unfamiliar larger dimensions of everything, and started to appreciate the similarities, and differences, of maintaining heavy vehicles when compared to cars. Even with Robin ensuring that he was satisfied with James's contribution at each stage, the entire service was completed within two hours. They had told the driver to expect to be waiting for three so James had to walk up to the café to find and tell the driver that his unit was already ready to take away. He had been easily recognisable in the crowded café, still wearing his Crossbow Transport blazer, and James had to interrupt his egg and chips.

'I don't suppose we'll be seeing that guy again for a while,' James said to Robin after the second lorry had left and as the pair of them were eating their lunchtime sandwiches. '30,000 miles is a pretty big gap between services'.

'You'd think so wouldn't you,' said Robin, 'but just think about the maths. Some of those guys are covering maybe 400 miles every day, maybe even more, and some of the lorries can be shared between a couple of drivers. As soon as one driver finishes for a day, another guy might take it out on the road again overnight. The engine never goes cold. At that rate, it could need a full service every couple of months. So, what with that, and interim services at 15,000 miles, and those PMI checks constantly needed every six weeks, it's not going to need much of the fleet calling in here to keep us on our toes. They may have hundreds of lorries, but we can still only handle the fraction of them that are regularly heading past our front door. Talking of which, we've got three more due in this afternoon. I may even let you hold the grease gun next time if you make a nice cup of tea now.'

James took the hint and scooped up the two mugs from the bench as he rose from the stool and headed towards the kitchen.

'I'll have one too please,' called Larry from where he had just appeared at the garage entrance. 'Two sugars.' Without another word, he walked straight to his office, but left the door open so that James could deliver the tea when it was ready.

Once he had set down the unexpected third mug on Larry's desk and sat back down with Robin, the chief mechanic leaned closer to him and whispered. 'You'd have thought that the blokes at Clancey's wouldn't have let The Great Bustard leave with lipstick on his cheek,' he said sarcastically. 'I told you. Seeing his bit on the side.'

James had not noticed Larry's failure to wipe the tell-tale sign from his face when he had just left the sugared tea on Larry's desk but was now more interested in the nickname that had been used. 'Great Bustard?'

'Not to his face or within earshot, but we all call him that behind his back. You just wait and see how moody the bastard can be sometimes. You'll understand why then.'

James was slightly confused by the subtle differences in Robin's pronunciations of the derogatory terms that he had used when referring to their boss. He again put it down to the man's strong, unfamiliar, regional accent. Any sign of a mood swing from Larry would have to wait for another time, however, as it was not long before the first of the afternoon's units appeared for their scheduled work. Robin and James did not see Larry again for the rest of the afternoon as they were too busy constantly working on the lorries. As they worked, they constantly talked, sometimes about the job in hand but mostly about Frank and the history of the earlier regime. Like clockwork, each vehicle appeared outside just before they had completed the work on the preceding one. Even when they did steal a few minutes for a break, and a cup of tea, they noticed that Larry's office door had been shut again and neither wanted to risk, or bother, disturbing him with the offer of an afternoon beverage. As in the morning, all the drivers simply left Robin and his new assistant to it while they took a well-deserved breather in the nearby café.

By the time the last one had left, it was early evening on James's first day. As they shared some squirts of Swarfega to remove the oil and grease from their skin, Larry suddenly reappeared from his bolt-hole and, with nothing more than a quick farewell to the pair of them, scuttled out of the building towards his Audi again. Robin seemed to find it quite amusing that Larry had to swerve around the approaching artic on the forecourt as he sped off to his unknown evening pleasures.

'I thought we were done for the day,' said James, indicating the advancing lorry.

'We are,' replied Robin, continuing with his cleansing routine.

Unlike all the other lorries that James had watched come into the garage that day, this one circled around the forecourt and slowly reversed into the building, complete with its trailer still coupled, until it occupied the far side of the expanse. As the driver climbed down from his cab, Robin walked over to greet him, closely followed by James, who he had motioned to follow him.

'Hiya. Good run?' said Robin as he approached.

'Not bad, matey,' replied the driver. 'Bit of a hold up on the M6 but that's the way it goes. Who's this?' looking straight at James.

'My new right-hand man, this is James,' said Robin, accepting the role of the one to have to introduce his apprentice, now that Larry had effectively delegated it to him by his sudden absence. 'James, this is Jackdaw,' he continued, with a slight, albeit unintentional, pause between the two syllables.

The two shook hands and smiled at each other, neither of them saying anything immediately. James, because of that pause, naturally assumed it to be the man's full name. 'Hello Jack,' James said eventually.

'No, it's not Jack Dawe, James. It's Jackdaw,' the man

corrected him, 'as in the name of a bird. You've heard of one, presumably.'

'Yes of course I have,' said James, totally confused now, 'but never as someone's name I'm afraid.' James was thinking that it was an unfortunately unusual name for someone's parents to selfishly choose, without consideration for the confusion it would undoubtedly cause later in life. Especially for someone, like himself, looking not much older than their mid-twenties. Jackdaw had long brown hair parted to the left and looked, to James, like a man well-suited to the heavy lifting required of his profession. His biceps bulged under the tight sleeves of his official company blazer.

James was just about to try to engage in some small talk to get to know his new colleague a little, when the sound of another approaching diesel engine pierced the air. The three of them stood aside as a second lorry, a four-wheel rigid type this time, reversed alongside Jackdaw's artic and parked at the same angle.

This driver also required an introduction and, again, it was Robin who performed the honours when a man with long sideburns joined them.

'Hi Raven, this is our new man, James.'

James couldn't help his reaction. 'Raven?'

'Ah yes. Maybe I should have explained something before now,' said Robin. 'We are all part of a bird flock here.'

'Bird flock?' James was now totally bewildered.

'Well, as I told you this morning, Frank Bird used to run this place, starting it from scratch about five years ago. He took on these guys, and two others, as he expanded it.'

'He could have done a lot worse,' interjected Jackdaw.

'It became a regular thing for all the crew to hit the pub after finishing on a Friday. Still do, actually. Anyway, apparently, one night someone came up with the idea for them each to have bird-oriented nicknames. Frank, already being a bird, was the only one allowed to keep his own name.'

'It seemed a perfectly reasonable idea at the time, especially after downing about a gallon each,' said Raven, thinking back to the drunken night that Robin was referring to. He reflected that ideas, and decisions made, immediately after drinking at least eight pints of beer were not necessarily good ones.

'So, suddenly there was Raven,' said Robin, jerking his thumb towards the man with the dark eyes, jet-black hair and sideburns, 'and Jackdaw,' moving his thumb sideways to gesture towards the other driver, although not revealing the reason for the choice of nickname. 'There's also Sparrow and Magpie, who should both be getting back here any time soon. There was also once talk of getting pictures of the individual birds painted on everyone's cab door, but Frank drew the line at that. I don't think that it was because he thought it was taking the piss out of his name so much as the cost for the artwork. So, when I joined, I had to have a bird name as well, of course. I ended up being christened Robin at my first Friday pub night. Something to do with me wearing a brown jacket over a red T-Shirt that night.'

So, thought James, it is definitely Robin, and not Reuben. Thankfully, he had been able to avoid using the word all day and now he had discovered his teacher's correct nickname without revealing his earlier misunderstanding.

'Robin is not your real name, then?' said James.

'No, of course not. Do you think I look like a Robin?'

James shrugged his shoulders, unsure why someone named Robin should look any different to someone with any other name. 'I just assumed it was.'

'A lot of people do these days,' admitted Robin.

'It all just kind of stuck,' Jackdaw said, picking up the thread. 'Real names are now totally banned between us, and so you'll not hear any ever used, other than Frank himself or Larry Mason. Even then, Mason is secretly known as The Great Bustard, another bird. Not that he knows anything about it.' The boss's nickname, that he had already heard Robin use earlier in the day, now made much more sense to James.

'Only behind his back,' added Raven. 'You'll have to come up with a bird name for yourself, Jim. Either that, or one will soon be chosen for you'.

'James, please,' corrected James, not at all happy that he might be forced down this childish alley of adopting such a nickname. He decided he would resist accepting one for himself for as long as he possibly could.

Contrary to the unwritten workplace rule, Robin rapidly announced everyone's real names, including his own and those of the absent drivers, for James's benefit. James had already realised it would be easier, and only necessary, for him to remember the nicknames and follow the accepted convention.

The four men were still stood talking ten minutes later when Frank drove up with the refrigerated trailer, causing all heads to instinctively turn in his direction. The sudden break in conversation served as enough of a reason for Raven and Jackdaw to leave the small gathering. With friendly farewells, and waves, they walked to their respective cars on the opposite side of the forecourt to where Frank was busily uncoupling the trailer for another week. Robin led James across the forecourt for yet another introduction that day, this time with the man with the ginger hair.

Frank was in a sour mood, having been delayed on the road past his permitted hours again and thinking that he was destined for another dressing down by Larry. When Robin told him that their mutual superior had already left for the day, Frank noticeably relaxed in the knowledge that he could shave some time from his hand-written log and no-one would be any the wiser.

Even so, the first brief meeting between Frank and James was somewhat subdued and strained. James was the first new recruit that Frank had not personally hired into his former garage and so, as they talked, he kept wondering whether he would have approved the employment offer if he had been consulted on the subject. James, for his part, was able to keep his composure whilst in the man's presence, albeit with his rather hostile demeanour, trying to assimilate everything he had already found out about this patriarch of the small bird community.

After Frank had finished uncoupling his unit from the refrigerated trailer and reversed it into the garage to couple up to his usual box trailer, he grunted his farewells to the two mechanics and drove off, leaving them to wait for the returns of Sparrow and Magpie. Robin had suggested that James might as well meet everyone on his first day, if he could, and had figured that neither of them should take much longer getting back.

As it turned out, the slight holdup on the M6 that Jackdaw had referred to had become a two-mile stationery tailback and so it was a further hour before the remaining two drivers eventually appeared, within ten minutes of each other. Magpie was first, a man similar in stature to Raven and sporting similar sideburns, though not quite as far down his face. Sparrow was the shortest of all those new people James had met that day, which James assumed accounted for his assigned nickname.

With those last introductions completed, followed by a few minutes of more friendly forecourt banter, James sensed that he was finally being allowed to leave for the evening. He got into his Capri, now standing on hardened mud after the evaporation of the puddle in the warmth of the day. As he drove off, heading for his lodgings and a welcome bath, he waved to the three men still on the forecourt, undoubtedly with Robin now telling the other two birds exactly how he felt the day had gone with his new aide.

James walked through the front door and was immediately greeted by his landlord, as desperate as a doting parent to hear the news of how his first day on the job had gone.

'They seem a good bunch, I guess,' said James. 'A bit of a strange bird's nest you could say.' He smiled to himself at the thought of them all in their bird personas, and at the confused look on his landlord's face. 'A bit of friction going on here and there, but I suppose you get that in most places.'

The collection of staff found at most jobs do indeed often include personality clashes, in varying degrees and for a multitude of reasons. However, it is unusual for there to also be underlying, murderous intent.

10

It was warm and sunny on the Friday morning as Robin drove onto the forecourt. Being the last to arrive for work that day, he immediately saw that his parking place was to be the mud patch. As was usual for a Friday, all five lorry drivers had all been scheduled for early starts and Robin knew that they would already be many miles away on their respective jobs. Larry's Audi occupied the sixth position, with James's Capri alongside that, the left to right order of the seven cars being testament to the order of arrival of their owners. It was the first time that Robin would be parking at the garage without concrete under his wheels, that particular honour being implicitly reserved for James until that day. Thankfully for him, though, the ground was still hardened, and no muddy puddle had formed underneath the driver's door, due to the lack of rain since the weekend before.

As he walked into the garage, the sight was unsurprising. As he had expected, all of the lorries had vacated the expanse earlier that morning. James, already in his overalls, was sat at the workbench with his back to him. He was leaning over one of the workshop manuals from the small collection, his left elbow on the bench and his head resting against his left hand, apparently reading up about some aspect of lorry maintenance. There was a mug of steaming tea placed on the bench to the top right of the open manual and there was another, further to the right, on the bench in front of Robin's stool.

'Thanks,' said Robin as he approached the bench, referring to the beverage that had already been prepared for him by his apprentice in anticipation of his arrival.

The sudden voice in the early silence of the day, coupled with being engrossed in the manual, made James visibly jump in his chair. The distinctive accent meant that he knew who it was before he turned round. 'Morning Robin, didn't hear you come in,' he said as he regained his composure. 'I was a bit earlier today so I thought I'd get on with a bit of reading until you got here,' he continued, pointing down at the manual.

'Fair enough,' said Robin, sitting down alongside him. 'Really, though, you only need to check those books when it's an unfamiliar job to do. Speaking of which, the first one due in today isn't one of the usual services. Apparently, the compressor is starting to play up for this guy, taking ages to get the air pressure high enough. It can be slightly awkward for a driver when the brakes don't work properly.'

'I saw it on the official copy of the schedule,' said James, sarcastically referring to the first entry on Robin's scruffy, hand-written list on the far side of the bench. 'So, my chapter for today is the one on air brakes systems.' Robin saw, for the first time, the subject matter of the page that the manual was open at, and was impressed at his apprentice's proactive initiative. 'It's a bit different to a car, isn't it?'

'Aye, you can forget everything you know about the way cars use brake fluid to stop when it comes to these big boys. It doesn't say caution, air brakes, at the back for nothing. If the driver clears off to the café for long enough, I should be able to show you around the rest of the system before he takes it away again. Those manuals are fine as far as they go, but you know there's no substitute for seeing it for real. The photos and diagrams always show you parts of a pristine, new vehicle, without all the inches of oil, grease and road dirt all over the place. It'll also say things like to just simply remove a particular nut, maybe as the first stage of a job. It won't ever mention that it could easily take you over an hour of hammering to release the damn thing that's welded itself to a thread after tens of thousands of miles on the road. They leave out little details like that and then the bosses think that you're skiving and taking much too long on a job when they happen to read those easy-sounding instructions for themselves.' Robin waved a careless gesture towards Larry's open door, not really caring if Larry could hear his minor rant from inside the office.

James realised he may have inadvertently struck a nerve relating to a possible incident in the recent past with his seemingly innocent choice of reading material. He tried to deflect and calm the situation by getting their thoughts back to the imminent work.

'Shall I open up the pit so that we're ready?' asked James.

Robin seemed to calm down as quickly as he had tensed up. 'Yes please. The guy is due about half past.' With that, Robin picked up his tea and drank slowly while James removed each of the planks of wood that covered the inspection pit ten feet from their bench. He stacked them at the end of the workbench as had done at the start of every day that week. For safety, the pit was always covered over when not in use, including each evening after all maintenance or servicing work had finished for the day.

Rectangular in shape, the pit was narrow enough for the wheels of a lorry to straddle it yet long enough for an entire tractor unit to be inspected, or worked on, without the need to reposition it. It had been excavated in the floor of the garage soon after Frank had hired Robin and had attempted his on-site maintenance approach. Allowing entry by concrete steps leading down from one of the narrow ends, a mechanic, or two, could stand in the depression and easily access the underside of a tractor unit and the inner edges of all wheels, including the brakes.

Along the inner edges of the two longest sides were integrated ridges, set about an inch below ground level. On these could be rested the inch-thick planks of wood, which were all cut to the same length as the width of the pit. When all planks were in place, the entire pit, including the steps, was fully covered allowing it to be safely walked, or driven, over. Many inattentive garage workers had fallen into open pits in workplaces throughout the country. Robin was determined that his would not be one of them and had always insisted that the pit was properly covered when not in use.

James had just finished removing and stacking the final plank when he heard the approach of the anticipated lorry with the faulty compressor. He did not even have the chance to pick up his cold mug of tea from next to the newspaper that Robin had been reading at the bench up until then.

'You timed that well,' said Robin, oblivious to his assistant's thirst and rising from his stool to make his way to the far end of the pit to guide the driver to park in position over it. He made it clear that he expected James to now forgo his first cup of the day and follow him, and so James did.

An hour later, the faulty compressor had been replaced and tested. With the driver still enjoying a late breakfast at the café, Robin had, as promised, taken every opportunity during its fixing, and afterwards, to give James a brief overview of the workings of a lorry's air-brake system. After the driver had returned from his meal and left in his repaired vehicle, Robin and James were sat back at the bench enjoying another cup of tea when Robin suddenly declared 'Oh well, at least it's Poets Day'

'Pardon?' queried James, never having heard the workplace term before.

Robin expanded the acronym for the benefit of his younger sidekick. 'Piss off early, tomorrow's Saturday,' he said. 'Why else do you think we haven't got a late one coming in today?'

'Hadn't really thought about it,' said James, thinking about it for the first time now.

'For all his faults, Larry does at least try to let us get away earlier at the end of the week. Frank used to do it before him, so that's probably where he got the idea. All the drivers get early starts, at least where it can be arranged, meaning that they finish earlier. A quick wash and brush up at home and then it's all out for a gallon at The Groom, not that Larry knows about that part of it. I don't think anyone has ever bothered mentioning it to him.'

'Gallon at The Groom?' James was having trouble keeping up with the unfamiliar terms that Robin was suddenly expressing.

'Happens every Friday night at The Horse and Groom pub in Clayborough town centre, just off Wilson Road. Has done for years. All the boys get together for a beers session from eight o'clock. At least a gallon each, or you have to pay the bill for the Chinese meal afterwards. So, are you up for it tonight?'

'Yeah, sure,' answered James, although the thought of six truckers and him each drinking eight pints of beer, or more, sounded like a recipe for disaster. He knew that he was never comfortable in large social gatherings. However, he also knew that it would be a perfect opportunity to get a bit closer to some of the team, especially as most of the time they were all out on the road leaving just him and Robin at the garage.

With only a minimal break for lunch, Robin and James worked constantly for the rest of the day with two pre-arranged 30,000-mile services and one PMI check. Although they knew he was there, they only quickly saw Larry a few times. It was usually when he was just on his way to or from the filthy toilet housed in the far corner of the garage. He spoke only a few words to them both all day, and it seemed it was only when he felt obliged to, as if his mind was preoccupied with other things. Although the door of his office was open for most of the time, that was more associated with the warmth of the day rather than suggesting an open invitation for random interaction with the two mechanics. Occasionally they would hear his office phone ring and, as was his habit, he would close the office door before answering it, only opening it again and wedging it in place once the call was complete. They had no idea what may be putting him in such a quiet mood for the day, but neither of them minded being left to get on with things.

By 4pm, the last of the day's visiting lorries had left and so Robin and James closed up the inspection pit, each of them replacing half of the planks and taking turns to drop them into place. James let the final one fall near to the last remaining gap and tapped it with his foot until it neatly dropped the inch into position to be flush with all the other planks.

'Here endeth your first week,' said Robin whilst walking towards the tub of Swarfega hand-cleaner on the end of the bench. 'You've done well James, and I'm certainly glad to have your help now. It was getting a bit much on my own with all the extra work coming in.'

'Thanks,' replied James, not sure what else to say to this unexpected praise. He had just decided to make some follow-up comment about how he was enjoying it and was pleased to be there when a lorry pulled up to the garage entrance and parked with a hiss of brakes. James did not need to squint to see into the cab through the sunshine reflecting off the windscreen. Being the only four-wheeler that was based there, he knew immediately that this was Raven arriving back first from his day's run. Having already specifically memorised all four of the registration numbers of the larger, otherwise-identical, articulated lorries which had formerly been part of Wazzo Haulage, he would have been able to similarly identify whoever it had been without any need to actually see the driver.

The dented front bumper, and the fresh scratches in the new company's paintwork, partially pre-announced what

Raven was about to say to them as he jumped down from the cab with a stern look on his face.

'Some bastard in a knackered old Datsun thought he could cut me up on the M6,' explained Raven as he approached them, pointing back at the recent damage to his lorry.

'What's the story?' asked Robin, pleased to see that Raven was apparently unscathed by the incident, at least.

'I was just passing an exit. Inside lane. Then this prat, who was overtaking me, decides that's the turn-off that he wants to take. He cut right in front of me and then suddenly slammed his brakes on to try to make it in the last few yards before the grass bank. He didn't.'

'What damage?' asked James.

'He walked away from it, but the back of his car is a mess. Probably a write-off, especially given the age of it.'

Robin and James both breathed a collective sigh of relief that Raven's accident had not been more serious. Vehicles could be repaired or replaced, after all. With people, though, it was a potentially different story.

'A Japanese bloke, as you might guess in a Datsun. Got all his details, though.' Raven fluttered the piece of paper that he had been holding in his left hand.

'You're okay though?' asked James.

'Yeah sure. A poxy Datsun is no match for one of these,' said Raven, waving his hand towards his lorry. 'A lorry is so powerful, you don't even feel any resistance. I'm just really annoyed. Even though he shot across me like he did, insurance companies always blame the guy at the back.'

Robin walked the few steps to the front of the lorry to inspect the damage more closely. 'Looks like it'll just need a new bumper,' he said after a cursory look.

'That's what I thought too, but that would still cost more than Mr Lau's ancient Cherry. Could you park it up for me please Robin? The Great Bustard isn't going to be pleased, and I'm the one who's got to tell him all about it.' With that, Raven headed towards Larry Mason's office, clutching his piece of paper containing the personal details of the unfortunate Datsun driver. He knocked, entered and closed the door behind him.

Robin climbed up into Raven's driver's seat and started up the lorry again. As he manoeuvred it into its overnight position in the garage, clearing the entrance to allow for the other drivers' returns, he realised that it was lucky it had only suffered such superficial damage. At least the lorry could still continue to be used in the meantime, whilst the insurance companies did battle and eventually agreed for the repairs to be done.

Once parked, he climbed down again from the cab, leaving the door unlocked and the keys in the ignition ready for Raven's next drive. The entire garage was always securely locked and alarmed overnight, so no further precautions were ever thought to be necessary. With Raven's unlocked lorry now potentially vulnerable for a few minutes, he and James stood and waited until the next driver, which turned out to be Sparrow, arrived five minutes later. With a background of Larry's voice rising in volume from his office, ranting about the sudden increase to his paperwork and still audible through the closed door, Robin casually reminded James of the regular weekly arrangement for the evening.

'Don't forget. Eight o'clock at The Horse and Groom,' he said.

'I'll be there,' said James.

11

At 8:45pm, James walked into the unfamiliar pub and looked around him. The taxi had dropped him, as he had requested, at the top end of Wilson Road. He had easily found the unimaginative sign, portraying a man leading a horse along a country road, swinging in the slight breeze. He had walked around the block a few times, though, delaying his entrance. The later he arrived, the less volume he would be obliged to drink with these experienced drinkers. Eight pints of beer still sounded excessive to him, so he was hoping to be able to miss the first few, drinking only maybe five or six alongside them, without losing face.

Even though it was a town centre pub, the building had the charm and character that would not be out of place in the middle of a small village or out in the countryside. With its low wooden beams and a multitude of alcoves, the old, listed building boasted a rare, relaxing atmosphere for the town. The man working behind the bar saw James's seeking expression and, knowing that he had not seen him in his pub before, simply asked 'are you looking for the feathered freighters?'

The expression amused James, having spent the whole of the past week referring to grown men by names associated with various wild birds. 'Yes, I guess I am.'

'Just round there on the right,' said the barman, pointing to an opening that obviously led to one of the alcoves. 'It'll cost you a tenner to get in, though,' he continued, waving a pint glass containing various notes and a few coins.

James was a bit confused at first but added a ten-pound note to the glass after the barman explained that the money represented the beer kitty for those birds. He was pulled a pint and the barman took out one of the pound notes for payment, dropping the change from the till into the glass as he replaced it on the shelf behind him. James carried his drink to the entrance of the alcove.

'James! There you are!' said Robin from the far side of a large table occupied by all six former employees of Wazzo Haulage. 'I told Danny we were expecting a new member tonight,' he said, referring to the barman, 'and you've paid into the kitty already I see.' Robin lazily pointed to James's full glass.

'Off and running,' said James as he looked around the group, wondering how many drinks each of them had already had. Probably not many, he thought, given that he was only forty-five minutes late but they still all seemed to be in a very relaxed, happy mood.

As the evening wore on, James felt more and more welcomed into the fold, with the drivers including him in the conversations, asking him more about himself and seemingly taking a genuine interest in what he had to say. Apart from feeling a little embarrassed for once getting the nicknames of Raven and Magpie the wrong way round, he was enjoying the evening. Each time that any glass was emptied, it was immediately replaced, automatically, with a full one by the observant bar staff. The appropriate cost was simply extracted from the glass on the shelf each time.

After an hour, the effects of the alcohol had helped to fully relax James and any earlier misgivings had dissipated. At one point, the background music, that had been constantly playing, included the latest release from ABBA, *Knowing Me Knowing You*. It prompted an unrehearsed collective 'A-ha' from the whole table, joining in with each chorus.

'So, which one of the two does everyone fancy the most?' Magpie asked the group when the track had finished.

'Definitely the blonde one, Agnetha,' said Sparrow, without hesitation. This was greeted with a chorus of approval from another three.

'I actually prefer Anni-Frid,' said Frank. 'Much more my type.'

'Mine too, actually,' agreed Raven.

With the poll split four to two, the only one of the group to have not voiced an opinion was Magpie, the originator of the question.

'So, what are you thinking?' Raven asked him. 'Which one of the two do you fancy the most?'

Magpie pretended to ponder his answer before he finally said, in a fake, and exaggerated, camp tone that accurately emulated TV personality Larry Grayson, 'well I've always thought the one with the beard looked the cutest.'

At this, everyone around the table collapsed into howls of laughter, exacerbated by the amount of drink that had been imbibed.

'You'd better watch your back Robin,' said Sparrow, indicating the chief mechanic's beard. More communal laughter.

As the latest frivolity was slowly dissipating, Larry Mason appeared at the entrance to the alcove in which they were sitting.

'Hello boys,' he said.

There was the briefest stunned silence before Sparrow broke it. 'Hi boss. What are you doing here?'

'Just thought I'd call in for a few with you. I was on my way home from somewhere. Anyone fancy another drink?'

Despite the intrusion being largely an unwelcome surprise, the majority of the birds accepted Larry's offer. It was not through any feelings of comradeship, though. Rather, they all silently felt he would probably be earning a much higher wage than any of them, all undeserved and on the back of their collective efforts. A drink was the very least they were entitled to from him. No-one told him of the existence of the kitty behind the bar, including the barman, Danny, who had invited James to partake earlier.

While Larry was standing at the bar and ordering the round of drinks, it was Jackdaw who whispered the question that they were all thinking of. 'So, who invited that wanker down here tonight?'

They all shook their heads in denial, but then Robin had a thought.

'I bet he heard me telling James about it at the garage this morning. Aye, that'll be it. Now he's come down here to mix with the troops and try to prove that he's just one of the boys. Sorry guys, but I may have let a cat out of the bag.'

There were sighs of dismay from around the table. However, as Larry returned with a tray of drinks for those who had accepted his offer, there was an unspoken consensus that they should at least give him the chance to socialise, despite being such a dictator in the workplace. After putting the tray on the table and pulling up an extra chair from another table for himself, he sat down and raised his glass to the group. 'Cheers, then, everyone'.

Some, but not all, responded appropriately.

'So,' began Raven, 'what brings you out tonight Larry?'

Larry had always thought that his best chance of endearing himself to his workforce, which was the main point of him calling in to the pub, was to talk at what he presumed would be their usual level, and subject, of conversation.

'I've just been spending the evening with a lady friend, shall we say. One that's always ready for it whenever I go round there. I've only had to leave now because her husband is apparently due back home soon,' Larry said, truthfully. The resultant drunken laughter was louder than Magpie had achieved with his reference to Benny Andersen of ABBA, and it successfully served to break the icy atmosphere. Most around the table suddenly, and perversely, started to see Larry in a more favourable light. With his honesty and apparent proof of being a 'real man' after all, maybe he could be regarded as one of the boys, at least when outside of the working environment. Even Robin also started to warm to the man, now that his suspicions about Larry furtively seeing someone had been confirmed.

Within a further hour, helped by still further alcohol consumption by the attendees, Larry had skilfully manipulated the conversation topics to make him appear as just another one of the bird flock. He was sure that, in order to get some measure of workplace loyalty shown to him from this crew, he needed to gain their friendship, and it seemed to be working. By the next round of drinks, they had even informed him about the kitty and he had been seen to readily contribute an extra ten pounds to the glass. Having already purchased an extra round, he figured that, by next week's outing, he would hopefully be fully accepted by them all at last.

The subject of Raven's accident that day came up, raised by Sparrow. Sparrow had seen the damage to the front bumper but not had the chance to talk to Raven about it before leaving the garage earlier that night. Raven recounted the same story that he had told to Robin, James and Larry to the wider audience.

'I guess that means you took Mr Lau's cherry,' joked Robin, when he had finished. Robin had been hoping to use the pun, relating to the model of the car involved, ever since he had arrived at the pub.

'Datsun drivers are all like that,' said Magpie. 'I had one do the same thing to me last year, if you remember.'

'Here's an idea,' said Robin. 'The one who's had the most serious accident doesn't need to put into the kitty the next time it needs topping up.'

'Sounds fine to me,' said Magpie who then gave further details of the way that he had managed to plough into the back of that other Datsun after it had unexpectedly tried to fit between his lorry and the one in front, at 60mph.

'Very similar to Raven's, really,' said Robin, having declared himself judge and jury for the competition. 'No clear winner yet.'

Sparrow gave his best story next, telling how he had once inadvertently backed into another lorry which had parked out of sight behind him after he had stopped in a lay-by. 'It may not have been as spectacular as your Datsun incidents, but it would have certainly cost an insurance company a lot more money,' he offered as his candidate to win the prize.

Larry's story involved him hitting another car whilst driving his own, supporting Frank's theory, albeit incorrect, that Larry could not drive a lorry. It was immediately obvious to everyone that the other incidents declared so far were more worthy of the exemption to the kitty next time.

Frank had been sat at the end of the table with his head down, not saying anything for some time. It was clear that he was now suffering the effects of the drinking more than any other at the table, as tended to be the case every Friday. He slowly lifted his head and everyone could see that his eyes were glazed.

'I can beat all of those stories,' he slurred morosely. 'I managed to kill almost a whole family in one go.'

The table fell into sudden silence, the jovial mood immediately dispelled. Larry, James and the birds all sat there, open-mouthed.

'It was over ten years ago, one quiet night. I was running late, close to the limit of the hours. I went through some traffic lights and suddenly this car was coming across from the side. I made a sandwich of it against the building that was opposite.' A few of them noticed that Frank seemed to smirk at the memory. 'It's quite amazing just how easily a car can crumple, especially when you've got fifteen tons of potatoes strapped on the back.'

'So, who's fault was it?' asked Sparrow who was, like them all, suddenly sobered by the revelation from their former employer.

'Well they must have come through a red light, so it was their own fault. The post-mortem said that the bloke who was driving had been drinking as well, so I was in the clear. I think only a couple of small kids, who were in the back, survived. A boy and a girl who went off to live with relatives afterwards.'

'So, you went through on green?' asked James.

There was a momentary hesitation from Frank, but then he said 'yes, of course. I even had to swear to it at the inquest and, without any witnesses, they had no choice but to take my word for it. It was green. It had been green for a while, and I was blameless. That was the official verdict.' He took another large mouthful from his latest pint before openly laughing about it all, in an unsuccessful attempt to lighten the mood again.

'Do you know any more about the family, like even their name?'

'No. Don't know if I was ever told. If I was, I can't remember it. I just wasn't interested. Certainly not interested enough to ask.'

James continued his questioning. 'Don't you feel anything for that family? Doesn't it make you sad that you know that you did that?'

'No, not really,' said Frank, still with a laugh. 'Never did. I was quite annoyed, actually, as it put my lorry out of action for a week and my car insurance premium went through the roof. They shouldn't have been there, and they cost me. Just one of them things guys. You can't let such things bother you. Shit happens and you move on. So, do I get the prize?' He looked at the seven surprised faces around the table, but no-one answered.

Despite the array of those stunned expressions, they were not all genuine. Frank's tale had not been a complete surprise to everyone. Not everyone was working for Crossbow Transport because they had simply wanted a job. Frank's workplace had been consciously targeted, with murderous intentions, with the sole purpose of being able to get close to him. Frank's glib attitude had effectively sealed his fate for there was another who had already known the most intimate details of that fateful night in 1965.

He had been there.

12

The sun had just risen on the following Monday when Jackdaw arrived at the garage. He parked his car in the leftmost space, being the first driver of the day. He had been scheduled for the longest run and he knew that he had to be over 200 miles away, ready to be loaded up with goods from the factory in the South, before mid-morning. After locking his car, he walked to the main entrance of the garage and used the second key on his personal keyring to unlock that door. Everyone who worked for Crossbow Transport had a key to the main door of the garage, as any one of them could be scheduled to start work first on any given day. Furthermore, unless someone else had arrived before the previous one had left, the garage would always need to be fully locked up again.

Jackdaw was immediately greeted with the audible warning tones of the alarm system, as he had expected. He calmly entered the four-digit security code onto the keypad just inside the doorway to deactivate it. He completed the action just before it would have otherwise burst into a cacophony of ear-piercing sounds and flashing lights to announce the potential presence of an intruder. He actually doubted whether any locals would be at all concerned about the possibility of the nearby haulage company being turned over. The residents had made no secret of their disregard for a noisy operation so close to their homes, signing petitions against the original planning permission application being just one example. They would probably just be rather annoyed at any disruption to their sleep.

He pushed the large red button on the wall and the sound of the electric motor of the large metal folding doors accompanied the squeaks of those doors as they slowly opened. Like curtains opening at the start of a theatre or cinema presentation, it allowed the sunlight to stream into the garage and reveal all five outward-facing lorries that formed Crossbow Transport's Northern Region. Parked closely side by side within the confines of the garage, their combined frontage matched the width, and height, of the doors that had now retracted.

Without giving it a second thought, Jackdaw climbed up into the unlocked cab of the centre lorry, his lorry, and picked up its key from where he had left it on the centre console. Under Larry's rules, all keys had to be left inside their unlocked vehicles in case any other driver needed to manoeuvre it in their absence. The main garage's alarm system was considered to be enough security to keep out any would-be thieves or vandals. Frank, when he was in charge, had always had a similar policy but, in his case, all lorry keys had been kept on hooks in his locked office, with each driver carrying copies of the office keys. In contrast, Larry had insisted that no-one except himself would have access to what was now his office and so the ignition keys were now left in the lorries instead.

Jackdaw turned the key and the large diesel engine fired into life. He had to wait until the loud buzzing of the air-brake low-pressure warning had stopped, and the gauge confirmed that sufficient air pressure had been built up, before he moved off. He slowly drove the large articulated vehicle the few yards out onto the forecourt and parked it clear of the garage doors. Its empty box-type semi-trailer was already coupled to the tractor unit, as he had left it on the previous Friday evening.

He filled out his start-time in the appropriate box of his driver's log and then, rather than walk around the vehicle, inspecting it for any obvious faults as he was meant to before every run, he just sat alone with his thoughts for a while. He thought again about the conversation of that last Friday evening at The Horse and Groom, and what it had revealed. Such thoughts had consumed him all weekend as he had replayed every word in his head and now his silent turmoil was causing his head to ache.

Even when he had first met him, he had immediately detested him. Since then, he had found it increasingly difficult to hide the fact and maintain his external composure. He had always had to carefully maintain a constant façade in front of all the other drivers in case his deepest feelings had been exposed to their scrutiny and possible interrogation.

Jackdaw had uncharacteristically managed to patiently wait until he had finally heard confirmation that he had always suspected the correct man. Everything had finally become clear to him and that had started the increasing pressure of his vengeful feelings to build over the weekend. Like the gradual rising of magma within an active volcano, the unstoppable eruption of his anger was imminent. He knew that it would inevitably be difficult, maybe impossible, to cover up, but he would not be able to live with himself if he did nothing.

He looked around the forecourt in front of him. His own car to his left, and Frank's uncoupled refrigerated trailer to his right. A thought suddenly struck him. If he were somehow able to lock his unsuspecting nemesis in there, how long would he survive? On any day other than a Monday, when it was always used for the abattoir job, it was usually left locked and idle for up to a week. However, that would mean him delaying any action for at least another day, and Jackdaw was not sure that he could now wait even that long.

He climbed down from the cab and walked back towards the garage, leaving the driver's door wide open and the engine still running. He did not care about the possibility of some opportunist lorry thief suddenly appearing from the bushes and jumping in to steal the valuable vehicle while his back was turned. They would not know that the trailer was empty, but the artic itself would still be worth a fair bit, if only for parts. If it happened, it would not be his problem and, besides, it would save him from having to drive the 450-mile round trip that he was now facing.

He closed, and secured, the massive garage doors from the inside, reset the alarm with the same four-digit code and walked out through the main entrance. Whilst locking that door he could still hear the rhythmic sound of his lorry's engine running and was disappointed to think that his lorry was still there, untouched. Even the criminals are asleep at this ungodly hour, he thought with an ironic smile as he walked back to the open cab door. Before climbing back up and setting off, he looked around the forecourt once more, at Frank's refrigerated trailer and at the front of the garage, with all its doors now closed again. He realised that he had now worked there for nearly four years. With such vengeful intent now incessantly burning in his heart, he knew that he definitely would not be working there for very much longer. It was time for him to act. Preferably before the day was over. He would work out the precise details of what he was going to do while he was out on the road.

Jackdaw uneventfully reached the motorway within fifteen minutes and joined it to head South, just as he had done on countless previous occasions. At such an early hour, the local roads had been mostly clear of other traffic and, initially, the motorway also had predictably far less people using it. So, as he drove further, he was more and more confident that there was little chance of him running behind schedule. Jackdaw always preferred this time of day for his professional driving. Having to sleep the previous night in the spare bedroom, with his alarm set at a time that his wife would, understandably, object to if it were to wake her, was a small price to pay.

Hold-ups and queues infuriated him enough when he was in a car. The cumulative effects of such delays when he was in his lorry could, because of those maximum permitted daily hours laws, mean the difference between being able to complete the job in time or not. He hated it whenever he was forced to spend nights in his cab in a layby or at a motorway service station. Whenever he had the option of an early start, like today, he could ensure that he got a few hours down the road, maybe even to his first destination, before the world and his wife woke up and started filling the roads. With such a head start on the commuters, he had a very good chance of getting back to his own depot before those permitted hours ran out. Laws or not, though, he was determined to get back today.

It was shortly after 9am when Jackdaw pulled into the loading bay of the factory and gingerly reversed his trailer to the loading dock that he had been advised of by the guard at the security gate. The factory worker standing at the dock whistled and thumped the side of the trailer with his palm, to indicate that he was in a satisfactory position, and so Jackdaw applied the handbrake and killed the engine.

He had suffered a slight delay on the short road between the motorway and the factory that was caused, he felt, by too many Southern commuters that could have surely left their cars at home and just walked their journeys quicker. Even so, as he filled in his timesheet, he was pleased to note that he was still ahead of his usual schedule for this particular run. He climbed down from the cab and stretched his aching limbs before walking the length of the trailer to greet the factory worker and have his first proper interaction with anyone that day. That did not include his loudly-expressed opinions of the questionable driving ability of so many of the car drivers, from his open cab window, during his southbound leg.

'Hi Jackdaw,' said the factory's foreman. 'Good run down?'

'Pretty good thanks Dave,' replied Jackdaw with a smile, successfully hiding the distracting dark thoughts coursing through his mind. Then, whilst handing the foreman his paperwork for checking and signing, 'I've got to take a big batch to your Preston depot apparently.'

'That's right, it's all here ready for you,' said Dave, waving his hand towards two rows of brown cardboard boxes that had been arranged on the dock earlier. 'We've had a crew putting them all together in the right order for Preston's system since daybreak.'

'I've not just got out of bed myself,' said Jackdaw, opening the large doors at the rear of his trailer.

'Yeah, but we've actually been busy here. Not everyone can sit on their arse all day listening to music and call it work.'

'These things don't load and unload themselves you know,' replied Jackdaw.

It was all light-hearted banter and said with smiles between the two who had known each other for years. This factory had always used the services of Wazzo Haulage, and now the successor Crossbow Transport, when their own distribution arrangements were stretched. That is, in as much as anyone could ever know someone else when they have only exchanged a few similar greetings during a loading session. 'How much help have I got today?'

'I can give you four pairs of hands,' said Dave.

Jackdaw was pleased to hear that. Including himself, that meant five men loading up his trailer and, with such cargo, that was probably the optimum number for the task. Fewer men would take longer and often, perversely, so would more, as they tended to just get in each other's way. He calculated that he should be away within the hour and then, with good road conditions and similar help to unload in Preston, he should easily be able to return to the garage with time to spare.

Dave waved over four of his workforce to assist Jackdaw with the boxes and signed the docket. He removed the carbonated third copy and folded it into his top pocket, whilst returning the remaining forms to Jackdaw. 'I'll see you later,' said Dave, as he walked to the adjacent loading dock to check on the progress of the preparations for the next lorry expected to arrive for its consignment.

Jackdaw and his four helpers formed a human chain into the open box trailer, with Jackdaw himself at the enclosed end. With the boxes passed along the line, and Jackdaw stacking them to the roof, the trailer gradually filled with the relatively light cargo. As Jackdaw had silently predicted, the loading was completed in less than an hour and the four helpers from the factory received his courteous thanks for their collective efforts.

The four disappeared through a side door, presumably to partake in what they felt was a well-deserved tea break, while Jackdaw closed the back doors of his trailer and walked up the right side of the artic to his cab. As he started the engine, he saw the foreman, on the opposite side of the loading bay, now supervising the unloading of some raw materials from another lorry. So, as he drove towards the exit and when he was near to him, he wound down the window and waved a farewell.

'See you next time Dave,' he called. However, with the vicious revenge that he had in mind for later that day, he knew that it was very unlikely that there would ever be a next time.

Jackdaw drove northwards back up the motorway towards the client's distribution depot near Preston, now hauling the latest load from the factory. He fully understood that the contents of his trailer would eventually be further divided and delivered from there to their nationwide network of shops, using the client's own smaller vehicles. In some instances, that would mean the goods would end up returning down the same stretch of motorway as he was now on, but heading South. Such logistical inconsistencies were not his concern. He was simply paid to load, unload and drive.

As the monotonous miles rolled underneath his wheels, Jackdaw quietly thought back over the pertinent events that had led him to his current violent thinking. After serving two difficult terms in Northern Ireland, he had bought himself out of the armed forces earlier than his original contracted length of service. That was where he had first learned to drive large vehicles. Since then, he had always enjoyed feeling like an important cog in the nation's supply chain of goods, rather than of weaponry. Like Frank, his first and only employer since his days with the military, Jackdaw had relished in the freedom of the open road once he'd had a taste of it. Unlike Frank, his temper could easily be fired by the slightest of traffic annoyances. That personality trait was not restricted to events on the road, either. Today, he fully intended to use another talent that his few years of serving Her Majesty had given him. That of unarmed combat.

After thinking of little else during the return drive North from the factory to the distribution warehouse, by the time that Jackdaw pulled into the loading bay on the outskirts of Preston, his mood was infinitely darker than it had been earlier in the day. Whilst unloading, he threw the boxes down the line of his second group of helpers with such force, anger and speed that the first receiving man dropped a box, with its fragile contents, more than once.

'Take it easy Jackdaw,' he said on the second occasion that

a package, probably now destined to become an item returned by a customer, hit the floor of the trailer. Jackdaw was single-mindedly only concerned with getting back to the garage and what he was going to do to the man who had destroyed his life.

The trailer was emptied quicker than it ever had been before and, without a further word, Jackdaw closed the doors on the empty trailer and just handed over the docket to the supervisor. The receiver of the delivery, puzzled at the unusual attitude of the driver, but just as silently, signed the carbonated paperwork and returned the top copy to Jackdaw.

Jackdaw ran back to his tractor unit and, with a quick check of his watch, knew that he should still be able to get back to Clayborough well within his driver hours. More importantly, he would be able to get back in time for the showdown that he planned.

13

Jackdaw turned off the main road and on to the approach to the forecourt of the garage. He could immediately see that the timing of his return could not have been better. The refrigerated trailer was stood in its usual position on the far side, meaning that Frank had already completed his Monday abattoir run. Furthermore, there were only two parked cars on the forecourt. That meant that everyone, other than himself and the object of his hatred, had finished work and had left for the day. There would be no witnesses.

Even so, by now Jackdaw's rage was blinding him to any possible repercussions for his intended confrontation. With or without witnesses, he would be easily identified as the one responsible for what was to come. He drove the lorry across the forecourt, past the cars, and turned it in a tight arc in front of the refrigerated semi-trailer. As he straightened up and accelerated towards the car that was parked next to his own, he felt in total control of his own destiny, for the first time in years.

The boot of the Audi crumpled like paper under the momentum of the lorry and the wrecked car lurched forward onto the grass beyond the concrete of the forecourt. Jackdaw stopped his lorry, jumped down from the cab and ran towards the garage which still had its massive doors wide open. Once inside he saw, as he had expected, that the other four lorries were parked in position, side by side and facing outward, ready for the next day. The space on the left of them, which had been left for his own lorry, was where the maintenance pit was, covered by the planks which Robin and James would have placed when they finished working.

Jackdaw reached down for the first plank and in the same movement as tossing it aside, under Magpie's lorry, he put his foot on the first of the revealed steps leading down into the pit. Grabbing the second plank, in front of his shin, he similarly disposed of that. He walked down the steps, and along the length of the pit, progressively removing each of the planks until it was fully open. Then he retraced his steps up and out of the trench and made for Larry's office door.

Without even trying the handle, he kicked his boot at it and the door swung open. The rotten wood of the door frame had easily splintered away from where the dead bolt had been. Larry, who had been deep in concentration, had heard neither the recent fate of his car nor the extraction of the planks from the maintenance pit. He had been sat behind his desk, contemplating the papers relating to the next day's collections and deliveries. His head shot up in surprise at the sudden intrusion.

'Jackdaw! What the fuck are you doing?'

'You bastard,' said Jackdaw, as if that explained it all.

'What?' asked an incredulous Larry.

'Karen,' Jackdaw said, again expecting his superior to understand.

'What about her?' asked Larry, as he began to wonder how one of his drivers could know the name of his secret lover.

He knew that he had certainly not referred to her by name at any time during the Friday night at The Horse and Groom, straight after he had just spent a passionate hour in bed with her.

'My wife, Larry. Do you think you can get away with shagging my wife behind my back and making a big joke of it in front of me and my friends?'

'Your wife?' For the first time, Larry realised just whose toes he had been treading on. 'How was I supposed to know she was your wife? I just met her in a pub on a Friday night. The first Friday after I moved here. She was alone and seemed lonely. All she told me was that her husband was out of town most days, working, and he always went out with his mates to another pub on Fridays. Besides, she said that her husband's name was Mark.' Even as he said it, Larry suddenly understood where he had missed the chance of making the connection before now. Jackdaw's real name was Mark. Larry had only been told it once, on his first day in the job. However, as no drivers used their real names in the confines of the garage, he had never thought of him as such.

'Look, Jackdaw. Mark,' said Larry, almost pleadingly. 'I didn't know. Honestly. Let's just talk about this like two reasonable men.'

'But I'm not a reasonable man, Larry,' said Jackdaw with a sudden manic look in his eyes. 'That, I am told, is part of my problem. Does your blazer feel a bit loose?'

Larry was taken aback by the unexpected question about the garment that he was wearing.

'You see,' continued Jackdaw, 'mine is a bit tight under the arms. At least it has been for the past week.' He pointed a finger at one of the armpits of the matching blazer that he wore himself. 'Last Monday it was a really warm day and I'd forgotten to wear it for work. So, knowing how much of a stickler for the rules you are, I called home for it as I drove past my house before getting back here. I found what I thought was my blazer in a crumpled heap next to the bed. My bed, Larry. But it was your blazer next to my bed wasn't it. Now why would that be? I thought it was strangely tight at the time, but I just put it down to a bit too much beer at the weekend. When you shot out of here, heading back to my house, you even almost drove into me on the forecourt. You hoped to get there before me and get yours back, but you ended up with my one. She eventually found it in the wardrobe for you. Remember? She's told me all about the pair of you and how she hadn't even realised that we worked at the same place until you showed up in your blazer that day. We had quite a few discussions on the subject over this weekend, in fact. I know everything now, and now you're going to pay.'

With that, Jackdaw launched himself across the desk and punched Larry full on the jaw. Immediately dazed, Larry fell back off his chair against the far wall and tried to regain his balance. Jackdaw had already steadied himself on Larry's side of the desk, though, and followed his initial attack with a rapid jab of his elbow into the bridge of Larry's nose. As Larry attempted to speak, he formed bubbles in his own blood that was now running profusely from his nostrils.

Jackdaw jabbed his stiffened fingers upwards into Larry's solar plexus, under the breastbone of his ribcage, temporarily paralysing his diaphragm and causing him to collapse to the floor, gasping for air. Jackdaw then, slowly and calmly, bent down and grabbed a handful of Larry's hair at his crown lifting him onto his knees with the strength of a man possessed. Larry was dragged around the desk and out through the shattered door into the expanse of the garage as he gradually regained the ability to breathe. Next to the open maintenance pit, Jackdaw finally released his enemy, who groggily got to his feet to face him.

As Larry attempted to say something through the blood that covered his mouth, Jackdaw ignored his pleas and took a swift large stride to his right and then kicked out sideways, and low, with his left leg. The vicious karate kick to the outer edge of Larry's left knee shattered his leg and he keeled over again, screaming in pain.

Jackdaw reached down and grabbed the lapels of Larry's company blazer. The same blazer that had originally been issued to Jackdaw when Crossbow Transport had first taken control. Pulling his adversary up so that his nose was just inches from his own, Jackdaw shouted directly in his face 'You think you can come in here with your flash motor and trample over other people's lives? You're just scum Mason'.

With that, and still holding the lapels, Jackdaw quickly twisted his body so that his back was towards Larry. With a well-practised bend of his upper torso and a thrust of his hip, he raised Larry over his pelvis, somersaulting him into the pit. The standard judo throw was designed to place someone on their back on a floor. Instead, with the tumbling of Larry's body into the depth, it was his right ankle that hit the ground first, breaking with a sickening crack, before his head also bounced off the side wall.

Jackdaw looked down at Larry lying motionless at the bottom of the pit. At first, he thought he may have killed him, but then he noticed the rise and fall of Larry's ribcage as he unconsciously drew breaths. Without taking his eyes off his adversary, Jackdaw slowly took off the tight-fitting company blazer that he had been forced to wear all week.

'Consider that as being my resignation,' said Jackdaw as he tossed it down on top of the beaten man and walked out of the garage to his car on the forecourt.

14

James was astonished to be confronted with the sight when he arrived for work the next morning. Two police cars were parked alongside one of the lorries which itself was parked at an unusual perpendicular angle on the forecourt. There was superficial damage to the lorry's front bumper, but Larry's smashed car sat five yards in front of it, on the surrounding grass. As he drove closer, he recognised the lorry's registration number as being Jackdaw's.

He parked where he could and walked to the open garage doors, through which he could see that none of the other four vehicles had yet left for the day. Five of his seven workmates stood together, all in their company blazers, and there were three uniformed policemen stood slightly to the side and talking amongst themselves.

'What's going on?' asked James to the group.

'We've had a break-in,' said his bearded mentor in his full Geordie accent. 'Looks like The Great Bustard was still here and disturbed them. They beat him up pretty bad and dumped him in the pit. Raven found him first thing when he arrived.' The man with the sideburns nodded from behind Robin and moved forwards.

'I called an ambulance, obviously,' continued Raven, 'and they've taken him to the hospital. He should be okay, they say, even though he's still unconscious. Not sure what they hoped to get, though,' he said looking around the garage. 'All your tools are still here and the trailers are all closed up. They took Jackdaw's lorry but, as you can see, they didn't get very far in it. Not even as far as the road.' He indicated the scene on the forecourt. 'I always said it was a stupid idea to leave the keys in the cabs. I guess they found out the hard way that they didn't know how to handle it after all. There was nothing in it, anyway, and all they've done is make a mess of The Great Bustard's car.'

'Strange thing is, there's no sign of Jackdaw so far, even though he was due to be away from here more than thirty minutes ago,' added Magpie. 'These cops have talked to all of us already, not that we know anything more. They were waiting for you and Jackdaw to get here to see if you had anything worth adding.'

'Well I don't know anything else,' said James to both the group and the policeman who was now approaching. 'I left at the same time as Robin and that was before Jackdaw got back here anyway. Before Frank, too, in fact.'

James repeated his short testimony for the policeman as he wrote the details, including approximate times, into his notepad. As he did, another man appeared who James had not noticed until that moment. Since before James's arrival, he had been dusting for fingerprints in Jackdaw's cab. He had also performed the same duty in the disarrayed office before that.

The police were satisfied for now and had other calls to answer. They prepared to leave and simply asked the group to get the remaining driver, the one who would normally drive the lorry that was nearly stolen, to be in touch when he did finally make an appearance. Although the focus of their enquiries would fundamentally change as soon as Larry Mason regained consciousness and gave them his version of events, the attempted burglary explanation was, for the moment, the most plausible.

With Robin, James and the four drivers also oblivious of Jackdaw's assault, they unanimously decided how to proceed. Raven, Magpie and Sparrow would each get out on the road immediately. Robin and James would prepare for the arrival of their first maintenance job. Frank, as the former head, was the one nominated to make the difficult phone call to head office to advise them of what had apparently happened. Hopefully, it would then be the responsibility of someone else at head office to phone the day's waiting clients to explain the situation, as minimally as they could. They could be left to apologise profusely for the minor delays, and assure the clients that their transport was already on the way to them. As for Jackdaw's scheduled client for that day, they would probably have to be compensated somehow. Even though his lorry looked to be serviceable, Jackdaw still wasn't there to drive it and Robin, even though he could, was needed at the garage for the servicing.

By the time Frank emerged from the office, the three other drivers had left, leaving just Frank's lorry in the garage. Robin had collected up the scattered planks from the pit and James had made some tea.

'They weren't happy,' Frank said to the pair.

'Hardly surprising,' replied Robin.

'They're sending up a relief manager to take The Great

Bustard's place for a while. Should be here sometime tomorrow.'

'They can't just leave us alone to get on with it, then?'

'Apparently not. Doesn't bother me, though. I'd rather be out on the road than sat in that poxy office all day answering moaning phone calls, which is what I was afraid they might suggest. Speaking of which, I'm already two hours late.'

Frank opened the door of the remaining lorry and climbed up into the cab. This morning was the first time that James had seen Frank since their social evening at The Horse and Groom. When James had arrived for work the day before, Frank was already out with his refrigerated trailer. After James's work was completed, he had left with Robin, long before Frank's return. When Frank had eventually got back, he had uncoupled his refrigerated trailer before reattaching his usual one in the garage. After that, he had gone home himself, leaving Larry alone in the office with just Jackdaw still left to return.

James now silently watched the back of Frank's ginger-haired head as he climbed in and shut the cab door behind him. Once he was ready to leave, Frank turned, smiled and waved as he pulled the lorry forward and across the forecourt, swinging around Jackdaw's abandoned vehicle before heading for the exit. James waved and smiled back when he knew that Frank was looking at him, but his hand dropped to his side and his mask of an expression morphed into a hateful stare as the lorry pulled away.

James had never reviled anyone as much as he did Frank. For years he had despised even the thought of him being alive, somewhere. He had also recently heard, first hand,

Frank's flippant recollections of the events that had turned his life upside down. With such a total lack of any responsibility felt by Frank for the fatal accident in Hartview twelve years before, James's hatred had deepened even more.

James watched Frank's lorry disappear from sight and thought about the family he had lost that night, including the father he had adored. He was working at Crossbow Transport for only one purpose and he knew how near his years of planning now were to completion. He was finally close enough to his nemesis to be able to get his full revenge, sometime soon. During the years since the accident, he had kept his father's memory alive by always insisting, to everyone, that he wished to only ever be referred to by his middle name instead of his first. His middle name that had been the same as his father's first.

James's actual christened, full name was Paul James Pearce.

15

It was mid-afternoon when the garage phone rang once more. As he had been doing all day, Robin interrupted what he was working on and rushed to the office to answer it before it stopped. When he returned to the pit, a few minutes later, his ashen expression told James that it had not just been another irate client or head office wanting to check a few facts.

'That was the cops,' Robin told him. 'The Great Bustard's woken up and talked to them. He seems okay, apart from a couple of broken bones.'

'So why the sour look?'

'It turns out that it wasn't a burglary at all. It sounds like Jackdaw totally lost the plot and went for him, for some reason. It was Jackdaw that beat him up, not some intruder. I guess that explains why we haven't seen him all day. The cops have already pulled him in and charged him with GBH and criminal damage, or something like that. They say that they'll want to talk to us all again here in light of this, as they put it, new evidence.'

James was deeply worried about this new development. He had no feelings, either way, for either Larry or Jackdaw but he could do without the police looking more closely at the operation and the people who made it up. His own plans involved more than simply giving Frank a beating. He intended to kill him, and hopefully by making it look like a simple accident. With them being mistaken about the apparent facts once already, the police might be suspicious enough to look a little too deeply into any second incident involving the garage so soon afterwards.

He could not afford to wait until a later time, though. He knew that the longer he stayed working at the garage, the more likely it was that his false, untraceable National Insurance number would be discovered. Each passing day increased his chances of being found out. Robin's words rocked him out of his train of thought.

'I suppose I'd better move Jackdaw's bruised lorry in here and out of the way, then. I doubt it'll be going anywhere soon.'

'After that I presume it'll be time for a brew,' said James, forcing a smile to disguise his worried thoughts.

'Aye, it certainly will.'

As he waited for the battered kettle to boil, hearing the reversing of Jackdaw's lorry outside, James agonised over what he should now do for the best. He was not a qualified car mechanic as he had always claimed and it was surely only a matter of time before that was exposed. That was not a heinous crime in itself, and the worst he could expect would probably be to be sacked on the spot. Alternatively, if he left the job of his own accord now, it would leave no suspicious trail and he would still be within reach of his objective. However, he mused, he would never again be in such a good position, on the inside, to be able to execute his scheme.

At least he was now certain that he had finally found the correct target. The lorry driver involved had only been referred to as a Mr F. Bird in the 1965 inquest report and, for many years, that was all the information that James had known about him. James had previously wasted six months tracking down, and eventually managing to befriend, Felix Bird, a lorry driver from the Midlands who regularly drank at a particular pub in the evenings. That time, James did not have the advantage of getting a job with the driver. He could only, apparently randomly, run into him in the pub occasionally. James had ensured that he was often in the same bar and he'd had to gradually check that man's personal history by using friendly, carefully crafted conversations over a few drinks.

Eventually, a significant revelation had suddenly convinced James that Felix simply could not have been the one involved in 1965 and that he had been tracking the wrong man. Felix had been in prison at that time. James had been fortunate enough to discover the man's effective alibi during their final meeting, before his plans had advanced beyond the crucial point. James never saw him again after that particular evening. Felix Bird did not go into that pub at all during the remaining two weeks that James had stayed in the area. James had needed to tie up some loose ends, but had still frequented the same pub each night, before returning home to start his searching again.

As the kettle switched itself off, James decided that he would only remain working at Crossbow Transport until the end of his second week, just three more days. After that, he would suddenly quit the job before his deceptions were revealed. He would reconsider his plans and wait for an alternative opportunity for his revenge. He would stay in the

Clayborough area, hopefully still in friendly contact with his former workmates, but able to keep well away from the scrutiny of the garage itself. Just three more days to see if he could still find a way to get close enough to Frank to be able to dispatch him in the manner he originally intended.

As it turned out, just one more day was sufficient.

Frank arrived back at the garage first, while Robin and James were still working, and reversed his lorry alongside Jackdaw's before parking it for the night. James successfully resisted the urge to reveal any of his inner thoughts as the ginger-haired man approached, simply smiling at him instead. It was left to Robin to explain the situation regarding Jackdaw and, when he had, it took Frank a few moments to digest the news.

'I wonder what made him attack him like that. I didn't particularly like him either. I know he came swanning in here like some sort of Emperor, pissing on everyone's chips, but I wouldn't have tried to beat the crap out of him over it.'

'Jackdaw always did have a bit of a temper on him,' said Robin. 'Maybe The Great Bustard just pushed a few wrong buttons after he'd had a bad day.'

'Perhaps. Anyway, changing the subject, I need to pinch your man for the day tomorrow. I've got a big load to pick up and I'll need someone riding shotgun to help me with it.'

James almost recoiled at the thought of having to spend any time alone with the one who had ruined his life. He was still trying to think of an answer when Robin interjected.

'No way Frank. I need him here tomorrow. We've got a lot of inspections coming in and I'll never get through them on my own.'

'If I don't get a hand,' explained Frank, 'I'll never get back here within my hours tomorrow night. I can't take any of the other guys with me as they've got their own runs to do. With Jackdaw now out of the picture as well, it's even more important that the others take their own lorries on the road.' There was still a little business thinking in Frank's head, it seemed.

'Why just tomorrow?' asked Robin.

'I've got to pick up a load from the fence panels place on the hill, but the guy who works there and usually helps out has called in sick this week.'

'That bloke is always crying off sick. I had to spend a day with you because of the same thing only two months ago,' said Robin.

'I know, I remember. Larry told me about it on Monday night before I left. He said it'd be okay to use James this time.'

'Well how convenient it is that Larry isn't here to back up your story,' said Robin sarcastically. 'What about at the unloading end of the run?'

'Actually, there's not a problem there. There's a couple of guys that can help at the other end. I just need the extra help at the pick-up.'

'How about a compromise, then? James can go with you and help you load up. I'll meet you there and drive him back here to help me once the pair of you have finished that part,' suggested Robin.

Frank thought about the idea and liked it. He was never particularly keen on having anyone with him in his cab when he was working. This way, it meant he would only have to put up with his necessary passenger for the half-hour or so it was going to take to get to the region's supplier of fence panels.

'Okay, that'll work,' he said and then, to James, as he walked off towards his car, 'I'll see you here at 5am.'

James, who'd had no input to the discussion, felt like a negotiated commodity. He was stunned that he had suddenly been ordered to be at work at such an early hour. Despite that, he kept his composure and realised that it was unlikely that he would get a better chance. This might just be the opportunity he had been waiting so long for.

The 4am alarm jolted James from his slumber but he successfully resisted the urge to just roll over and fall asleep again. As soon as he had sat up in bed and placed his feet on the floor, his head filled with clear thoughts of the upcoming day and what it might entail. It was the day that he had anticipated, and planned for, for twelve years. The day to start avenging his family.

In the ten minutes before he left for the garage, he found the inquest report at the bottom of his holdall and read it all. Wherever he had been, he had always kept it close. He had read it countless times over the preceding decade, ever since he had managed to obtain a copy. By now he could probably recite its contents verbatim, in the same way as an actor might recall a long speech from a script. As was usual, he paused at the paragraph that had always confused him on the third page and the same burning question entered his thoughts. He read on and felt the rising anger as he read the sworn testimony of the lorry driver.

As he drove onto the garage forecourt, he saw that Frank had already driven his lorry out of the garage and was at that moment securing the large garage doors behind it. Although wearing his official blazer, Frank was easily distinguishable from the others, even at that distance, by his distinctive ginger hair. James looked over at the man that he hated more than anyone as he parked his Capri next to Frank's car on the edge of the forecourt. The overnight rain had re-formed the mud puddle and he was pleased that he did not have to negotiate that on this, of all mornings. He took a deep breath as he got out and locked his car, forcing himself to appear, sound and act in a normal way.

'Morning Frank,' he shouted across to the senior driver.

'You're only just in time,' Frank called back curtly. 'Jump in then,' he continued, pointing his finger down the length of the nearside of the artic.

James reached up to the door handle on the passenger side of Frank's lorry and climbed in as Frank entered from his side. When they were both seated, Frank removed three cans of cola drinks from a bag behind his seat and placed them between them on the centre console. At first, James thought he might be being offered one, but then he realised that Frank had not said anything and all three had been positioned on Frank's own side of the console. He concluded that Frank must simply have a liking for fizzy drinks when driving and was not generous enough to share. Not that he wanted to be offered anything by this horrible man, anyway.

The engine had been running ever since the lorry had first driven out of the garage and so Frank now just put it into gear, released the handbrake and drove them towards the exit. That handbrake was just a small lever, a few inches long with a sphere on the end of it, the size of a golf ball. It operated an air valve which disengaged the lorry's parking brakes. The handbrakes on lorries were totally different to those on a car. On a car, a handbrake lever pulls on strong cables to apply the brakes. The higher and harder the lever is pulled, the greater the brake pressure. On lorries, equipped with air brakes, it was simply a case of the brakes being fully on, or fully off, controlled by a short lever that can only sit in one of two possible positions. The footbrake, whilst also operating air valves, did have a similar effect to a car's. Greater foot pressure resulted in more-open valves and, thus, stronger braking. Unlike a car, where the system contains hydraulic fluid, there was no resistance to be felt underfoot in a lorry. It was possible to depress the pedal all the way to the floor, resulting in the wheels locking up.

Frank turned on his radio-cassette and the loud music of Queen, coincidentally James's favourite band, filled the silence. He turned left out of the exit from the garage and on to the main road, suddenly talking to James and shaking him from his thoughts about the braking system.

'So, how are you finding the job and working with Robin?'

James was in no mood for small talk, especially trying to make himself heard over Brian May's unique guitar sound, but he realised it would seem odd to not respond and chat as expected.

'Yeah, it's going great,' he shouted back. 'Robin is quite a character too.'

'I met him in a pub a while ago. Luckily, I was looking for a good mechanic at the time,' he lied, or misremembered. 'Turned out that he was available.'

'He's a good mechanic and a good tutor,' said James.

'Don't you want to actually drive lorries rather than just fixing them up?' asked Frank.

James, given his personal history, could not think of anything worse for him as an occupation. 'Maybe,' he lied. 'One day.'

'It's not for everyone,' said Frank. 'The only job in the world where you can get into trouble for working too fast or for too long.'

They continued talking for just a further ten minutes before their conversation petered out and the atmosphere in the cab was totally dominated by Frank's home recording of the *A Day At The Races* album. James heard Frank occasionally singing along to well-known chorus lines but tried his best to detach his thoughts from the presence of his companion.

In contrast to the volume in the cab, they drove along the eerily quiet morning roads towards the fence panel factory. James allowed himself to think more of the brakes and what he had originally planned throughout his teenage years. From the moment he had resolved to get revenge on the anonymous lorry driver who had torn his life apart, he had imagined himself tampering with the man's brakes to cause another fatal crash. He wanted to make the man suffer and die as he should have, alone, in 1965.

As a teenager, James had originally had visions of cutting an airline, or maybe damaging a compressor or air tank so that air leaked from the system. The insufficient pressurised air would surely disable the brakes, he had logically thought. He reasoned that would then result in a driver having no brakes at all, pushing his foot ineffectually to the floor while he and his heavy load careered helplessly down the road.

In reality, such scenes were uniquely the staple of action movies. The function of the air is actually to keep the brakes disengaged, not push them on. If too much air pressure is ever lost, the brakes get applied by virtue of a set of strong springs. A lorry will simply not move if the compressed air is not there. Even if a lorry is in motion when the air is suddenly lost, the brakes will engage and it just stops.

Since first discovering that, James had always found it difficult to accept, thinking that there must surely be a way to bypass this safety feature. However, last week with Robin, and having also closely studied air brakes for himself, he had come to the infuriating conclusion that there was indeed no way of simply sabotaging Frank's brakes in that way.

It had been the following day that he had realised that there was still a very simple alternative sabotage. An idea that had actually first occurred to him years before, but which he had originally rejected as it had always required him to be able to be legitimately in the cab of the lorry beforehand. Now he found himself in the cab, having even been personally asked to accompany the driver to a pick-up. This was his most perfect chance. He would not get another as good. Doing it the way he was now thinking would no longer be possible after leaving Crossbow Transport, as he was intending to at the end of the week. It was those details that were running through his mind when Frank suddenly did something that made James's blood run cold.

16

The traffic lights at the junction ahead of them were red and Frank started slowing down, changing down through the gears. He had started slowing much earlier than James would have expected he might. When the lorry was down to about 5mph, Frank released the brake pedal and just let it chug along at that slow speed. As at most traffic lights, there was a black, pneumatic rubber tube running across the carriageway, about ten yards before the junction. As a car driver, even though he had noticed such hoses, James had strangely never realised their purpose. Very soon after Frank's wheels went over this air-filled pressure sensor, the lights started to change in their favour, firstly showing both red and amber. The instant that it did, Frank accelerated the lorry across the intersection, passing the solid white line of the intersection before the light had advanced to green. James rarely criticised anyone else's driving, but he was astounded at the move Frank had just made. He had been taught, rightly, that a red and amber combination still meant stop.

'That was a bit risky,' he said, as calmly as he could, hiding the realisation that was rapidly forming in his mind.

'Not really,' answered Frank. 'During the day, lights tend to work on a timer. When it's quiet, though, like now, they tend to change to where the traffic is. If I'd stopped, I'd have had to get this beast moving again from scratch, changing up through a lot more gears.' He paused while he changed gear, as if to emphasise the point. 'Doing that has saved me about three unnecessary changes of the very low cogs. Besides, it would have been red the other way.'

James was no longer listening. His thoughts belonged to twelve years before. He had always known that his father had driven past an amber light, not a red. A signal that had replaced green at the last second. He had seen it himself. There was also a passage in the inquest report that had revealed that those particular traffic lights had been shown to have a secondary problem. They had potentially allowed an amber light to be displayed in both directions simultaneously. Amber showing one way, when in the process of changing from green to red, whilst at the same time a red and amber combination, in anticipation of green, in the other direction. It had been ruled as irrelevant at the time of the inquest because of that sworn insistence, by Mr F. Bird, with no witnesses to say otherwise, that his light had been green for some time. The documented implication that his father had driven through a red signal had always haunted James. Now having seen, first hand, Frank's driving habit, James concluded with absolute certainty, for the first time, everything that must have really happened.

He was still assimilating his thoughts when he hardly noticed Frank slowing down again. With a large red brick house to his left, James watched Frank swiftly turn the steering wheel to turn off the main road and onto the road to their right. Almost immediately, they started to climb the hill that Frank had presumably been referring to when he had first mentioned the collection of the awkward fence panels. Frank alternated between high and low gears as he negotiated the incline.

'Welcome to The Cresta Run,' announced Frank.

'Why call it that?' asked James, shaking himself from his dark thoughts for a moment.

'Just try coming down here in the winter and you'll understand why.'

At the brow of the quarter mile winding hill was an open vehicle entrance. There was no barrier or security point, just a gap to drive through. So, they drove through it, without stopping or slowing, straight into the loading bay of the fencing suppliers. Frank swung the artic round in the available space and then slowly reversed his trailer towards the loading dock. James realised that his enforced time of sharing Frank's cab was nearly over. They had only been driving together for half an hour, maybe fifteen or twenty miles on the non-motorway roads, but, to James, it had felt like an eternity.

'I'll just sort the paperwork with those monkeys over there,' said Frank as he fully stopped the lorry. 'Then I'll be needing you to help load all those panels.'

Frank left James alone in the cab, while he carried his papers over to the side building bearing a sign which indicated it to be the office. James sat and thought about his situation. He was convinced that he would never again get as good a chance as this for his intended revenge. He was justifiably in Frank's cab and, without any way of disabling the brakes as a mechanic after all, as he'd always wrongly assumed he could, he was now within a short reach of using his simple alternative idea from so long ago instead. If he could jam something, anything, under the brake pedal, Frank would be unlikely to notice it whilst starting up. Looking ahead, at the exit to the loading bay, James reasoned that Frank would not need to touch the brakes at all until after he was heading back down that hill. The hill that he had called The Cresta Run. Rather than the complication of sabotaging the braking system itself, this would also be much more likely to appear as just an unfortunate cause of an accident. A cut airline or a punctured air tank, even if it would have had the desired effect, would immediately lay suspicion on the last mechanic to work on the vehicle. It was about as easy and perfect as it could get.

James then thought about the potential damage of an uncontrollable, runaway lorry. He had seen the results of Jackdaw's simple shunt of Larry's Audi, and had heard Raven's description of the unintentional damage he had caused to the Datsun Cherry. Could he now risk that there would not be an innocent party further down that hill, even on a quiet early morning such as this?

Further conflicting thoughts struck him. He wanted his own revenge, of course, and had always pursued it. The temporary move North, to Clayborough, to find Mr. F. Bird. The false CV and references. The fictitious, untraceable, National Insurance number. Applying for, and getting offered, the apprenticeship. It had all been for this one opportunity. It would avenge his father, mother and sister and they deserved his unwavering action. This was his chance to start to redress the balance. If he now lost his resolve and allowed Frank to live, Frank would undoubtedly continue to drive recklessly. It would surely only be a matter of time before he had another big accident. James hated the notion of another family having to suffer the same torment as he'd had at Frank's blood-stained hands.

It was now or never. He drew a deep breath and made his decision.

17

Frank was calling up at him from outside the cab.

'Come on lazy. Get your arse in gear.'

James climbed down from the passenger side and walked with Frank to the back of the trailer. Frank opened the rear doors and pointed across to the small mountain of nearby fence panels that they now had to load into it.

'That lot needs to go in here. Now you can see why I couldn't do it on my own.'

Without a further word between them, James moved to the first stack, followed by Frank, and the two of them started gradually filling the trailer with the wooden structures. An hour later, at 6:30am, the loading was complete. James was soaked with sweat caused by the exertion and was sat on the tailgate, whereas Frank showed no such signs of strenuous activity and had calmly walked back to the factory office to collect his paperwork.

'Now you know why I didn't volunteer to drive up here earlier and do it with him instead,' said a familiar voice, with a Geordie accent, from the corner of the trailer. 'That, and wanting a lie-in myself.' Robin seemed to have appeared out of nowhere but James realised that he could not have possibly seen Robin's approach from where he was sat. His only view was of the now-empty loading dock.

'Hi Robin,' said James. 'Frank's in their office. He'll be back soon.' He had only just finished the words when Frank suddenly returned, appearing at the other side of the trailer.

'Hello Robin,' said Frank. 'I could have guessed you'd show up as soon as all the lifting was finished.'

'It's a gift,' said Robin.

'Time for me to hit the road, then,' said Frank, jerking his thumb over his shoulder to indicate that James should get out of the trailer. 'Thanks for your help this morning James.'

James jumped down from the trailer and followed Robin to his car, which he had parked on the opposite side of the loading bay. Frank was left to close the tall, heavy trailer doors. As soon as James had closed the car door, Robin drove through the gate and down the hill, heading back to the garage. Frank had not even returned to his cab when they left.

As Frank turned the ignition key, Freddie Mercury's singing picked up from the point that the cassette tape had reached when they had arrived and the engine had been stopped. However, it failed to completely drown out the sound of the buzzing of the compressor warning whilst the air tanks filled to the required pressure. As he waited the short amount of time before pulling away, he habitually picked up one of the two cola cans that were beside him and removed the sharp ring-pull. Tossing it out of the open window beside him, he looked down at the one remaining unopened can and deduced that James must have cheekily taken the third can for himself at some point. It was part of Frank's daily routine to drink a can of fizzy drink after loading, another once unloaded, and a third on returning to the garage. He always had to drink the contents of entire cans, in one go, and when stationary. The bouncing of a cab on the move, especially with a heavy load bearing down on the fifth wheel behind him, would soon discharge even a half-empty one. Today, he would have to forgo the final one, thanks to that thieving little sod.

The first can was swiftly emptied and, like the ring-pull before it, was discarded out of the window. The buzzing having now stopped and air pressure gauges showing all was well, Frank put the lorry into gear and released the handbrake lever. With such a heavy load in the trailer, he had to use all of the lowest of the twelve gears as he drove across the loading bay. He had reached third gear before reaching the exit opening. Changing to fourth as he drove though it, without stopping or even braking, Frank sailed over the brow of the hill to the start of his short Cresta Run down to the T-junction at the bottom.

He had built up enough speed and momentum by the time he reached the first slight bend that he needed to touch the brake, just to slow down slightly. However, as his foot tried to lightly press the pedal, he realised to his horror that it felt solid, with no movement in it at all. He instinctively pressed slightly harder as he pulled the wheel to the right, successfully staying on the road but still without any effect from the brakes.

Even without Frank touching the accelerator, the lorry started to gain speed due to the momentum of the weight it was carrying. Frank pushed down on the brake again, much harder this time and with as much intensity as would put the pedal to the floor, and lock the wheels, under normal circumstances. It only felt as though it moved a minimal amount, and that was still not enough to apply any braking.

The third can, firmly jammed under the pedal, had only slightly dented and was fulfilling its intended deadly purpose. As Frank approached the next slight bend to the left, still gaining speed, he could feel the panic rise and raised himself off the seat to push all his weight onto the intractable pedal. With still no effective braking, it took all of his strength to pull the wheel to the left and continue to follow the road round.

He desperately tried to slow down by changing down through the gears but, because of the incline and the heavy load, the clutch depression actually allowed the lorry to freewheel and increase its speed slightly. Even so, he managed to force the gear lever into a lower position, against the resistance of the synchromesh transmission. The engine screamed in protest at the mismatched gearing revolutions that he had enforced, and he instinctively knew that it probably would not be possible to change down again until the lorry had slowed some more by other means.

All that now remained straight ahead of him was the T-junction and the red-brick house at its apex. He stamped down three times on the brake pedal, but still the unseen, defiant can resisted. Through the panic he somehow suddenly remembered the basics of air brakes and reached for the handbrake lever. When the handbrake lever was engaged, the powerful springs would apply the brakes and stop him. However, as he now pulled back on the short lever with his left hand, he found that too was somehow jammed. A short metal screw had been carefully left leaning against the lever a short time before. It had fallen down into the small space above the lever's pivot point when Frank had pushed it forward to release the parking brakes back at the loading dock. The screw was now lying in that space and preventing the lever from being returned to the applied position. Frank, with his terrified eyes firmly fixed on the road ahead of him, had no way of knowing that the simple obstruction was there.

With him frantically pushing down on the brake pedal and simultaneously pulling in vain at the lever, Frank now had thoughts of running the tractor unit against the low stone wall running alongside him in an attempt to slow it down. He tried, but it had little effect and he rapidly ran out of road. As the lorry careered across the T-junction and into the house directly opposite, Frank let out a frightened yell that no-one else could hear. There was no Austin 1100 to absorb the impact this time.

The collision crushed the front of the cab, throwing Frank forward and bending him double over the steering wheel which splintered under his weight and momentum. Similar to those fatal injuries that he had caused to James Pearce Senior years before, it was possible that this is what killed him even before his face was shredded by the exploding windscreen and his body was helplessly thrown into the brickwork of the house wall. The momentum of the laden trailer following behind sheered the fifth wheel assembly and the trailer's kingpin under the sudden force of the crash. It continued forward, crumpling the cab from the rear and forcing Frank's torso into an impossibly small space.

The subsequent post-mortem would be unable to determine whether it was the splintered steering wheel, the trauma to his front, or the crush from behind that had killed

Frank. All it would ultimately report was that death was commensurate with injuries sustained in the accident. Within a second, the entire heavy vehicle had halted, but the top of the tractor unit had been bent to a grotesque, unrecognisable shape. The fateful small screw had been thrown from its unsecured position at the base of the handbrake lever and onto the floor of the mangled cab. Even if it were to be found, no subsequent accident investigator would ever associate this random screw with playing any part in the incident. The unopened can of fizzy drink remained securely under the brake pedal which was now being tainted crimson red by Frank's blood.

18

Oblivious to the carnage behind them, Robin and James made the return journey to the garage noticeably faster than it had taken Frank's lorry to drive the distance in the opposite direction. James also saw that the traffic lights which had revealed Frank's dangerous habit earlier, were already in their favour as they approached them. He noticed, again, the rubber sensor strips which served to change the lights at non-busy times. James reflected that, although he had often seen such installations in the roads near to traffic lights, he had never properly understood their function until now.

Robin had thought that James had been uncharacteristically quiet during their drive back to the garage. When he questioned James about it, James had just said that he was tired because of both the early hour and the fact that he had already spent a lot of time doing heavy lifting that he was not used to. It was still before 7am, and the roads had still not filled, when they pulled on to the garage forecourt and saw the last, vacant parking positions that were available on the concrete. The drivers had all come since James's earlier arrival and were already out on the road in their lorries. With Larry still in hospital and Jackdaw possibly still in police custody, the parking facilities were adequate for all, at least for now.

'When the new boss gets here, he can have the bloody mud patch,' said Robin with a smile, parking at an awkward angle so that his car occupied both of the remaining two spaces. He had seen that the overnight rain had converted the improvised extra parking space to a quagmire once again. With everything else that he had been contemplating that morning, James had completely forgotten about the expected arrival of Larry's temporary replacement that day.

'Right,' said Robin, 'we've not got the first one due in until nine-thirty. So, you can either go back home for another couple of hours' kip, or you can make me another one of your excellent cups of tea and help me to set up here.'

'I might as well stick around as I'm up now,' replied James. The thought of returning to his rented room to sit alone, and reassess the thoughts and emotions that had been tumbling around his mind since he'd first woken, did not appeal to him. He knew that his landlord was out of town for a few days and so he would not have even had the chance to join him for a distracting chat over a breakfast, as he normally might. Besides, if the relief manager appeared before he returned, then James would inevitably be the one who would have to negotiate the small, muddy lake.

The expected arrival time of the relief manager had not been advised to any of them at the Northern Region of Crossbow Transport. At least, Frank had not mentioned any firm arrangement when he had first announced the company's intention to send him. So, Robin and James just spent their extra time, before the scheduled arrival of the days' first lorry to be serviced, drinking tea, opening up the inspection pit and casually ensuring that their environment looked reasonably tidy and professional.

It was approaching 10am when the new man finally did appear and they were both working on the lorry that had arrived at its earlier allocated time. The driver, like many others before him, had chosen to use the break that it afforded him to eat an early lunch at the nearby café, leaving Robin and James to it. It was James who first saw, through the open garage doors, the taxi pull on to the forecourt. He alerted Robin.

'Looks like we've got one who likes to be chauffeured around now,' said James.

Robin looked out from the pit, across the concrete that was at his eye level, averting his gaze from the head of his ring spanner that was, at that moment, loosening a sump plug. 'Bugger,' he said, as he realised that their new superior would not be stepping into the muddy waters after all. 'I was hoping he'd be looking like an idiot for his first impression with us lowly workers.'

'A bit like my first day, then?' said James.

Robin was about to try reassuring his apprentice when the sump plug, with a slight extra movement of the unwatched spanner, slipped off the last of its thread, and released warm oil over Robin's neck and shoulder.

'Shit!' exclaimed Robin as he quickly moved an oil bowl under the stream.

James, for all his suppressed dark thoughts of the day, could not help but collapse into fits of laughter. This was the scene that greeted Larry's temporary replacement. He was carrying the suitcase that he had brought with him on the train as the taxi pulled away from behind him. Robin climbed up the steps of the pit to at least be on the same level as the approaching man.

As they introduced themselves, Robin instinctively held his hand out to shake that of his latest superior. However, the other man declined Robin's oil-covered appendage with a smile and a wave of his own hand. As he had with James the previous week, Robin gave the new man a quick overview of the garage, and its history, and then he led him to the office. James, as much as he could, managed to keep mostly silent throughout.

After a few more minutes, and leaving the new man to settle into his adopted office, Robin returned to James. Just as he did so, they both saw a police car pull on to the forecourt.

'It's all action here today,' said Robin, expectantly watching the police car park alongside the line of drivers' cars. As the policeman got out and stepped into the puddle, Robin openly laughed at the sight of perceived authority looking foolish.

'He copped it,' said Robin, laughing again, this time at his own pun.

The policeman cursed under his breath and pulled on his flat hat with its chequerboard trim as he turned to face the open garage.

'He's one of those who was here yesterday, when Larry got beaten up and we thought it was a break-in,' said Robin, recognising the officer. 'Probably a load more silly questions that they want answering.'

James only had eyes for the approaching uniform and had not recognised the policeman. He sensed that the purpose of this visit had nothing to do with the assault on Larry just two nights before.

Still walking towards them, but close enough to be within earshot, the policeman loudly asked them which one was in charge of the garage. Even though it had been neither of them for only the past ten minutes, they were thankful to be able to direct him toward the office at the back. Neither of them particularly relished the thought of speaking to the local constabulary, under any circumstances.

It was very soon afterwards that an ashen-faced manager, followed by the policeman now holding his hat under his arm, reappeared from the office to include them in what he had just been told. Although only minutes into his new position, the relief manager now had to tell some of his new staff, and also report back to head office, that one of the Northern Region lorries had been involved in a serious accident. The driver, Frank Bird, who he had never had the opportunity to meet, had been killed and the lorry was badly damaged.

James and Robin's cheerful expressions dropped to match the shock and seriousness of that on the face of their boss.

'Where?' asked James, after a tangible silence while they each gathered their thoughts and digested the news.

'At the bottom of Threshers Hill, about twenty miles from here, apparently.'

'The Cresta Run,' whispered James, mostly to himself.

'Shit,' said Robin with an expulsion of breath. 'We were both with him just before he would have gone down there.'

'You were?' said the officer, immediately more alert and reaching, automatically, for the small notepad in his top pocket.

'He picked up a load from the fencing factory at the top. We'd both helped him because the panels are too big for one man to handle on his own.'

James did not contradict his mentor over the accuracy of his loose definition of assistance.

'We both left him to it after he was loaded up and came straight back here,' Robin continued. 'He couldn't have been more than a couple of minutes behind us.'

'I presume you didn't see or hear anything at the time?' said the policeman, frantically writing.

'Of course not,' shouted James. 'Like we would have just ignored anything like that, whether we knew him or not.'

'Calm down please sir,' said the policeman in a steady, unemotional tone. 'I'm just trying to ascertain the facts.'

'Sorry,' said James, and then, more composed, 'was anyone else involved? Anyone else hurt?'

'No, nobody, and no-one has come forward as a witness either,' replied the policeman. 'Our initial understanding is that the lorry seems to have run out of control down the hill, crashing into the house at the bottom.'

'Why would he lose control?' said Robin. It was not really a question, more a spoken thought, but the policeman answered it anyway.

'Early indications are that a full can of fizzy drink had rolled under his brake pedal and so he simply couldn't stop.'

'Aye, he always did drive with cans of drink next to him,' observed Robin after a moment of thought. 'One must have fallen over onto the floor without him realising.'

The policeman scribbled his notes to reflect Robin's supporting theory, and specifically his confirmation of

Frank's liking for canned drinks.

After giving the new manager the details of where the wrecked lorry was being taken and the next steps expected of him, the policeman offered his condolences and left the three stunned men to their thoughts. The manager continued probing the two mechanics for more details about Frank and his lorry, and superfluously asking them to repeat all that they had just told the policeman. Everything had already been said in his presence, but he was trying to delay the inevitable, awkward first phone call to head office. He would have to combine the report of his safe arrival at the Northern Regional Depot with the news that Frank had been killed whilst performing his working duties. Furthermore, one of the company's lorries had been badly damaged, probably past the point of viable repair, and required a thorough examination by the police. Already having been one driver down, in Jackdaw, The Northern Region would now be running at significantly lower capacity for some considerable time.

Eventually, he could delay the unavoidable no longer and retired to the office to make the call. At that moment, the driver from the Southern Region returned from the café to wonder why his servicing was not as close to completion as he had expected. As Robin started to explain the delay, James backed into a quiet corner and his private thoughts whirred around his head.

Frank Bird was dead. The man who had ripped his life apart was finally dead. James was secretly elated whilst having to force the outward appearance of being reverential about the man. As he had always planned and hoped for, Frank had died in a manner appropriate to his part in James's family's tragedy. It was the only reason that James was even there, in Clayborough and at that transport garage in particular.

If only Frank had perished that way, or any way, more than twelve years before, he mulled. He wished so much that Frank had died back then, sometime before 1965. Alone, and not with a family car crushed between him and his destiny. If he had, then James's father could have driven safely across that junction without Frank's lorry bearing down on him, and James's world today would be so very different.

19

The rest of the day passed in a numb blur for those at the garage and, as each driver eventually returned from their days' runs, they were also told the news. The end of the working day, and into the evening, was dominated by mourning thoughts of Frank Bird, for most of them. James, however, was consistently smiling to himself during his return drive to his rented room. He felt like a soldier with a mission successfully accomplished.

He had searched for years for Mr F. Bird, spending hours in the reference section of his local library and making various phone calls. All he had known was the initial and surname of the man behind the wheel of the lorry in 1965. Eventually, and by pure chance, he had discovered the name of Frank Bird as the owner, and director, of Wazzo Haulage Limited amongst the registrations of limited companies in the UK and it had immediately sounded so likely to be the right man. Fortunately, he had made his breakthrough just a month before the recent takeover by Crossbow Transport. If he had not made the connection when he had, amongst active company names, it would have been much more difficult, perhaps even impossible, to furtively track down his intended target.

He had temporarily relocated the 150 miles to

Clayborough, the same town as the organisation that he suspected was being run by the man he sought. However, once there and with somewhere inconspicuous organised to live, he had been unsuccessful when he had tried to surreptitiously find out any further details about the proprietor. After only a few days, he had realised that he would have to find some way to get even closer.

The timing and availability of the apprentice position had fallen perfectly for him. He had known a reasonable amount about general car maintenance as his cousin was a trained mechanic who had often helped, and guided, James to successfully keep his Capri serviced and on the road. So, he had produced an impressive, but entirely fictional, CV that told of a past in the motor trade, together with some false references. He had simply hoped that they would not even bother verifying any of his claims. After sounding knowledgeable enough during his interview, Robin had hired him on the spot and, exactly as James had predicted and hoped, had blindly trusted in what he had presented without feeling any need for further confirmation.

As he parked the Capri outside the empty house that he had shared with his landlord since his move to Clayborough, he felt the tensions of the day starting to manifest themselves as one of his migraine headaches. Although he knew his landlord was not at home, he did not take advantage of the solitary comforts of the lounge, as he normally might. Instead, after a brief detour via the kitchen for yet more paracetamol, he went up the stairs and straight into the room that had been his small domain since his arrival in the town.

In his room, he pulled down his holdall from the top of

the wardrobe and quickly packed it with the few items that he owned. It took him longer to write the two notes on some notepaper that he always kept beside the bed. With one intended for his landlord and the other for the man who had been his boss for less than a day, he wrote essentially the same thing to each of them. He sincerely apologised for the total lack of notice but explained that he had been urgently called back to his home town to help deal with a family emergency. Unfortunately, he would have to leave immediately and, furthermore, probably would never be returning.

For his landlord, he enclosed money equivalent to two week's rent within the note, folded once. Although he was only required to pay for a one week notice period, as agreed when he had moved in, he felt that he owed the man more thanks and respect than that. He would leave it in front of the carriage clock on the lounge mantelpiece on his way out. That way, his landlord would undoubtedly see it as soon as he returned home, expected to be sometime during the following day.

For the message to the garage, he added an addendum that, as he had not worked there long enough to reach even his first pay day, that he would like any outstanding wages that he may be owed to be given to Robin instead. That way, he figured, he could omit the need for any forwarding address, assuming they would indeed feel obliged to pay him anything at all after quitting so suddenly. The news would give the new man yet another problem to deal with so soon after his new appointment, so it could well be that he was forfeiting his unwanted wages anyway. Not that he had ever been interested in receiving any pay.

He genuinely hoped that Robin would benefit financially, though. He was giving him an undeserved big problem by leaving the maintenance and servicing function so short-handed again. He regretted that. He had really liked Robin and, although he had only known him for a brief ten days, would always remember him as a friend. One of the very few people that James thought of as such.

However, that alone was not a good enough reason for him to stay at Crossbow Transport any longer than necessary. The longer he stayed, the riskier his situation would become. The new boss might suddenly decide to check up on past references and the claims he made on his CV. Furthermore, if he was still working there when the monthly pay-day came round, his invented bank account number and his fictitious tax references would immediately highlight that there was something not genuine about him and shine the light of suspicion. James felt that he had no choice but to take the risk of his sudden disappearance potentially looking irregular, especially with it being so soon after Frank's sudden death and him being one of the last people to see him alive.

If he stayed a while longer, he may have still been there at a time when the police accepted that it was indeed an accident. That would be increasingly precarious, though, and he had no other reason to stay. He had meticulously planned the nature of the accident. Frank Bird was now dead. It was time for him to disappear.

Carrying his holdall, and having left the sanctuary of his small room for the last time, James left his front door key with the note for his landlord by the carriage clock. Being a Yale type, the front door locked behind him as he walked down the two steps to the garden path and out to the road. He tossed the holdall into the boot of the Capri and sat down in the driver's seat. He just had one more thing left to do in Clayborough, and then he would be gone.

The garage was locked and deserted for the night when James pulled onto the forecourt, parking his car next to Frank's refrigerated trailer. For the first, and last, time he used the key that Robin had given him on his first day to unlock the main door. As he passed it, he entered the four-digit security code to silence the alarm. The office door in the far corner was ajar as it had still not been repaired since Jackdaw's single kick, and James walked straight in to leave his hand-written resignation, and false explanation, on the desk. Without a second thought, he walked back across the garage expanse, across the planks of the inspection pit, reset the alarm and back out of the door.

Once it was locked again, he dropped the key through the letterbox for the first driver of the next day to find and walked to the Capri. He started the engine and drove away from the garage for what he knew would be the last time, turning left at the exit. The start of his 150-mile drive to Birchstead, his real home.

20

During the journey, James gradually felt the weight of his recent false persona lifting from his shoulders. James the experienced car mechanic was disappearing from the world forever. Even if an accident investigator was called upon to examine the wreckage of Frank's lorry, and found something suspiciously wrong, this James would have effectively vanished overnight. He was confident that the trail of forged references and personal history, combined with the false surname that he had provided, would simply lead them nowhere.

Three hours later James was driving down his street in Birchstead. His main car, his Mercedes with what he liked to think of as his personalised number plate, was still parked on the road outside his house. It was not the kind of registration number that would ever be immediately noticeable, or memorable, to anyone else. It simply included his initials, PJP, as part of the identification, along with three random digits and an extra single letter to indicate the year it was registered. For James, though, it had been enough reason for him to buy the car when he had first seen it for sale on a forecourt.

He had purposely left it in front of his house so that he could drive the Capri straight into his garage on his return. He had not wanted to leave the Mercedes in the garage and risk that the battery might have gone too flat to start it when he got back. He'd had no idea when he had left how long his lethal mission might have taken. Being unable to start the Mercedes in his garage would have forced him to leave his Capri, complete with its false plates, outside for a while. With his overly observant neighbours, that could have been disastrous.

After removing his holdall from the boot, he pulled down the garage door to hide his second car from view. As he did so, he looked down at the false registration plate on the back of the car. He vowed to swap that, and the corresponding one on the front, back to their true plates as soon as possible. He had seen the originals in the glow of his headlights, as he had driven in, still where he had left them on the floor at the far end of the garage. Once that little job was done, he would probably take the Capri to the nearest scrap yard anyway, as he had no further use for it. His Mercedes had been his main car for the past two years, after all.

Through an open window, he could hear the Westminster chimes from a clock owned by one of his neighbours as he inserted his front door key. So, without checking his watch, he knew it was 11pm when he finally walked back into the familiar environment of his home. He stepped over the accumulated letters on the mat, momentarily visible in the dim light from the street, and habitually turned on his hallway light before closing his front door behind him. He quickly looked into each room that was immediately accessible from the hallway and saw nothing out of place. The rooms were, unsurprisingly, exactly as he had left them three months before.

He would work his way through the waiting post in the morning, he decided. There would be nothing there so important that it could not wait a few more hours. He felt the toll of the eventful day, his recent long drive, and the tiredness caused by his early morning rise, all hit him and suddenly drain his energy. So much had happened, and changed, that day, yet he had hardly had an opportunity to take stock of it all. He dropped his holdall onto the lounge floor, sat comfortably down onto his sofa and, with his eyes closed, drew a deep, satisfied breath. He reminded himself that Frank was dead, crushed in the remains of his own lorry, and the thought of it brought a smile to his face once again.

He had another sudden idea, opened his eyes and moved to his case of vinyl albums in the corner. It did not take him long to find what he was looking for. His own copy of Queen's album, *A Day At The Races*. The same album that Frank had been playing in his lorry that morning. James had heard the familiar tracks during the entire drive to the fence factory and knew exactly where Frank's tape had stopped when he had parked in the loading bay. So, he now put on, and played, the second side of the album on his turntable. He sat back down, patiently listening up to the same point before musing that what immediately followed would likely be what Frank had started listening to as he had driven away straight after the loading. As *Good Old-Fashioned Lover Boy* broke into its first chorus, James calculated that it could well have been the music that would have been ringing in Frank's ears as he finally met his deserved end.

As the album continued to play to the end, James checked around his home. His house, and the Mercedes, had been paid for by the sizeable inheritance and life insurance disbursement that he had shared with his sister, Rebecca. It had been held in trust for them both until adulthood and had undoubtedly provided each of them with a reasonable start in life, financially at least. He would have traded it all, in an instant, to have all his family still with him, though.

After retrieving his toiletries from his holdall, he went to the bathroom to wash his face and brush his teeth before bed. As he looked at his own reflection, he decided that it would be safest for him to finally get his long hair cut short and maybe even grow a beard, or at least a moustache. He would go to the hairdressers on the corner first thing, even before swapping the number plates on the Capri.

Such a radical change to his appearance would hopefully prevent him from being recognised if there was ever a nationally issued photofit picture of him on the TV news or in the national newspapers. He could not discount the possibility that the police may yet suspect foul play and be desperate to trace him. Yet, as he had been gradually realising throughout the day, ever since the moment that the policeman had arrived at the garage to break the news, he would still be able to solemnly swear that he had nothing to do with it, if necessary.

He had certainly always hated Frank and, years ago, he had vowed to kill him one day. He had meticulously planned how he would murder him, and Frank had indeed died that day, exactly as he had always intended. However, James had to now painfully admit to himself that he had no recollection of placing the cola can under the brake pedal. He really wished that he did, if only to complete the picture for himself, but there was a definite gap in his memory. Whilst not actually providing him with a proper alibi, it did mean that he could truthfully claim, perhaps to a questioning detective in the future, that he could not remember anything of sabotaging the lorry.

The brain injury that he had suffered at such a young age had caused him numerous problems over the years. Frequent headaches and occasional blurred vision being just two of them. He had always suffered in silence. He had never admitted to having the symptoms to any doctor because then he would be unlikely to be allowed a driving licence, for one thing. Sat in his lounge that evening, listening to Frank's final Queen album, he concluded that there was now a new problem that could also be attributed to the hidden damage.

He could certainly remember looking across at the can while he had been left alone in the cab that morning. It had been on the centre console where Frank had placed it. He had thought, then, that it would be a perfect, innocuous choice of obstruction for him to put underneath the control. He remembered the doubts that had then crept into his mind, wondering if he really was capable of such an act and thinking of the potential damage a runaway lorry could cause to innocent people. He had thought about the Datsun that Raven had hit. He had remembered the state of Larry's Audi. He remembered considering that it was still very early in the day, with little else using the roads. After all that deliberation, though, he still had absolutely no memory of setting the trap. All he could remember was that turmoil in his mind just before Frank had suddenly called him down from the cab to start the loading.

There was, admittedly, an infinitely small possibility that it really had all been a coincidental accident. The drinks can really could have rolled under the pedal and into the very position that he had planned to put it, and on the very same day. However, that was all so unlikely as to not be a serious consideration. He simply must have been responsible, he concluded. It was just that his subconscious had erased all memory of his actions from his mind. Some kind of selective amnesia.

James had learned to live with, and compensate for, all the other problems that his head injury had caused. So, he should also be able to accept a very brief spell of memory loss. Frank, the one who was most responsible for the tragic turn that his life had taken, was dead. That was ultimately the most important thing.

Everyone must pay, and they must pay with their lives. He had so often repeated the phrase in his mind. It was his vengeful mantra. Now, he felt no remorse that one of them finally had.

PART THREE

1981

21

James awoke with a start to find that it was still quite dark, the dawn chorus outside only just beginning. The alarm of the Goblin Teasmade had roused him just as its kettle had boiled and it was now loudly playing the radio station that he always had it set to. He sat up in bed for a few minutes before reaching for the pot of tea that the appliance had automatically brewed for him during his final minutes of sleep. He poured half of its contents into the nearby mug that he had primed with some milk the evening before. The sudden rush of blood as he had been forced from his slumber had made his head start to ache, so he reached for the paracetamol that he still always kept next to his bed.

When the contents of the mug had cooled sufficiently, he swallowed one of the tablets with the first mouthful. To complete his morning ritual, he closed his eyes against the rapidly-increasing sunlight and leaned back against the headboard to relax for a few more minutes. He still held the half-empty mug near to his chest as he contemplated what the day ahead may hold in store.

The disc jockey on the radio was announcing the next song that he was about to play. James was immediately focused on the programme and smiled to himself. He reacted the same whenever he heard, or knew he was about to hear, any song by Queen. As well as still being his favourite band, it always, inevitably, made him think back to that day at the fencing suppliers. Even though he had never remembered anything of actually sabotaging Frank's lorry, he did not have any doubt that he had been responsible. Today's particular upcoming song was being introduced as 'a blast from the past' by the morning's DJ. *Don't Stop Me Now* had been released more than a year after Frank had died. However, ever since he had first heard it, James had always humorously thought that the title of the song might have formed a much more appropriate soundtrack for Frank's uncontrolled descent of the Cresta Run that day.

As the song faded out to be replaced by another, inconsequential track by another group, James put down the empty mug on the bedside cabinet and swung his legs out of his lonely double bed. He turned off the radio as he passed it, on his way to the bathroom. As he looked at his own reflection in the mirror above the basin, he was momentarily shocked to notice the absence of the moustache that he had become so accustomed to over the previous four years. He had shaved it off the evening before, having finally decided that it was no longer necessary for its original, intended purpose.

The feared, and anticipated, knock on the door had never come. Despite his sudden, unexpected, and possibly suspicious, departure from Crossbow Transport, there had been no nationwide manhunt. Not one that he was aware of anyway. No photofit images of his face, potentially composed from descriptions obtained from the 'birds', had been circulated via the press. He deduced that it must have eventually been ruled as a straightforward, tragic, fatal accident. Either the authorities had not looked close enough at the wreckage or, as he strongly suspected, and hoped, they had simply not suspected foul play in the first place. Even if they had, they had certainly been unable to trace him even after all this time. His efforts to conceal his identity had either been unnecessary or had been successful.

He had been extremely careful to cover his tracks just in case he had subsequently become a suspect. The false employment references and the fictitiously-claimed past work as a car mechanic had been necessary to secure the job as Robin's apprentice. Later, the false National Insurance number would have been an impossible lead for even the brightest of detectives to follow. Along with the invented surname and the fake number plates on the Capri, it had meant that all those at Crossbow Transport had effectively known nothing of his true identity and would not have been able to provide any helpful leads to trace him. As the weeks had flowed into months, he had begun to gradually rest easier until now, years later, he was confident that he had gotten away with the murder of Frank Bird.

Frank had not been the only one responsible for the fatal crash in 1965, though. There were others who had yet to meet their fate.

James dressed and left his house, pulling the door closed behind him until he heard, and felt, the familiar click of the Yale lock. He walked straight past his Mercedes, now beginning to show its age as far as the corrosion of the bodywork was concerned. There was a particularly distinctive rusted area on the front wing, about five inches across and humorously resembling the shape of Australia. One of his neighbours had even once commented that he had immediately recognised the car from that single feature when James had unknowingly, and coincidentally, driven past him along Oxford Street during a visit to London, over fifty miles away.

He also often had difficulty getting it started on cold mornings. As usual, it was parked on the road opposite his terraced house rather than in his garage, in the block to the rear. There was plenty of room for the car to be stored in the garage, as he kept hardly anything in it. The Capri was no longer housed in there, having been consigned to the scrap yard years before, but James still found it more convenient to just park on the road. That way, whenever he used the car, which was not that often, he would not need to be bothered with the unlocking, opening, closing and locking up of a garage door each time. Today, being a Sunday involving alcohol, he had no need for the Mercedes.

Within five minutes he reached the house where he had lived as a child, at least until just before his thirteenth birthday. He paused and stood outside, as he did whenever he passed, unable to see in but just looking at the net curtains that had been chosen by the current owners of the property. He imagined himself inside, firstly as a child, playing with his various toys on the lounge carpet, so close to the other side of those curtains. Toys that he may possibly have received for his thirteenth birthday if he had not been consumed with grief and attending the funerals of his family around that time.

Then he imagined an alternate version of himself in the

present, where he would perhaps be visiting his parents, still living in this same house on this day. What additional family memories would he have had to look back on from all those missed years? Without his all-consuming quest he might have met someone to settle down with and have had children of his own by now. This very Sunday he might have been bringing them to visit his own parents, their grandparents. Brenda, his older sister may have had her own children too, and purposely coincided a visit of her own so that they could all have a day, or at least a morning, together. The potential for all of this had been cruelly ripped away from being reality, James's reality, by the actions of Frank Bird and the others.

James wiped away the uncontrollable tear from his eye and walked on to the bus stop. He had often wondered what his life would have been like without the heart-breaking events of 1965. Each time he saw the house, it invariably channelled his thoughts down the same path. He and Rebecca, his younger sister, had been taken in by Uncle Ray after the accident. His parent's house had been sold. There had just about been room for them all at Ray's, but Auntie Bea had been unable to cope with the extra strain on her fragile relationship with Ray. She had apparently found the new situation even more intolerable and had left him, and his expanded family, within six months.

James had shared a bedroom with his older cousin, Tom, for six years until Tom had found a place of his own and moved out. James had been eighteen, and Tom was twenty-three, at the time. Rebecca had always had the smaller, third bedroom, and they had both continued to live with Ray until Rebecca was also old enough to receive the inheritance and insurance payments from their parents' estate. Although he loved Ray, and fully appreciated what the man had forfeited for him, James had bought, and moved out to, his own house soon after. At the same time, he had bought the second-hand Mercedes with the original intention of replacing the Capri that he had owned for a year. After thinking more about that, he had retained both cars for a while, having realised that the Capri might serve a worthwhile, more inconspicuous purpose in the future.

The number 18 double-decker bus appeared from around the corner and James flagged it down by raising his left arm to the customary outstretched, horizontal position. After paying his fare, he settled back for the ten-mile journey which, allowing for routing away from the most direct roads and stops to pick up passengers, he knew would take around forty-five minutes. It was impossible to sleep on the loud, rattling bus, but he kept a relaxed position with his eyes closed for most of the journey, avoiding the need for any eye contact with his fellow passengers. When it finally arrived at the town which was his destination, he got up and made his way to the door, indicating to the driver that he wished to get off.

As the bus pulled away without him, from the bus stop at which he now stood in the small town of Hartview, he zipped up his bomber jacket against the cool breeze and strode down the street towards his girlfriend's house. His customary two taps with the door knocker was soon answered, and the front door swung open to reveal the smiling brunette, with her typical 1980s bubble perm, who he had met two months before.

'Well now, that is a bit of a change,' Sue said, referring to the lack of facial hair above his top lip.

'I told you it was coming off, so I got out the garden shears and set about it,' replied James.

'Makes you look younger somehow,' she continued, stepping back so that he could step into her hallway. 'I think I prefer you without it. What made you grow it in the first place?'

'Just thought I'd have a very quick experiment to see what it looked like at the same time as I suddenly decided to have my hair cut short, about four years ago,' he answered, only partly truthfully, as she led him into the lounge. Then, deflecting the subject as they both sat on her sofa, 'so, how have you been?'

'Oh, you know. Same old routine at work all week, constantly dreaming of the weekend. It's a shame you were busy last night and couldn't come round. I really wanted to see you, and you could always have stayed over to save you setting your alarm this morning.' The tone, the smile and the twinkle in Sue's eyes confirmed the meaning of her words. It would not have been the first time that he had accepted the hospitality of her bed, but he'd had other things on his mind the previous night and had wanted to be focused.

'Couldn't be helped, I'm afraid. Just a bit of business that couldn't wait,' he said, non-specifically.

'I could always have come over to your place instead, to be there with you when you were finished with whatever it was,' Sue suggested.

At this, James felt he was being pressured and so he tensed slightly. Sue had never been to his house in Birchstead, nor even knew precisely where he lived, and he wanted to keep it that way. He wanted to avoid the potential complications of her suddenly appearing, unannounced on his doorstep one day.

'You wouldn't say that if you'd seen the state of the flat where I live. It's an absolute hovel,' he lied, 'and the three piss-artists that I have to share with aren't particularly civilised company. You really wouldn't like it there. I much prefer coming here to be with you.' It was all a believable excuse for never inviting her to his home, and Sue accepted it at face value.

'Speaking of company, Julie will be back any minute,' said Sue, getting off the seat and making her way towards the kitchen to put the kettle on. Sue had shared the house with her older sister ever since they had bought it together the year before. They had realised that each on their own, with their respective modest salaries, were unable to afford much from the rapidly-rising property market. That was even with the generous mortgage offers that were available.

'What time are you meeting him today?' Sue called back from behind the kitchen door where she was filling the kettle with enough water for three mugs.

'Not until half-twelve,' said James, realising that meant he had two hours with Sue before meeting Richard in the Queens Head pub that was only ten minutes' walk away. 'So, we've still got a little while to do anything you may want to do,' he said, in the most suggestive voice he could muster.

'Don't go getting any fancy ideas,' shouted back Sue, crushing his rising libido in an instant. 'I told you that Julie will be back any moment. She's only gone up to the paper shop. It's one thing you staying here overnight occasionally, when we can shut my bedroom door, but even I think it's a bit much to risk her walking in on us, bonking on the sofa on a Sunday morning.'

James had always found her forthright approach to be refreshing. He had met her in the Queens Head, the same place where he now planned to meet his recent friend, Richard, for their regular Sunday lunchtime drinks. It had been early on a Friday evening, when the bar was already quite full of patrons and all of the tables had been occupied. James had luckily managed to secure one of those tables and that was where he had been sitting alone, with his first drink, waiting patiently for Richard to arrive. Sue and her sister, Julie, had appeared, having called in for some drinks themselves, straight after work. The only remaining, available seats had been at James's table. They had politely asked if they could use the two chairs opposite him and, as that would have still left the fourth seat unused, and therefore available for Richard, he had offered them gladly. As was confirmed later, he had correctly estimated that they were both in their mid to late twenties.

After a brief expression of thanks, Julie had sat down while Sue had turned to retrace her steps to the bar to get the two of them some drinks. James had immediately noticed that Sue's very tight-fitting jeans showed off, and complemented, her curvy figure exquisitely. Without properly thinking about any potential consequences, he had involuntarily made one simple, quiet remark under his breath. An openly expressed thought, as he had an unfortunate habit of doing sometimes, that had really only been intended for his own ears.

'Just how do you get into a pair of jeans like that?'

Sue, with her impeccable hearing, had heard the candid remark and had quickly spun back to face him. He had thought he was about to be given a mouthful of abuse for his chauvinistic attitude. Instead, she had just smiled and said 'well, for a start you could try buying me and my sister a drink.'

With the ice broken, and genuine friendliness all round, James had readily left both women at the table while he had forced his way to the crowded bar to purchase their requested drinks. At his turn, he had ordered those, together with a refill for himself and one for Richard who was, by then, expected imminently. Richard had finally arrived after James had ordered, but while he was still waiting for the four drinks to be prepared.

'I think I may have pulled for us tonight,' James had said, confusing, and exciting, Richard immediately. By the time the two men carried two drinks each back to the table, Richard had been fully briefed of the situation and was full of smiles and eagerness for the unexpected female company.

Although things had been friendly enough, Julie and Richard had simply not found a romantic connection, and nothing more had come of that evening for them in that regard. James and Sue, however, had gotten on very well for the remainder of the night and had agreed to see each other again later in the weekend. Straight away, James had known that she would be perfect and, ever since, he had often been catching the number 18 bus to see her in Hartview.

22

When Julie returned from the local paper shop, her mug of tea was already waiting for her on the small table in the centre of the lounge. Sue had sat back on the sofa beside James and was comfortably leaning close to him with her feet up on the remainder of the far cushion.

'Hiya James,' Julie said as she entered. At maybe an inch shorter than her younger sister, Julie sported the same, fashionable bubble perm as Sue. James thought that the style suited Julie's blonde hair slightly better than Sue's darker locks, but he knew better than to ever say such a thing to either of them. As Julie sat opposite the couple, on the armchair, with the mug on the table between them, she suddenly noticed the different appearance.

'It's gone,' she exclaimed with a smile, pointing at James's bare top lip. 'You finally shaved it off.'

'Yes, I thought it was about time.'

'Makes you look younger,' continued Julie.

'Sue said that,' said James, smiling at his sofa companion.

'Yeah, makes you look about forty instead of fifty,' joked Julie, knowing that James was still on the younger side of thirty. 'I never understood what made you think your nose was so special that you had to underline it anyway.'

Sue laughed, almost snorting the latest mouthful of tea

through her nostrils. James laughed at the remark as well. It was the kind of light-hearted banter that the three of them had often shared, with each of them capable of giving as much as they got and never taking things to heart. James thought, correctly, that the mention of his friend's name might successfully deflect from the hilarious subject of his newly absent facial hair.

'I'm meeting Richard for a couple of beers soon. He always asks after you. Anything that you'd like me to pass on from you?' James had remembered that, even though the first night that they had all met had not gone as well for the other pair as it had for himself and Sue, it had still all been very friendly.

'Well you could always give him a passionate kiss and tell him it was from me, if you really wanted to.'

'That's not quite what I meant.'

'No, I know. He was nice enough James, but one Cinzano and lemonade is never a solid foundation for a relationship. I'm seeing someone else now anyway.'

'You are? Who?'

'His name is Ian, and he'll be round later. You can meet him this afternoon if you're coming back here. Please don't bring Richard back with you if you do, though.'

'Scouts honour,' said James, raising the middle three fingers of his right hand to his temple with his thumb pushing down on his little finger across the palm. He had never been part of the scouting movement, but he still knew the traditional salute.

'Thanks, and as a token of my appreciation I'll leave you two love birds alone while I go and read my paper.' Julie finished her entire drink in one motion, picked up her newspaper with her left hand as she put down the cup in her right, and left the two of them alone in the lounge.

James and Sue sat together on the sofa for the remainder of the morning, talking generally and making vague plans for a possible evening at the cinema later that day. At one point it was explicitly suggested, by Sue, that James would be welcome to stay the night with her afterwards, especially as the Sunday buses did not run late enough to match the timing of the last film showings. What was also mentioned was that Sue and Julie would both have to leave early for work the next morning. So, if he were still there when the sun came up, he would most likely have to let himself out and lock up, just as he had done a few times in the recent past.

Eventually, the clock on the lounge wall silently informed James that it was nearly time to meet Richard, as they had arranged the last time that they had seen each other.

'I'll see you in a couple of hours, then,' he announced as he rose from the sofa.

'Only have a couple of drinks please James. I don't want you coming back here all pissed and embarrassing, especially if you're going to be sharing my sheets tonight.'

'Scouts honour,' he repeated with the same salute as before.

'I'm serious. I don't want to be eating my Sunday lunch while you collapse, face first, into yours.'

'Fair point,' said James pulling on his jacket. He leant down, kissed her and left her to start preparing their lunch.

Just off the High Street, the Queens Head was a traditional pub with low oak beams and a friendly atmosphere. James had purposefully arrived slightly earlier than their agreed meeting time, so that he was at the bar, already ordering their first two pints, when he saw Richard's tall outline appear from the direction of the doorway. Towering above the crowded throng, Richard had immediately seen James from the other side of the room.

'Hi James. Mine's a large one,' called Richard, loudly, across the heads of a number of surprised drinkers.

'Yes, Richard. I'm sure it is,' replied James, more quietly, as Richard reached the bar alongside him. They were smiling broadly at each other, but James was thinking that the imbedded joke of Richard's habitual pub greeting was, by now, wearing somewhat thin.

Their drinks were placed on the bar in front of them. After James had paid, and received his change, they carried them away to the nearest vacant table where Richard sat down first. As he looked up at James, who was about to sit down himself, Richard suddenly adopted a surprised look.

'The 'tache has gone. I'm sure you had it last time. When did that come off?'

'Just last night,' replied James.

'Makes you look younger.'

'Oh fuck off,' he said light-heartedly and with no trace of any venom. By now he was wondering if the change really had shaved a few years, as well as coarse hairs, from his appearance.

Richard shrugged off the comment with a laugh and continued with the moustache theme. He was going to milk the subject for as long as he could. 'I suppose you'll now have to find another way of tickling Sue's fancy.'

It was in the same vein that their light-hearted, often lewd, banter continued as a few more beers were consumed. Eventually, the shiny bell hanging behind the bar was rung by the barman indicating that he could only accept a further ten minutes of drinks orders. Richard used this time to order one more drink for each of them, but James had only managed to finish half of his before the bell had been rung a second time and the allowed further twenty minutes of drinking time had also passed.

The pair walked out of the pub into the cool, early afternoon air and Richard immediately looked longingly at the closed chip shop next door.

'I could really do with some chips right now,' he said. 'I'm really hungry. Any chance of coming back with you to Sue's for a bite. I could have another go at impressing Julie.'

'I don't think so mate, sorry' said James, himself wistfully looking at the shop. 'This used to be a toy shop you know.'

'So what?'

'Just saying. Things always seem to change, that's all. No matter how much you might want things to stay the same.' He was thinking of the night that Rebecca had stood with her nose pressed against that same pane of glass, staring into the dark abyss of the shop. He decided that the time was now right for him to ask Richard his burning question. He would find out, one way or the other, today.

They walked to the High Street and then along it towards the traffic lights. As they approached, James watched them changing, taking specific notice of the timing of the sequence. He noted that there was a definite delay between a red light being shown, after amber, and the start of the signal starting to change, from red, in the opposite direction. They had changed three times by the time they reached them, at the crossroads where they would be parting company. Richard would be walking to his house in one direction and James would be continuing to Sue's in the other. They paused on the corner, as was usual for them.

'Fancy doing the same next Sunday?' asked Richard.

'Bit awkward for me next weekend, actually. How about in two weeks' time?' suggested James, anticipating the answers to his next questions and not wanting to be obliged to have an unnecessary drinking session with Richard.

'Okay, two weeks it is. I'll see you then.'

Richard was about to walk on, but James had decided that he wanted their parting talk to continue for a little longer today. Having often wanted to ask, but always getting cold feet at the last moment, he now summoned the courage required to confront his suspicions and find out for sure.

'Have you ever worked on traffic lights? I've often wondered, what with you being an electrician.'

'I have done, yes, years ago, but not any more. I've rigged them all over town, including these very ones. Not something that you have to do every day but there was once a time when the council wanted every junction upgraded, or something like that. So, they subcontracted the job to the company where I was. I'd only just started working for them at the time. It was my first job straight out of school. Actually, thinking about it, these are probably the ones that I got slightly wrong and had my knuckles rapped over.'

James felt his heart skip a beat. 'That sounds rather dodgy.'

'I wired together the wrong logic circuits. Rather than

showing red both ways before changing, they showed amber lights on all four poles. I think there were a couple of prangs over the next few days, but it wasn't until there was a fatal crash that the Council's Highways Department had a closer look and found my little mistake.'

Although it felt like his blood was suddenly boiling, James kept his composure, inwardly disgusted with his companion. However, he was pleased that the alcohol seemed to have loosened the man's tongue, exactly as he had intended. 'You were responsible for a fatal crash?'

'No, thankfully not. They found that the guy who was killed must have jumped it at red anyway as the other vehicle, a lorry, had come through green. All it did was make them look closer at the sequence of lights and then they found where I'd got it wrong. Nearly lost my job over it, but I'd only been doing it a short while and someone should really have checked my work. Thinking now about the crew I was with at the time, they were probably all in the pub. I just got sent back to the tech college one day a week for some extra training, for a while. The earlier prangs were maybe a little to do with me, in theory, but then no-one should go through on amber anyway.'

Just as he said it, and as if to illustrate the point, the driver of a car took his chance, accelerated and drove through an amber light in front of them. James caught his breath at the sight.

'I'd better get off now, anyway, I'm bursting for a piss,' said Richard, starting to walk towards his house. 'I'll see you in a fortnight, then.'

'Yeah, I'll see you in there,' replied James, turning to face his intended direction and not expecting to ever need to see Richard again after his revelation.

It had taken James a few months of feigning friendliness and drinking in the man's company. He'd had to endure hours of the man's sexist comments and his distasteful general outlook, but now his efforts had paid dividends. He had finally heard the confirmation of Richard's part in his personal tragedy. As he had done with Frank, years before, James had waited for Richard to verify his involvement.

James put his hands deep in his jacket pockets and walked towards Sue's house. His mind was racing with thoughts of Richard's admission and what that now meant for his longer-term plans. He had been painstakingly waiting for his suspicions to be substantiated, ever since first meeting Richard in the Queens Head three months earlier. He had always understood that he would have been unlikely to get Richard to admit to such an episode from his past without first gaining his friendship and, ultimately, his trust. So, he had patiently nurtured the friendship until today, when it had finally felt like the time was right to find out for sure if Richard was indeed the person he sought.

Now he knew, beyond doubt, that he had the correct man in his sights.

23

James's hunt for Richard had started slowly ten years before, on the same day that he had also first started attempting to trace Frank Bird. Each quest had presented its own unique problems. As far as Frank was concerned, the inquest report had only quoted an initial and a surname. However, due to the nature of lorry driving, James had soon realised that the driver could have potentially come from anywhere in the country. It had taken many hours of phone calls and checking of public records, all the while trying to avoid specific enquiries that may raise suspicions, to find matching details amongst the thousands of holders of HGV licences. Even once he had accumulated his short list, he had then had to check for their possible involvement by referring to such things as their ages and then, finally, had still needed a final confirmation. If he had not been so meticulous in his checking, then Felix Bird from the Midlands may have been prematurely, and wrongly, terminated as part of his revenge. James often reflected that, although he had effectively wasted six months with that particular fruitless pursuit, at least that man was still alive, blissfully unaware of how close he came to an untimely end.

Tracing Richard had been a totally different process. All James had known of him was that there had been some question raised about the effectiveness of the traffic lights' wiring. There had been no name given in the inquest report for this aspect since all blame for the accident had been attributed to his father. Frank Bird, although decreed to be blameless, had only been mentioned because of his direct contribution to the collision. So, all that James had been left with was his understandable assumption that an unidentified electrician may have wired the lights in a dangerous way, albeit inadvertently. Unlike with his concurrent search for Frank, he'd had no name to start from, but it had been a reasonable notion that whoever it was would have been a local man. He would likely have been working for a local company or, if not, the local branch of the Electricity Board.

Although he had known from the outset that it would be a massive task, James had always clung to the hope that he had a slim chance of finding him somewhere in Hartview. It was a relatively small town and therefore James had reasonably believed that his quarry could, potentially, still be living relatively close to the road junction that had been the birthplace of so much of his emotional pain.

So, James had frequented many of the pubs in the area whenever he could, which usually meant at weekends, striking up conversations with strangers every time he found an opportunity. Standing at a bar or sharing tables on busy nights, he often found that a friendly comment was enough to trigger a casual exchange. Unsurprisingly, countless times he had failed to find anyone useful to him, and had often despaired close to the point of giving up.

However, his enforced absence while he was in the Midlands, followed by the successful spell in Clayborough soon after, had meant that he had returned to the area with renewed enthusiasm for his overall mission. Although he did not properly resume his search until more than two years after Frank's death, still fearful of possible repercussions, he had eventually restarted his weekly hunt. At a time when he felt he had exhausted every possible pub and conversation opener, and it had all felt futile once again, he'd had the good fortune to meet a man who had restored his faith in his unorthodox approach.

That man had been standing at the bar, apparently on his own and awaiting his turn, when James had taken up position next to him. Easily in his late sixties with grey, thinning hair, he had not been a typical target of James. Even so, James had figured that it was still not beyond the realms of possibility that he could have been a traffic light engineer some seventeen years before. James had initiated an innocent-sounding conversation.

'Are you being done?' James had asked, apparently not wanting to jump his turn to be served when the barman reappeared.

'I think everyone is at these prices sonny,' had come the friendly reply, encouraging James to continue the exchange. James had smiled and half-laughed to, hopefully, endear himself to the stranger.

'That's Thatcher's Britain for you,' he had said, being the first thing that he could think of to reply. He had instantly regretted putting a political slant in to the talk. The man might have been a paid-up member of the Conservative Party for all he knew and could have immediately taken offence.

'Doesn't matter which one is in charge. Beer and fags still

keep on going up and that's all that pisses me off these days,' the man had replied, whilst pulling a cigarette out of a packet for himself. James had declined the offered second cigarette with a thanks. The man had lit his own with a flourish, as if to openly demonstrate his rebellion against the policies of ever-increasing taxation.

James had been relieved at the man's apparently neutral political stance, especially after revealing too much of his own viewpoint before. The barman had placed a single pint in front of the man, which James had correctly assumed was proof that he was on his own and so, maybe, would be receptive to more friendly conversation. After the man had paid for his drink and taken a first sip from it, James had ordered his own, pleased to see from the corner of his eye that the man had not moved away from the bar. That would have meant having to follow him to restore the conversation after he had bought his own lager.

'There's more to it than that, though. Income tax for one thing,' James had said, having decided to stay political for a while longer.

'Doesn't affect me these days. I'm retired now. Left all that behind when I worked at the council.'

'The council? In this town?'

'That's right.'

'So, you know a bit about working for the government?'

'A bit, I suppose, yeah. If you can call the drudgery of sitting in the Highways Department for years *working for the government*. It's hardly like being a secret agent is it? Good chat-up line, though. I work for the government,' he had said with a wink.

James had hardly been able to suppress his delight at finally finding a potential lead. 'Highways?' he had asked, hoping for the man to expand, but he had already set off down another train of thought.

'Those were the days when you could go down to the typing pool and have your choice of the birds working in there,' the man had fondly reminisced. 'I remember there was one who was so easy you almost had to put your name on a waiting list.'

James politely, and patiently, then had to listen to the man's irrelevant and enthusiastic boasts of his many extra-curricular activities with the keyboard massagers. After two more drinks, both paid for by James, he had managed to calmly, and innocuously, direct the conversation's topic back to the man's former responsibilities. 'What did you do exactly?'

'Basically made sure the roads were all okay.'

'Like getting potholes filled?'

'That sort of thing, yeah. Not that the council ever did it themselves. Always sub-contracted out to the cheapest bidder, or maybe to your brother-in-law,' he had said, winking again.

'What about a bulb blowing in a traffic light?'

'Same thing,' the man had replied with a wide, reminiscing smile. 'Strange you should mention that. They used to blow all the time. That is, until I authorised a full overhaul of the town's lights in the sixties.'

James had suddenly felt like he had won a random jackpot. He had thought he might as well go for broke. 'I don't suppose you remember who did the work?'

The man's smile had grown even wider. 'Actually I do, as it happens. I have a really good memory of the, how should I put it, preferred suppliers that we used. Basically, those who stopped me worrying about income tax so much.'

'Who then?'

Suddenly the man had become suspicious. 'What does it matter to you?'

James had shrugged his shoulders and feigned disinterest. 'It doesn't. Just conversation.'

The man had looked unsure but continued anyway. 'It was Franklinford Construction that did the excavation type stuff and Princeberg Electrics that wired them up. Franklinford went out of business about five years ago, but Princeberg are still around. Probably the biggest outfit in town in their game these days. Greased all the right palms on the way up, obviously.'

James had been ecstatic when this unlikely man had turned out to finally be the one able to tell him some of the useful information that he had been so desperate for. Although he still did not have the name of an individual responsible, the conversation had propelled him so far forward in his search that he could almost taste it.

24

James had spent the following three weeks carefully contemplating his next move, deciding that any further weekend journeys on the number 18 bus would be unlikely to be beneficial until he had properly weighed up his options. He had concluded that the random pub conversations with strangers had, for now at least, served their purpose, prompting the need for a completely new approach. It could have even been the man's casual mention of a secret agent that had subliminally placed such an attitude, and such an audacious plot, into his mind. Whatever the cause, James had eventually devised what he considered to be the quickest, and most direct, method of getting his next piece for the jigsaw puzzle.

James had phoned his manager on the next Friday morning to claim that he was feeling too sick to work that day and would therefore not be going into his office again until Monday, at the earliest. For what he had in mind, waiting until the weekend was not really an option. With his employer always reluctant to allow single days of holiday, he had felt that he had no choice but to feign an upset stomach. Once off the phone, with his unscheduled absence authorised, he had showered and dressed smartly, just as if he was still going to the office. If anything, he had paid a lot more attention to his overall appearance than he normally would. That day, he fastened the top button of his shirt, rather than using his tie to pull the two edges of his collar together as was his habit. He had also trimmed his moustache of the occasional stray hairs growing at unconventional angles. He had even, unusually, polished his shoes before pulling on the trousers of his sharp business suit. Picking up his briefcase from just inside the front door, he had looked every inch the model of professional appearance. Outside, purposefully walking to the parked Mercedes, any casual onlooker could have easily mistaken him as one who was on his way to a job interview, keen to impress.

As he had started up the car, he was pleased to realise that he did not have the prospect of trusting the public transport to Hartview for a change. Alcohol did not feature at all in his plan for that day and so he was going to take full advantage of his chance to drive to the town himself. It would also give him the opportunity to become more familiar with the place, anyway, maybe seeing a few new prospective pubs for the future as he drove around. He had probably been concentrating too much on those that he had found within easy walking distance of the bus station for his enquiries, anyway.

Having arrived at Hartview, he had spent the second half of the morning either driving around the suburbs or sometimes parking the car and walking a few hundred yards to clear his head, thankfully numbed from his tension headache by paracetamol. He had driven across the intersection where his family had been cruelly split apart, and the painful memories had served to strengthen his resolve to successfully complete his intended day. Like an actor appropriately fuelling his emotions before delivering a convincing performance, James had been fully ready for his upcoming act by the time he pulled into the car park in front of the Princeberg head office, just after 1pm. The office occupied a small unit on an industrial estate on the outskirts of town and, at that time of day, there had been few other cars around. As he had correctly predicted, a Friday lunchtime was the most likely period that the office would be close to empty. Most employees, specifically any senior management, would have driven to a nearby pub for a liquid lunch, leaving only an essential skeleton crew to answer the phones until at least mid-afternoon. He had his own reasons for abhorring any drinking when driving, but the common cultural practice had played to his advantage that afternoon.

James, carrying his official-looking briefcase, had walked through the main entrance and straight up to the first desk that faced it.

'Can I help you sir?' the female receptionist had professionally asked. A petite blonde in her late twenties.

'Your electricians,' James had announced in as much of an official tone as he could.

'Sorry, sir. If you require the services of one of our qualified electricians, then you need to arrange it with one of our retail shops. I can give you the number of your local store if you tell me your area.'

'I don't need any services, thank you. I don't want a job done. I'm here to collect the personnel records of your electricians,' James had expanded, keeping the tone in his voice.

'I'm afraid I don't understand,' the receptionist had said, confused.

'I'm from The Inland Revenue,' James had falsely clarified. 'We called last week to say that we needed the details of all your electricians for comparison with our own records, as part of an investigation. All of them, past and present, going back at least twenty years. Are you not expecting me?'

'I'm afraid I haven't been told anything about it, and I'm the only one here at the moment. Could you maybe come back next week?'

'I'm here for them now, please. I do actually have the authority to look through your filing cabinets myself right now, but I'd rather we kept it friendly.'

The woman had been unsure of what to do, feeling threatened, and had shuffled uneasily on her swivel chair. 'How about waiting until this afternoon?'

'Look, I've been to a lot of places this morning collecting such details,' James had said in an exasperated breath and pointing with his left hand to the briefcase that he held in his right. 'I've got a lot more to do this afternoon, too.' The woman had started to look extremely worried, so James had then tried to soften his approach slightly. 'I shouldn't really tell you anything about it but, between you and me, it's not an investigation into Princeberg themselves. It's just trying to catch out any electricians who are doing a bit of extra work on the side without paying tax.'

That had seemed to do the trick. Past employees were no longer the concern of Princeberg Electrics and if any existing employees were indeed taking on extra jobs, contrary to specific company policy, then they only had themselves to blame if they were caught out. So, now without the fear that it could be Princeberg that she could be getting into hot water with the taxman, she had breathed easier. 'Wait here please,' she had said getting up and moving deeper into the office and out of sight.

James had stood and waited with his heart pounding, hearing filing cabinet drawers open and shut and the sound of a photocopier operating. After a further ten minutes, which had felt like an eternity, the receptionist had returned and handed him a small stack of A4 papers which he had promptly placed into the briefcase.

'That's every 'sparks' that we've ever had working here from the year dot,' she had said. Then, just as James was about to mutter his appreciation and leave, she caught him off guard with her next question. 'Could I take a note of your name please? I'll need to tell my boss that you've been when he gets back,' she had said, picking up a pen from the desk.

Concealing his sudden panic, James had instinctively responded to the unrehearsed scenario. 'James. James Harper.' It was the same pseudonym that he had used during his time in Clayborough, five years before. The intention was the same. A precaution of not leaving a traceable route back to himself after the entire task had been completed, should any subsequent suspicions ever be aroused.

Although he had desperately wanted to run, James had walked calmly out of the office and to his car, leaving the receptionist to wonder, and worry, about her turn to be left holding the fort while everyone else went out for a lunchtime drink. As James had sat down in his driver's seat, with the car door still open, the stress of the situation had manifested itself. He had suddenly leant out and vomited onto the tarmac.

Back in his house that evening, James had carefully sifted through the photocopies that he had been given. Effectively one page of details for each electrician who had ever worn the Princeberg logo. Those names that he could associate with his precise year of interest had formed a much smaller pile of its own once the irrelevant, later ones had been placed aside. Back in the 1960s, the fledgling company, as it was at that time, was still to be expanded to its larger size. One name had shone out from those few in that remaining pile, like a night beacon on a ship at sea. The ages of every other 1965 employee had suggested many years of experience for each, making them much less likely to make fundamental wiring mistakes, James had reasoned. There had been just one young apprentice, in his early twenties at the time, who James had considered to be the most likely candidate. His name was Richard Jennings.

Now that he finally had an actual name to consider, the pursuit had immediately become much more straightforward for James. The next day, Saturday, he had caught the number 18 back to Hartview once again. The phone book hanging in the nearest phone box to the bus station had advised him that there were just three R. Jennings listed as being in the area. The second entry of these three even had the occupation of the phone's owner included, in brackets. This additional note had presumably been specifically requested as a cheap, extra advertisement of his present self-employed services. Electrician.

James had bought a red-covered street-map book of the

local area from the newsagent near to the phone box. With trembling hands, he had referred to the index at the back to find the page number and grid reference of the street where the electrician lived. Within a day of his successful portrayal as a tax inspector, he had known exactly where his prime suspect was. A road just a hundred yards past the tragic junction, with the extra, obscene coincidence of being in the direction that Frank Bird had been heading on that fateful night.

25

Rather than simply knock on the man's door, unannounced, and without a seemingly good reason, James had concluded that it would be better for him to resume his approach of pursuing an apparently random meeting. If the man drank in pubs, at least occasionally, James had reasoned that he would eventually run in to him, at some time, if he waited long enough. If that failed to work, then he would still have the option of re-evaluating his strategy after a reasonable amount of time. He had forced himself to be patient, reminding himself that he had already waited years to get this close. It would be unwise for him to rush this last furlong, and raise the man's suspicion, by asking for electrical services when he did not even live nearby.

The main difficulty that he could foresee would be knowing how to recognise his prey when the time came. He had considered waiting outside the address to maybe catch sight of the man before any contrived encounter. He had soon discounted it as a viable option. Hanging around in a residential street, for potentially hours at a time, would undoubtedly attract the unwelcome attention, and suspicion, of the local curtain-twitchers. He had originally wanted to remain as inconspicuous as possible to everyone else unconcerned with his purpose.

After a quick check of the area, with his map-book in hand, James had determined that the nearest pub to the electrician's address was The Queens Head. Appropriately next door to what had once been the town's only toy shop, he had decided that he would initially await his target there.

For each of the following five Saturdays, James had caught the number 18 bus into the town and had spent many hours sipping slowly at pints of beer in The Queens Head, striking up conversations with men in their thirties at every opportunity. Behind his back, many of the locals were soon talking and laughing, assuming that this new stranger was gay. That conjecture, in itself, had not bothered him other than it meant that many of the men avoided any further conversation, or interaction, with him, effectively reducing his chances of successfully finding the man he was looking for.

On the fourth Saturday, halfway through the lunchtime opening session, he had begun to feel that he had exhausted all possibilities in that venue. He had started to seriously consider trying an alternative pub from the following weekend, when he had seen the unfamiliar tall man walk in. James had instantly known for certain that he had not seen him in there before. He had been immediately distinguishable by his excessive height. Furthermore, James had judged him to be in his mid to late thirties, making him immediately of interest.

After the experience of so many disappointments, it was only once the man leant on the bar, close enough for him to see, that James's heart had skipped a beat. He had realised that he would not have to waste time with his fruitless ritual of casual conversation this time, finally culminating in either asking the man's name or occupation and taking care not to appear disappointed when the answer was neither Richard nor an electrician. This time, he had already known those answers. The man had been wearing a green fleece jacket embroidered with yellow thread above the left breast pocket. It was his usual working jacket, being specifically also worn at the weekend to attract any casual enquiries. It had proclaimed both his name and his occupation. James had finally found Richard Jennings, the electrician.

'Who's next?' the barman had asked, turning to face James and, next to him, Richard.

'This guy,' James had said, nodding his head sideways towards the man on his left.

'Thanks,' Richard had casually acknowledged, before ordering his pint. Both had known whose turn it was to be served but, as any drinker knows, there are many who would have grasped the opportunity to get their next drink a minute or two earlier when confronted with the same query.

While the barman had been pulling Richard's drink, James had leant closer to Richard and whispered. 'Always annoys me when a barman doesn't bother to keep an eye out for the proper queuing order. It's like they think it's our job to know. That's part of their job. An important part and, if they don't do it, they're simply not doing their job properly.'

'I suppose so,' Richard had said, still watching the beer filling his glass behind the bar and avoiding eye contact with James.

James had persisted, trying to strike up a fuller conversation before Richard had received his drink and moved away from him. 'It's like you and your job,' he had continued, pointing to Richard's embroidery. 'You, presumably, wouldn't be asking a customer what colour an Earth wire is.'

Richard had looked down at where James's finger had pointed, realising that his careful hand-stitching had informed James of his trade. Richard had smiled at the thought of trying to do his job without knowing such basic information but was still cold towards James. 'I can't say that I've ever had to do that, no,' he had said, before turning back to accept the full glass of beer and hand over a five-pound note.

James had become desperate to hold the man's interest. Then he had thought of a way to hold on to the conversation for a while longer. 'Actually, I'm glad I ran into you. I'm having a bit of trouble with the lights flickering in my house. Are you available to have a look?'

With that, Richard's eyes had lit up at the thought of paid work and he was immediately more convivial with his new acquaintance. 'Yeah sure,' he had said, accepting his change from the barman as James quickly ordered his own drink. 'Where do you live?'

'Raphael Road,' James had lied, randomly saying the name of one of the roads that he had often walked along on his way from the bus station. It formed part of a new housing estate where the roads were all named after famous renaissance artists.

'I know it,' Richard had said. 'What number?'

James had thought quickly, and successfully sidestepped the question. 'Actually, I'm not going to be there for much of this week. Got to go away on business. Do you have a business card or something so that I can call you to arrange it when I'm back?'

'Of course,' Richard had replied, producing one of his cards from a top pocket and handing it to James. 'Call in the evenings, though, as I'm usually out with customers during the day.'

James had given it a polite, cursory glance, noting that the card included Richard's contact number as expected, and had put it in the back, left pocket of his jeans. In his right was still the folded page he had ripped from the phone book, also containing the same phone number. He had frantically searched for a line of conversation that might hold Richard's interest before he moved away. All he could think of had been the subject of electrics.

'As well as sorting out the lights, do you think you could also wire me up to next door's meter so that they pay my bill for me?' he had joked.

Richard had smiled, genuinely. He had heard this same hypothetical question many times over the years and always enjoyed perplexing the one asking with his superior knowledge of the subject. Unbeknown to Richard, however, James had already been fully aware of the answer. He had spent many hours discussing electrics, and how they worked, with the former electrician who had been his landlord during his time in Clayborough.

'You would think that would be an easy thing to do, wouldn't you, but, because of a process called phasing, your neighbour is most likely to be on a different cycle of electrical current to you. You can't just simply join the two circuits together.'

So James, pleased to have successfully found a way of

keeping their interaction going, had adopted the appearance of listening intently while Richard had continued to explain the fundamentals of how house electrics worked. They had still been stood at the bar, with Richard still lecturing, when they had both finished their first drinks. James had wasted no time in buying refills for them both. It had allowed the conversation to continue to flow as freely as the electrical currents that Richard was describing and had obliged Richard to stay with him for at least a while longer.

So, with those second drinks, Richard had suggested that the two of them moved away from the bar to sit together at a table to keep on talking. James had been sure that, as the man now seemed to be in his element with his pet subject, he now had him on his hook and line. All he had to do was to maintain the friendly conversation.

As the subject of electrics finally did start to dry up, James had progressively moved the conversation forward to the topic of musical tastes. He had initially changed the subject by introducing it with a comment that he had once had an electric shock from a record player and had successfully portrayed the façade of matching Richard's slightly older perspective and tastes. Having correctly guessed at Richard's own preference, he had lied that he personally preferred American Rock and Roll artists, such as Buddy Holly, Elvis Presley and Chuck Berry, to the later genres of the 1960s and 1970s.

James had continually contrived to build on the new friendship that was gradually forming between the pair. However, despite James's calculated control of everything, at the end of the lunchtime session it had been Richard, rather than James, who had taken the initiative to suggest them drinking together again in the future.

'Well, I had better be making a move now. I've really enjoyed talking to you today and it's been a pleasure to meet you,' Richard had said, getting up and extending his hand. James had shaken it firmly. 'In fact, do you fancy doing it again sometime?'

'Sure, why not,' James had replied, a bit taken aback, but pleased, that the invitation that he had intended using himself had been hijacked.

'I'm Richard, by the way, Richard Jennings,' Richard had said, forgetting that his name was embroidered on his jacket for everyone, especially James, to see.

'James Harper,' James Pearce had reciprocated. He had decided that he would continue to use the same pseudonym to save from confusing himself. 'Next Saturday lunchtime again?'

'Actually, I don't normally drink on Saturdays. I prefer to watch the football. Today was a one-off,' Richard had replied, effectively explaining to James why it had taken so long for their paths to cross. 'Are you okay for a Friday evening instead?'

'Poets day.'

'Indeed,' Richard had replied, apparently requiring no further explanation of the expression.

'Suits me. What time?'

'Seven o'clock?'

'I'll be here. See you again then.'

From then on, James had been regularly catching the number 18 evening bus to meet his new drinking buddy on

Friday nights, cultivating their friendship. The first time, they had spent the entire night discussing football, the conversation initiated by James, but prompted by Richard's parting comment the week before.

The night that they had first met Sue and Julie had been one such occasion. Meeting Sue had been an unexpected bonus for James. To maintain the charade as far as Richard was concerned, he had also had to tell her his false surname. That encounter had been just two weeks before James had successfully changed their regular weekly rendezvous to be Sunday lunchtimes instead. Not only did that allow him to see Sue for the rest of the day, it had also meant that he did not have to spend more than he had done on beer getting home in a taxi after the buses had finished running every Friday night.

As he now walked towards Sue's house for his late Sunday lunch, James reflected on his skilful tracing and entrapment of Richard. The man that he had sought for so long had indeed blindly taken his bait. He was firmly on James's fishing hook and all James had to now do was guide him to the shore.

And kill him.

26

Sue quickly checked the contents of her oven once more. Everything for the Sunday roast dinner was progressing well, with the potatoes forming a golden covering, the Yorkshire puddings rising, and the beef gradually browning. With a glance toward her kitchen clock, she calculated it should all be fully cooked and ready for plating up in ten minutes. James was expected back from his lunchtime drinks with Richard at any moment and, so long as he had not delayed his walk back, that would be perfect timing.

Julie's latest boyfriend, Ian, had arrived an hour before to join them for lunch as had previously been arranged. Those two were watching early afternoon Sunday television in the lounge, leaving Sue alone in the kitchen to prepare the meal for the four of them. Sue preferred it that way, enjoying cooking much more than her sister. She found that any extra help, no matter how well-intentioned, just tended to get in her way, made her nervous and often led to her forgetting an essential element of the meal.

As Sue closed the oven door again, the doorbell rang.

'Could you get that please Julie,' she called in the direction of the lounge. 'It'll be his highness expecting his grub.'

Julie opened the front door to find James leaning against the wall and smiling back at her with glazed eyes.

'You'd better not be pissed after all the effort she's put in for your dinner,' warned Julie.

'Nope. Just happy to see your pretty face again,' said James, maintaining the smile and stepping over the threshold.

There had been similar doorstep exchanges between them most weeks since the three of them had fallen into the regular routine of James's Sunday visits. Visits which invariably incorporated a lunchtime drinking session with Richard while Sue cooked a full roast dinner for them. Julie would always be the one who would have to answer the door on his return, while Sue increasingly scurried around the kitchen doing the final tasks of preparation.

James walked ahead of Julie and went straight up the stairs to the bathroom to wash his hands and face before the meal. When he came back down, he walked into the kitchen, put his arms around Sue from behind and kissed her on the cheek. Sue did not stop her stirring of a bowl of stuffing, but still kissed him back, similarly.

'It'll all be ready in about ten minutes,' she said to him with her face next to his. 'You're back just in time to make yourself busy and lay the table.'

'I'll make myself useful then.' He released her and made for the drawer where he knew the cutlery was kept.

'For four,' Sue added.

'Four?' queried James.

'Julie's new boyfriend, Ian. We told you he'd be here this afternoon.'

'He's here already? I didn't think she meant he would be eating with us,' said James, as he reluctantly picked up a fourth set of tableware. With what he had recently had confirmed by

185

Richard still whirling round his mind, he was secretly in no mood for meeting anyone new over a meal. It would be difficult enough to act normally with his usual Sunday lunch triangle.

James carried the knives and forks into the lounge and half-turned towards the dining table at the end of the room. Julie had sat back down on the sofa next to her companion, who now rose to formally meet James. James judged that this unfamiliar man was a few years older than himself. It was difficult for James to speculate accurately, since the man's traditional style of his short, wavy fair hair, parted to one side, served only to add to the perceived years.

'You must be James,' he said with an accent that James could not accurately place. He walked forward with his hand outstretched. 'I'm Ian.'

With only the evidence of six spoken words, James suspected that the man probably originated from somewhere close to Devon, possibly as far away as Cornwall. He wondered what personal history may have persuaded him to move Eastwards at some point. With all the cutlery still held in his left hand, James was freely able to shake Ian's hand with his right. 'Hello Ian,' he said with a well-practiced smile. 'Welcome to Sue's Sunday feast.'

James was not speaking sarcastically. He genuinely thought Sue to be the best cook he had ever shared a meal with. Just one of her many attractive features. Julie, suddenly feeling outnumbered by the men, chose to go back to the kitchen to see if Sue would appreciate any help with the arranging of the meal onto the plates.

'How long have you known Julie, then?' James continued

after she had gone. He was placing the knives and forks either side of the placemats that were always permanently left on the table, even between meals.

'Just a couple of weeks,' answered Ian. 'I already think she's great, though'. He spoke the aside at a lower volume so that Julie herself would not hear the praise from the kitchen.

Minutes later, when Sue and Julie arrived carrying two full plates each, the two men were already sat at the table, chatting like old friends and waiting to be fed.

As the four of them ate, James kept up the general conversation with Ian, the newcomer, preferring that to the alternative of silence. It was difficult, though, as he could not immediately find much common interest between the two of them. It was not particularly surprising. They were just two strangers that happened to each be dating the sisters, after all. Despite his constant, relaxed talking, Sue could sense that James was not speaking and behaving as genuinely as she knew that he normally did. Today he seemed a little contemplative, as if he was pre-occupied with something else on his mind. He did not seem to be properly listening to Ian's answers to his many questions for one thing.

More importantly, she also sensed some signs from Julie that, despite her mostly constant friendliness toward James, she actually disapproved of him in some way. There had also been a few other times in the recent past when there was just something in the way that Julie occasionally spoke to her about James that made Sue think that there might be a deep-rooted dislike, or distrust, of him. Today, Sue felt that subtle tension again, albeit only slightly, across the dining table. There was nothing that she could specifically, and consciously, pinpoint. There were perhaps just some sporadic, almost imperceptible, cold looks from Julie as James tried his best to be friendly with her new boyfriend. Eventually, Sue dismissed the feelings from her mind, explaining everything to herself as being a result of the unfamiliar dynamic of their Sunday meal.

After all plates were emptied, accompanied by expressions of appreciation and praise from around the table, Sue carried all four away to the kitchen and placed them in the sink to soak. She assumed, and hoped, that Ian and Julie would have washed those, together with the various pans and baking trays, before she and James returned. Within the hour, she intended to go out with James for the remainder of the afternoon, and into the evening, as was their adopted Sunday habit.

When Sue returned to the lounge, she was surprised to find that Ian was holding Julie's acoustic guitar and starting to remove the first of the strings by rapidly turning the tuning peg. Julie, sat beside him on the sofa, had bought a complete new set of six during the previous week and Ian, claiming to know all about such things, had been eager to demonstrate just how it should be done.

As he effortlessly replaced each string, one at a time, he talked constantly of how he had enjoyed playing in a rock band years before. By the time he came to replace the sixth, and final, string, he was starting to lose the attention of his latest captive audience. Having been with Julie when she had bought the new strings in the local music shop, and been asked at that time to re-string her instrument for her when he could, he had brought a small set of pliers with him. He pulled these from his top pocket and proceeded to cut the excess inches from the end of each of the strings, close to each tuning peg. Leaving strings at their full length so that they splayed from the headstock at all angles was a dubious practice that he felt should be reserved for those electric guitarists that were apparently trying to whip out the eyes of their bandmates on *Top Of The Pops*.

He dropped the six portions of metal guitar strings, of varying widths, into the small waste bin that was between the sofa and the armchair that James was sitting on. James briefly looked down at the latest contents of the bin before looking back at Ian's actions. Turning the tuning pegs, and rapidly plucking each associated string, Ian tightened every string of the instrument until each was at its correct pitch relative to the others. Once satisfied, he strummed a six-string version of a C-chord that rang out from the virgin strings, pleasantly and tunefully.

'Any requests?' he asked of his three spectators.

'Can you play *Over The Hills and Far Away*?' asked Sue, apparently unimpressed with the man's musical ability. Then, turning to James as she rose from her armchair, she asked 'shall we go then?'

'You bet,' replied James, also getting up. 'It doesn't start for a while yet but the earlier we are, the better seats we get.'

'Where are you off to?' asked Ian, genuinely curious.

'The new Bond film is out,' replied Sue on behalf of the pair of them. '*For Your Eyes Only*. It's on at the Odeon in town and James is going to talk all the way through it to explain to me why Roger Moore is so much better than Sean Connery.'

'I hear that it's really good,' said Ian, and he started playing the well-known James Bond theme on the guitar that he still held across his lap. Coincidentally, it had been one of the first tunes that he had ever learnt to play as an aspiring ten-year-old musician and so he knew it intimately. It was so instantly recognisable to most listeners, being part of the soundtrack of every film in the Bond franchise since the 1962 release of *Dr No*, and he often loved to play it. His way.

Having played every note perfectly for the first fifteen seconds of the tune, he purposely played the next note slightly off-key. It was only one semitone note away from what it should have been, so it was very nearly the correct pitch, but it suddenly grated on the ears of the listeners, as he had intended. He played the following notes precisely again, but then he did it once more. He hit more wrong notes, and more often, as the tune progressed. He had originally had the idea of this rehearsed party piece after once watching Les Dawson on a television programme. Dawson had been similarly playing well-known tunes on a piano but striking an increasing number of off-key notes for comedic effect.

James, Sue and Julie all agreed that the stunt was very amusing, laughing progressively louder at each apparent mistake. Ian gratefully accepted their applause when he had finished his rendition.

Sue grasped James's hand and, with a quick farewell to the others, they both left the house. Ian leant the re-strung guitar against the wall next to the sofa. He and Julie had been left alone for at least the next few hours, just as they had both been wanting.

As they stood, holding hands in the Odeon queue, shuffling forwards and closer to the ticket booth, Sue could not help feeling that James was still somewhat distracted. He had hardly spoken to her during their walk from her house to the cinema but had insisted that there was nothing wrong or playing on his mind. She was not sure that he was being totally truthful about that, as she knew him to never normally be at a loss for something to say.

Being naturally an insecure person, she desperately hoped that it was not a sign that he was starting to have doubts about their relationship. Then, forcing herself to think more positively, her theories moved in the opposite direction. Could he perhaps be thinking about moving their relationship forward, and that was causing the thoughtful demeanour? Could he even have a ring in his pocket and was searching for the perfect moment to produce it? For her part, she already knew that she loved him, and she hoped that he felt the same. Neither of them had ever openly expressed any such feelings to each other, but some things are just simply understood between a couple, she mused.

Their relationship had sometimes been quite difficult to maintain. They had only ever been able to see each other at weekends. That might, conceivably, have been what was playing on James's mind. When they had first met, that night at The Queen's Head months ago, James had explained to her that he lived quite a distance away and that he worked long hours during the week. That would inevitably restrict their future opportunities to see each other as well as James, strangely for a man of his generation, not being able to drive. He always had to catch the bus for them to get together, as

Sue's epilepsy had always prevented her from driving herself. Thankfully, he had already been making the journey to Hartview regularly to meet his good friend, Richard. All she knew of Richard was that he lived somewhere near and that he and James regularly went out for drinks together. She had never seen James's flat but, from his description of it and of the men he was sharing it with, that was probably a good thing. Hartview was small enough for them to walk to many of the types of places where they might want to go anyway.

She was not able to phone him during the week because he had said that he was not on the phone, either at home or at work. The only times that she did talk to him, between those days that they were able to spend together, was when he was able to call her from a roadside phone box.

He had a few strange ways and habits, as any man did, that were difficult for her to understand. He had always insisted that he did not want her to go to see him at his own home, just saying that he hated the thought of her travelling so far alone as well as it being an unsuitable place for the two of them. At first, such reluctance had made her suspect that he might already be married but, after a while, it had become clear to her that there was no other real evidence to support the notion. Sue had acknowledged, after she had confronted James with the theory one night in bed together, that no woman would let her man stay out overnight for an entire weekend without questions being raised at home.

Another peculiar aspect of him was that he always insisted on meeting her at her house, even for those times that they had planned to go out. He would always call round for her first, never arranging to simply meet her in a pub or outside a cinema. He had nonchalantly explained it by saying that he panicked at the thought of trying to locate her in a crowd, almost to the point of it being a phobia. She preferred to think of it as an indication of his gentlemanly nature, wanting to accompany her on even the shortest of walks, rather than expecting her to walk alone.

In spite of some of his odd ways, she loved him more than she had any man before and she knew that one day, and one day soon if possible, she wanted to be Mrs. Harper. Whatever it was that was troubling him, she dearly hoped that it did not signal the ending of their relationship. She prayed that it was the opposite or, if not, that it was simply something completely unconnected with their potential future together. James was still obviously reluctant to reveal or discuss it with her, though. So, if James was too afraid to risk moving their relationship forward, if indeed that was the direction he was thinking, then Sue concluded that it would have to be her.

Today, if possible.

27

James had been extremely distracted, ever since his last conversation with Richard at the junction. The overall situation had become crystal clear now that he was finally certain that Richard had been the one responsible for the incorrect sequence of signals. Even though he had never doubted his goal, he was now having trouble similarly focusing the finer details of his plan to achieve it. He knew that he probably needed some quiet time alone to determine the best way to execute his scheme. He had thought, and hoped, that the short walk from the junction to Sue's house might have been sufficient, especially after so many years of preparation. However, he had found that the day's latest leap forward would demand all of his concentration for much longer than that.

Despite his inner turmoil, he had managed to force himself to continue to act normally in front of his girlfriend and her sister. He had also been suddenly introduced to someone new and he'd had to respond appropriately. He had managed to call upon all of his recent experience of banal talking with strangers, acquired during his elongated search for Richard, to cultivate a friendly atmosphere with that unexpected fourth dinner guest. All the while, though, his main train of thought had been devoted to ensuring that he accomplish the victory of the covert battle ahead.

Although he knew that Sue was an excellent cook, he could not remember tasting the lunch that she had prepared for him and the others that afternoon. He had routinely chewed and swallowed between insignificant snippets of conversation while he had silently formulated his intended strategy. Watching the Bond film that evening, with his girlfriend by his side and holding her hand, he had not been at all aware of the dialogue and so had no idea of the plotline or any context to the many action sequences. He knew that Sue would not be discussing the finer points of the film after they left the cinema, and he was thankful for that. James was sure that Sue had only agreed to see this latest instalment in the franchise with him because he had expressed such an interest in seeing it himself. The world of espionage, gun battles and random explosions held no appeal for her.

As the credits rolled and the cinema lights brightened, they joined the throng of other filmgoers and inched towards the exit. Knowing that the nearest pub would already be populated by many of those who had either pre-empted the end of the film or managed to get through the exit before the human bottleneck had formed, they walked past it to the one further down the street. In here it was quieter, with tables available and no swarm of individuals at the bar, each waving money like flags in a feeble attempt to be served next.

James and Sue found a small vacant table, with two chairs, next to the far wall and then James left Sue there, backtracking his steps to order some drinks from the bar. When he returned to sit down, carrying Sue's Cinzano and a pint for himself, it was Sue who broke the silence that had been hanging over them for hours.

'What's on your mind James?' she asked. 'You've been quiet and deep in thought ever since you got back from meeting Richard.'

'Nothing,' he lied. 'I haven't been quiet at all.'

'Yes you have. You may have been talking to Ian a bit over lunch, but you weren't really listening to what he was saying. Since then you've hardly said a word, especially to me.'

'I'm sorry,' he said. 'I probably have been slightly switched off, now that you mention it.'

'Why?' she pushed, nervously taking her first sip of the drink that he had bought her.

'It's nothing to do with you, or us, if that's what you're worried about.' Sue hoped that the relieved exhale from her was not as audible as it felt in her head. 'I've just got a slight problem at work at the moment.'

'What kind of problem?'

'From next month they want me to work from the office here in Hartview rather than the branch near Birchstead, where I live. It'd mean even longer days and I'm not sure the number 18 runs early enough anyway.'

Sue suddenly saw her chance. 'That's not a problem,' she declared, brightly. 'It's an opportunity. An opportunity for us. Why not move in with me,' then, after a brief pause, 'and Julie, I suppose. It would be just down the road for you then. We could be together all the time, rather than living this weekend life.' James looked pleasantly surprised at her suggestion. 'We could even have a lie-in together each morning,' she added, seductively and with a smile.

'It would certainly make things a lot easier for me, and so

very much better for you and me,' he agreed, also smiling now, and genuinely, for the first time that day. He took a large mouthful from his drink before continuing. 'What about Julie, though? Wouldn't she have any objections?'

'She can't really say anything about it. We each own half of the house and, from the way she's been talking, I think she wants to have a man move in with her one day soon, anyway. If you move in with me, it'd save me from being the one feeling like a gooseberry. At the moment I guess it's Ian that is under consideration. There's plenty of room for four anyway. You know that it's a pretty big place.'

James almost choked back the lager that he was drinking at the very moment that she said it. This was a development that he had not anticipated.

'So, if Ian passes the test, a test that he doesn't actually know he's taking, when do you think that might be?'

'No idea. She's only known him five minutes, but she can be a bit impetuous sometimes. If I had to guess, I'd say that it'd probably not be for another month or so.'

James breathed easier again, anticipating that he would not need nearly that long to deal with Richard. The thought of another man living in the house that he had just managed to successfully manoeuvre his way into, possibly a man who would readily attempt some basic household maintenance, had unnerved him. Such a situation, if it happened too soon, had the potential to severely affect his latest plans.

'So, when can you move in?' asked Sue, relieved that her earlier fears had not been realised.

'Can we go for the first of next month? They want me to move office on the Monday after, and it's only a few weeks for us to wait. It'd give me time to sort things out and get my gear together from the dive I'm living in at the moment.'

'Sounds perfect to me. You're still staying tonight as well, aren't you?'

'If I'm invited.'

'Of course you are,' said Sue, smiling even more broadly than she had done earlier and giving the inside of his thigh a squeeze under the table.

They finished their drinks and left the pub, constantly smiling at each other and holding hands, talking more freely again now and walking in the direction of Sue's house. It was in darkness when they got back to it.

'They must have gone out somewhere,' said Sue as she turned her key in the lock. 'I keep telling Julie that it would be better to always leave a light on to put off any would-be burglar, but she says that would put up the electric bill.'

'I don't think you'd notice a bulb or two being on for a few hours amongst the amount of times she boils a kettle for cups of tea,' said James, following Sue into the dark hallway.

As Sue reached for the light switch and the door swung closed behind them, James reached around her waist and pulled her to him. He wanted her with all his being and now that they were in the privacy of the house, he could contain his desire no longer. She wanted him too and, after a passionate embrace, she abandoned thoughts of any further evening conversation on the sofa and led him to her bedroom. She had already been reassured that their relationship was still solid, and James had agreed to move in with her within weeks.

She was happier than she had ever been.

28

The bedroom curtains were cheap and much too thin, allowing the light of the morning to stream into the room as soon as the sun had risen. It had always woken James whenever he had stayed overnight at Sue's, and so he just lay there as motionless as he usually did. This time his mind was actively contemplating the immediate future and his few hours of respite passed extremely quickly.

Sue slept soundly beside him until her alarm rocked her from her slumber. She groggily thumped down on the button on the top of her clock to silence it, then rolled over and noticed that he was already fully awake. She smiled at her lover.

'Good morning,' she said. 'Have you been awake long?'

'Just a couple of minutes,' he lied, without any reason for the falsehood other than to avoid criticising her choice of drapes.

'Me and Julie are on the earlier shift today,' she announced as she stepped out of her side of the double bed. As James knew, the two sisters, working at the same place, always tried to coincide their working days so that they could commute together. 'Are you on your usual Monday late start?'

'Don't have to be there 'til lunchtime,' James confirmed, rolling onto his back and placing his hands behind his head as if to emphasise his slower start to the week.

'Well you can make yourself useful and get the breakfast together while I try to beat Julie into the shower,' said Sue, throwing her pillow playfully into his face as she walked towards the door.

The pillow bounced onto the floor beside him as James watched Sue's naked body glide beautifully through the doorway and head towards the bathroom. After she had gone, he pulled back the covers and got out of the bed himself, dressing in the same clothes that he had discarded beside the bed the night before. As he did so, he heard Julie's alarm ringing in her bedroom further down the landing. It was stifled within seconds and James knew that it would not be long before the two women were competing for the required facilities of the bathroom. His best course of action would be to get out of the way, downstairs, and await their appearance there.

Having stayed overnight with Sue before, James confidently knew his way around her kitchen. He primed the kettle with water, prepared three mugs with milk for tea and pulled three cereal bowls from one of the cupboards on the wall. The box of breakfast cereal was kept in the cooler cupboard under the stairs, so James left the kitchen to retrieve that. As James looked into the makeshift larder and reached for the box, he took the opportunity to have a long, hard look at the electricity supply for the house, with its various components screwed to the far wall.

Unsurprisingly, it was the typical three-stage arrangement that could be found in millions of houses around the country, with the same layout that had been used in homes for decades. The main power cable, direct from the street, rose from the floorboards and was wired directly into the first component, known as the cut-out. Sometimes also referred to as the 'head', this rectangular box contained the high-rated main fuse for the entire supply. From there, thinner, separated live and neutral cables were wired to the meter. Both elements were securely screwed to a separate backboard.

The live and neutral cables running from the meter, commonly known as the tails, were wired into the consumer unit, a dark brown Bakelite fuse box which, in turn, would be feeding the various circuits for the house. He was pleased to see that there was no isolator switch included between the meter and the fuse box. Although rarely fitted, if there had been one it would have complicated things for him as it would have allowed the electricity to be easily turned off from either that switch or the one included as part of the fuse box. He wanted there to be no choice.

James had purposely learned much about such electrical connections and the terminology whilst he had been living in Clayborough, waiting for his opportunity to work at Crossbow Transport. He also knew that no householder was permitted to interfere in any way with either the cut-out or the meter. The responsibility for these sections of the system rested solely with the electricity supply companies. That was why they were always located on a separate backboard. To underline the restriction, numbered seals, formed by small loops of wire, tended to be placed through any screws or access points by those companies. They prevented such screws from being tampered with, or undone, without noticeably removing their seals.

However, as James had also been reliably told by his former landlord, such seals can sometimes be mistakenly left off by an engineer in a hurry. As he looked at Sue and Julie's supply, James could see that the screw allowing access to the house's main fuse, contained in the cut-out, had no such seal included. That fell perfectly with his plan of preventing live electrical current from reaching the fuse box while he safely made the adjustments that he intended to. Sue had some screwdrivers lying around but, if a seal had been there, he would probably have needed to bring his small wire-cutters from his own house to remove it. He did not want to risk touching live electrical wires or terminals.

He did not want to risk electrocuting himself rather than Richard.

29

'Any chance of some breakfast for me as well?' asked Ian from immediately behind James.

'Shit!' exclaimed James, visibly jumping in response to the unexpected voice breaking through the silence before turning to face him. 'Do you always sneak up on people from behind in the quiet of the morning?'

Ian smiled back at James's surprised expression. 'Well I did try, but she said she had to get ready for work instead.'

James gave Ian a brief acknowledging smile for his attempted humour as he closed the cupboard door with the back of the same hand that was carrying the cereal box. Having regained his composure after his evil train of thought had been so abruptly interrupted, James stated the obvious. 'I take it that you also stayed last night, then.'

'Julie is quite a girl,' said Ian, leaving James to infer whatever he wanted from that.

The two men walked to the kitchen and James added another cereal bowl and cup to the collection that was already on the worktop.

'So, where did you two go last night?' asked James, adding a bit of extra water to the kettle.

'Didn't go anywhere,' answered Ian, as he sat down at the large kitchen table in the centre of the room. 'Just stayed here.'

'I didn't think there was anyone here when me and Sue got back. It was still quite early, but the place was in darkness.'

'Like I said, quite a girl,' said Ian, with more of a smirk than a smile. 'We just thought that we'd have an early night.'

Having now heard Ian speaking without his own inner voices drowning him out, as they had for much of the previous afternoon, James concluded, from his accent, that Ian was definitely from Devon.

'Tea? Milk and sugar?' asked James, acting the host in a house that was not his.

'Yes please. Two.'

James switched the kettle to boil and divided up the contents of the cereal box across the four bowls. He poured some milk, and spooned the requested sugar, into the additional cup. He preferred to use a traditional teapot in the mornings, rather than the modern alternative method of assigning a tea bag to each cup. Once the kettle had automatically switched itself off, he poured the boiling water into the waiting teapot and stirred it to encourage the tea to brew for a few minutes. As he also sat down at the table to wait for the tea to be ready, and for the women to join them, Ian launched into conversation.

'Julie suggested, late last night, that I move in here with her. That was a bit of a surprise to say the least. I don't know how it would work out, though, what with Sue also being here.'

However their cosy evening had progressed, it was clear that Ian had passed Julie's suitability test with flying colours.

'Now that's a bit of a coincidence,' said James, fully

realising that it was no such thing. 'Sue asked me the same thing while we were out.'

'Sounds like they both want a bit of male company, and with neither of them wanting to be the one left on the sidelines. I think these two sisters may be guilty of a bit of cunning planning behind our backs.'

'Are you going to?'

'Might as well. I'm sleeping on my friend's sofa at the moment and I'm sure he wants me out from under his feet. I'll probably leave it until the end of next week, though, for various reasons.'

So, James now knew the deadline for his plan, and it was even sooner than he had anticipated. In less than two weeks' time, this man would be moving into the house, with the potential to obstruct, or even prevent, his carefully thought-out murderous scheme.

Sue was the first to join them, dressed in her work clothes and with her hair perfectly in place. She was startled to find that James, who was the only one she had expected to see, had company.

'Oh. Morning Ian. Did you, er?' she began, not quite knowing how to phrase the question that she had intended.

'Yes. Yes I did,' pre-empted Ian, confirming his whereabouts for the previous night.

Julie soon appeared downstairs too, looking every inch as ready for work as her sister. Without further explanation of Ian's presence to either James or Sue, not that any was needed, she poured the brewed tea into the cups and the milk into the four bowls, over the cereals. It was always the acknowledged duty of the last arrival at the breakfast table, even when it had been just the three of them, so that all would eat at the same time.

'So, I hear that the four of us will all be here together soon,' said Julie, getting straight to the point as she distributed the breakfast items around the table. James and Ian both realised that there must have been some applicable extra conversation between the two women upstairs before either had come down.

'I guess so,' said Ian. 'So, here's to us four musketeers,' he continued, raising his cup of tea above the centre of the table and inviting the others to similarly raise their cups and chink them together in the manner of an alcoholic toast.

They ate their cereal and drank their tea, briefly talking about proposed house rules, household duties and financial considerations for their new arrangement. There was not much time for details as the women had to leave for work together as soon as the second cups of tea were drunk. Such was the tight timescale that resulted from the chosen setting of their alarm clocks.

'Please make sure the door is pulled shut as you leave,' said Sue, to James, as she pulled on her coat in the hallway, referring to the Yale lock. 'Thinking about that, I'll get a key cut for you during the week. How about you come over on Saturday to get it, and then you can stay for the whole weekend for a change?'

'Sounds great,' replied James, as he kissed her goodbye for another week.

Further along the narrow hallway, Ian and Julie were similarly finishing their own, private, farewell conversation. Once Ian finally released Julie from his arms, Sue and Julie left for work, leaving the two men in their house to tidy up the breakfast crockery and to get more acquainted.

James now felt uncomfortable, and annoyed, with just Ian for company. He had wanted, and expected, to be left alone for the rest of the morning so that he could have a proper, closer look at that fuse box, without any fear of interruption. He had even had thoughts that he might have been able to use the opportunity to make his intended adjustments. Instead, he now found that he was stood over a kitchen sink, handing over the cereal bowls, that he had just washed, to a man that he hardly knew. A man that had already found him suspiciously looking at the fuse box once already. A virtual stranger who was eagerly holding a tea towel next to him and showed no signs of leaving any time soon.

'So, you're not planning on moving in for nearly a fortnight?' asked James, idly making conversation.

'No, I'm busy next weekend. You know, things to do, people to see and all that. A weekend would definitely be a better time to shift my stuff in, though, what with Julie working during the week. So, that means it'll be in just under two weeks' time. How about you?'

'First of next month,' said James, absently. His mind was now racing over the timetable that he had just been presented with. 'So, you're not around here at all next weekend? I won't see you at all?'

'No. Like I said, other things to do.'

James conceded to himself that the following weekend, the one that he had just been invited to spend at the house, would now be his best, and probably his only, opportunity to set his intended trap for Richard. With that thought, he also realised that it was now no longer necessary for him to come up with a plausible way of getting Ian out of the house before him. As soon as the washing up of the breakfast things was completed, James mumbled something about not wishing to be late for work. Ian admitted that he, similarly, had no reason to stay in the house any longer, and so they both pulled on their coats and left together. James pulled hard on the door to ensure that the Yale lock clicked into place and the pair walked down the pathway to the street.

With a cheery goodbye at the gate, they parted company, Ian walking off in the opposite direction to James. James was heading in the direction of the bus station, his thoughts already firmly focused on the following weekend. Ian had said that he would not be around at all and James had already ensured that he would not be meeting Richard for their usual Sunday drinks.

Next weekend would be the pivotal time.

30

The Goblin Teasmade prepared his first hot drink of the day and then, with the help of his preferred radio station, announced the Saturday morning alarm to James, waking him from his fitful sleep. It had felt like a very long week, with many possible permutations of conversations and events for the upcoming weekend being considered. All that he knew for sure was that he would be spending this entire weekend with Sue. During that time, there were two main things that he had to accomplish, in either order. He needed to find some way of being left alone in the house with at least enough time to interfere with the electrics. It was also necessary to obtain Sue's keen agreement to a subsequent visit from Richard.

After an intense week of contemplation, it now felt like he had considered an infinite number of potential scenarios to navigate. He knew that, in the end, whatever happened would be largely dictated by circumstances outside of his control. Both Sue and Julie had to unknowingly behave and respond in one of the many ways that he had predicted for each situation. Also, Ian had to either keep completely away and out of the picture as he had said he would or, if he did appear, be at least stuck close enough to Julie for them to be regarded as one combined obstacle. Regardless of all his planning, he was acutely aware that he would simply have to be prepared to adapt and play it by ear when the times came.

Once he decided that the tea would have cooled enough to allow him to use it to swallow yet more of his strategically-placed paracetamol tablets, James sat up in his bed and picked up the mug with his right hand. Using his left, he picked up the inquest report, with its curled corners, that he had also purposely left on the bedside cabinet the night before. It was not that he felt he needed any reinforced motivation for the execution of his planned weekend. Rather, he wanted to just focus his mind on the main reason for his current existence and, as usual, he read it all.

As always, he paused at the confusing paragraph on page three and, as he had done ever since Frank's death, concentrated on what he perceived as the next most relevant section. This was the one which revealed that the traffic lights had been wired incorrectly, and potentially dangerously. Although absolved of any official blame for the tragedy at the time, as a direct result of Frank's perjury concerning the timing of the signals, everything was crystal clear to James. Richard had been responsible for the double-amber indication that had been an integral cause of the crash.

James returned the document to its former place on the bedside cabinet and rose from the bed. After a shower and getting dressed, he packed a few extra clothes and toiletries for the weekend into a backpack. As his kettle was heating up the water for his second cup of tea, he pulled out the small kitchen drawer where he kept a few tools and looked down at the screwdriver that was his intended weapon. He did not think that he would need to take anything else that he could see in that drawer. Even if he left the screwdriver behind, Sue would likely have one lying around that he could use instead. He had reasoned as much the previous weekend before being unexpectedly interrupted by Ian. Preferring to know for certain where his chosen instrument of death was, he placed his own screwdriver in the side pocket of the backpack as his kettle came to the boil.

James did not have to wait long for the next number 18 bus to arrive and he paid his fare with the exact money before sitting down for the familiar ride to Sue's. Being a Saturday, rather than his usual Sunday journey, there was more traffic on the roads and the ride correspondingly took slightly longer than he was used to. It did not particularly matter. No exact arrival time had been agreed between them and James knew that Sue would undoubtedly be waiting for him at her house.

Sue answered the door within seconds of James ringing the doorbell. It seemed to him that she must have been eagerly waiting for him with her hand poised above the latch. In fact, she had been upstairs making her bed when she had randomly glanced out of the window and seen him walking down the street. She had then descended the stairs and simply arrived in the hallway at the appropriate moment.

'Welcome to our weekend of fun,' she said as she threw her arms around his neck and kissed him.

'That sounds wonderful,' James answered, pondering what she may be meaning by the expression. 'Have you planned anything specific?'

'No, nothing. I just mean that we have a whole weekend together for the first time ever. Julie has even gone away, leaving us alone for two whole days.'

James was elated at the news that he would not have to somehow persuade both sisters to go out together in order to get the house to himself at some stage during the weekend. Although he had spent long hours contemplating how to achieve that situation, the problem had immediately solved itself. Now all that he needed to concentrate on was to persuade Sue that she should leave him alone sometime. 'Where's she gone?' he asked.

'Ian's taken her away for a dirty weekend somewhere, so we have the place to ourselves. She'll be back Sunday night, though.'

'So much for people to see and places to go,' said James, quietly, to himself.

'Sorry?'

'Nothing. Just thinking about something that someone once said. Shall I put my bag upstairs?' James asked, indicating his backpack, which was still hanging from his shoulders, over his coat.

'Yeah, sure,' said Sue, stepping back to allow him to pass her in the hallway. 'I'll put the kettle on and then you can tell me all about the week that you've had.' James stepped past her towards the stairs.

They spent the rest of the morning sat closely together on the lounge sofa, talking about their respective events of the previous days, usually concerned with work. James had already heard most of Sue's latest tales during his regular Thursday evening phone call to her two days before, but he did not mind listening to them again. Besides, this time she was able to embellish her entertaining stories of what her crazy boss had said and done during the previous week by enacting his accompanying movements across her lounge floor.

Lunch was at a nearby café, followed by a single quick drink in The Queens Head. They had only just managed to get there and be served in time before the final bell for the session had been rung. An afternoon spent shopping for women's clothes reinforced James's eternal dislike of the task. Wasting hours browsing around endless stores whilst clinging on to the vague possibility of seeing something worth owning was not his idea of fun. As far as he was concerned, shops only needed to be visited when there was something specific to purchase. He said nothing of his opinion to Sue as she strangely appeared to be revelling in the experience.

An early dinner at a local restaurant was followed by another visit to the Odeon cinema where they found that the latest James Bond offering had been replaced by a film that featured talking animals. The harmless flick concluded their long afternoon out together before they returned to Sue's house, hand in hand. As Sue turned her key in the lock, James checked his watch to find that it was nine-thirty.

'Bugger!' he said in response to the discovery.

'What's the matter?' asked Sue, concerned and confused, as the door swung open and she reached inside for the light switch.

'We've missed the start of *The Professionals*,' he said, with a tone of genuine disappointment.

'You like that programme?'

'What's not to like? Tough guys, with guns, beating the baddies every week.'

'Well, it's only been on for about a quarter of an hour. You can still watch most of it.'

After removing their coats, they sat down on the sofa in front of Sue's television and both watched what remained of the action-packed episode. Sue pretended to be interested and engrossed, purely for James's benefit, in the same way as she had during the James Bond film the previous weekend. James was genuinely enjoying the programme, but it was to a lesser extent than he had led Sue to believe. He was also devising the details of the next conversation he intended, which he began as soon as the credits began to roll.

'I would have liked to have seen the start of that one,' he said. 'I couldn't work out how Bodie and Doyle would have both ended up in that place at the same time.'

'Well, you should have said before that you wanted to watch it. How could I be expected to know what you liked to watch on a Saturday night? I've only ever seen you on Sundays until now. We could have easily left the cinema a bit earlier. It would have meant missing the end of the film, but I wouldn't have minded.'

'Or we could have had a video recorder here, taping it ready for when we got back.'

'Oh yeah, sure. We could have even got our chauffeur-driven limousine to pick us up when we came out of the Odeon.'

'They're not necessarily that expensive. I've been reading about them and quite a few people are getting one these days.'

'How expensive?'

'We wouldn't even need to fork out to buy one. You can rent them, by the month, from shops like Radio Rentals.' James was desperately trying to get her to take his bait.

'I'm not throwing money down the drain by renting anything.'

'I'll pay for it,' he said. 'It can be part of my contributions to the house.'

Sue conceded that it would be nice to have the new technology at her fingertips, especially if it meant being able to record some of those weekday afternoon programmes that she hated to miss because she had to work.

'Okay,' she said. 'You can organise it, though.'

'Fair enough,' said James. 'But you'll need a double socket put down there before it gets here. It'd need plugging in near to the set.' James pointed down at the single electrical socket that the television was plugged into.

'We can just use one of those adapters,' said Sue, but James had expected this counter.

'Oh, no. They look horrible with everything crammed together. It's a simple enough job. You simply change the socket to be a double one. It'd look much neater, and nicer, for the two things to be plugged in at once.'

'If it's so simple, you can do it.'

'I'd probably blow the place up if I tried. I'm no good with such things.'

'I'll get Julie to ask Ian, then. She says he's good with his hands.'

'I don't think that's quite what she would have meant,' said James with a wry smile.

Sue smiled too, acknowledging her possible misunderstanding of her sister's praise. 'I've never had any electrical jobs done here so I don't know of any electricians to trust. I guess there'll be some in Yellow Pages, though.'

James paused for a moment, apparently considering a solution. 'How about Richard? He's an electrician.'

'Is he? You've never said,' replied Sue, realising the sense of the suggestion.

James was already pulling Richard's business card from his pocket, the one he had been given when the two men had first met in The Queens Head. 'Here. Ring him now and see if he can come round this week and do it for us.'

Sue slowly took the proffered card, with a puzzled look appearing on her face. 'I thought you said when you called on Thursday that Richard wasn't around this weekend. That's why you're not seeing him for your usual beers tomorrow lunchtime.'

James realised the contradiction that had been revealed within his plans. Having told Richard the previous Sunday that he could not see him for a fortnight, in order to avoid an unnecessary drinking session, James had also lied to Sue that Richard had been the one to alter their regular arrangement.

'Oh yes, of course. He won't be at home. How about you keep the card and call him Monday, then?'

'Okay. If you still think it's worth messing around with it.'

'I do.'

'Maybe you'll say that to a vicar for me one day,' said Sue before properly thinking it through and causing a sudden, awkward silence between them.

Eventually, it was James that broke it, relieved that his own mistake had quickly been overshadowed. 'Maybe I will, one day,' he said with a smile and a reassuring kiss.

Sue turned off the television where the late news was just finishing. 'Time for bed,' she announced, with a glint in her eye. She was hoping that James would not be interested in *Match of The Day*, which followed it. He wasn't, and the two of them went upstairs to bed without a further word.

31

James woke with a sudden start to an unfamiliar ringing in his head. He drowsily reached for the bedside teasmade, that was not there, before he fully realised where he had been sleeping. He turned to look at his lover in the morning light that was streaming in through the thin curtains again, but Sue's side of the bed was empty. It was the first time that James had woken in her room on a Sunday morning and he had rudely discovered, much to his chagrin, that her house was close to a church. One with a bell which was now incessantly summoning the local parishioners to its walls for the morning service.

Through bleary eyes, he looked around Sue's room, wondering where she was. Suddenly, she appeared in the doorway, already dressed and, he noticed, very smartly.

'What's going on?' he asked, confused.

'I just thought I'd let you sleep on for a bit this morning,' she explained. 'You seemed so tired last night. I've had my shower and had some breakfast already, but I was just about to wake you to let you know I was going out for a while.'

'Out?'

'Church parade. We have it once a month in the Guides.'

'Church parade? Guides? What are you, an Akela or something?'

'That's the Cubs and Boy Scouts. It's Brown Owl in the Guides, and no I'm not. I just help out on meeting nights during the week. Have done ever since I was too old to be a Girl Guide myself. I'm not a leader, or any kind of owl. Not yet, anyway. I always go along to the parades, though, to stay a part of the movement.'

'How come you've never mentioned it before?'

'I've been a bit embarrassed about it, I guess, clinging on to my past and still needing to feel part of it. The meetings are Wednesday nights, and you've never phoned me then. Parades are every fourth Sunday, at ten o'clock. Most weeks you meet up with Richard before you come round here on Sunday afternoons, so it's simply never clashed with our plans before.'

'You're full of surprises,' said James. Then, with a wicked grin, and a change of tone, he asked, 'haven't you at least got some sort of a uniform that you could wear, though?'

Sue refused to react to his decadent suggestive question, not when she was just about to go to church. With just a smile and a goodbye kiss she said, 'I'll be back at about half past eleven.' After that she left him in the room, walked down the stairs and out of the front door.

After days of thinking through the numerous anticipated permutations and potential problems of being able to manoeuvre the situation, James suddenly found himself alone in the house without having had to orchestrate it in any way. He laid back on the bed for a few moments to gather his thoughts and accept his good fortune. Despite pondering on it for so long, he had not been able to think of a ruse that would have persuaded Sue to gladly, and unsuspiciously, go out and leave him alone. Yet, here he now was, with ample opportunity to perform the task that had been uppermost on his mind for years.

As a result of the information that his Clayborough landlord had unwittingly shared, James was confident that he knew enough to sabotage the electricity supply to the house, making it lethal to anyone else subsequently working on it. With her agreement to the idea of having an extra electrical socket near to the television, Sue had also agreed for that next person to be his target, Richard. All he had to do now was rewire the fuse box.

He showered slowly, with his mind contemplating aspects of the job ahead, and dressed purposefully in the change of clothes from his backpack. Once downstairs, he avoided the cereal from the cupboard under the stairs and instead just made himself a cup of tea, his first of the day. He tried to calm his increasing heart rate by sitting at the kitchen table, slowly drinking the beverage and watching the birds feeding at Sue's ornamental bird table beyond the window. As he finished the last of the tea, a robin landed on the garden accessory to accept its share of the seeds. The sight of it made James smile, suddenly thinking of the colleague, and rare friend, who had, with him, been one of the last to see Frank Bird alive before he had left him behind at the fencing factory.

'Hello Robin,' he said, out loud and towards the garden, despite there being no-one to hear or understand. 'Are you always going to show up when I'm about to set a trap for one of those bastards who took everything away from me?'

The outburst focused James's thoughts and he reached for his screwdriver that he had carried downstairs with him, having retrieved it from the side pocket of the backpack after dressing. He walked from the kitchen, pulled open the cupboard door under the stairs and gazed again at the components of the electricity supply. The cut-out box was positioned on the left of the backboard and next to the meter. He knew that, if he was extremely careful, he might have been able to achieve his planned adjustments to the circuitry, regardless of the wires being left live, and without any need to encroach in this section. However, he did not want to take the unnecessary risk of electrocuting himself, especially as he had previously discovered that there was no security seal on the cut-out to expose his actions. He unscrewed the small cover on the top left of the box, below the thick, red live power cable, and removed the high-rated master fuse that had been underneath. This effectively cut all electrical power to the house, the meter and, most importantly, the consumer fuse box.

He looked at the thick fuse that he now held in his left hand and took a deep breath before gently placing it on top of the cut-out box. He turned his attention to the fuse box, on the wall to the right of the meter. As he raised his screwdriver towards it, he paused as he suddenly felt a surge of doubts about what he was doing. In exactly the same way as had happened to him when his opportunity had finally come to sabotage Frank's lorry, just before the unexplained gap in his memory, James's head filled with simultaneous reservations and uncertainties.

He realised that he was completely reliant on Sue calling in Richard, rather than another electrician, to replace the socket that was near to the television. Richard might not be available or he may even be unwilling, especially given his failed history with Julie, to do the work. As a result, Sue might suddenly decide to entrust the work to an innocent individual instead, just to please him and get the job done. Finding willing electricians in the Yellow Pages was relatively easy after all. Alternatively, Ian might be persuaded to attempt it, or Sue might even recruit someone from the congregation at the church that he had not known, until recently, that she had any connection with.

He also realised that he would soon be subjecting at least one of the women to the grizzly aftermath of his actions. Strangely, even with all his meticulous planning of the other details, this obvious point had effectively eluded him until now. Sue, or perhaps Julie, or both, would have to be in the house at the time that Richard would be working on the socket. It would be unrealistic to expect otherwise.

Regardless of such contrary thoughts, he clearly remembered that, long ago, he had vowed to avenge the deaths of his family. This fuse box still remained his best chance to do that as far as the electrician responsible was concerned.

For a further ten minutes, James's head, and the top half of his body, remained inside the cupboard. The screwdriver was always in his hand, up until the time that he finally replaced the main fuse to restore the power to the house and he closed the cupboard door. His heart was pounding so hard by the time he returned to the kitchen and sat down again that his ears were ringing.

32

When Sue returned home from the church later that morning, she found James sat at the kitchen table with a cup of tea in one hand and her Sunday newspaper, which had been delivered, in the other. He appeared to be engrossed in an article to such an extent that he had not heard her come in. Her greeting shook him back to reality and he smiled back at her, visibly pleased to see her return.

James had been quite oblivious to his surroundings, and not concentrating on the newspaper at all. He had purposefully adopted the pose, knowing that Sue's arrival was likely to be imminent. His eyes had been unseeing, and his thoughts had been elsewhere, when Sue's voice from behind him had suddenly dispelled everything from his mind. He knew that he had to instantly jump back to normality, if only to prevent her suspicions from being raised.

'How'd it go?' he asked as he got up from the table to pour her a cup of tea from the pot that he had prepared only five minutes earlier.

'Fine. I was hoping that he would talk all about the sins of the flesh, if only so that we could maybe pick up a few tips,' Sue joked. 'Strangely, though, with the place half full of Girl Guides, Brownies, Cubs and Scouts, he simply concentrated on *Thou Shalt Not Steal*.' She had never been a religious believer, hence the frivolous attitude. Ever since being a young girl, she had only ever attended the church because it was a mandatory requirement of the organisation that she had associated herself with.

'My favourite bit of the book is when he loses his rag in a marketplace and wrecks all the stalls,' said James. 'I think that would have been really funny to see.' Like Sue, James was not religious in any way, but he'd still had to endure hours of compulsory Christian teaching at school and so he knew many of the stories from the Bible.

As he spoke, it was the sixth commandment, *Thou Shalt Not Kill*, that suddenly appeared clearly in his mind, causing him to catch his breath and pause momentarily. He quickly dismissed the thought, as he often did, justifying his thoughts and actions to himself under the guise of honouring his father and mother, the preceding commandment.

Unaware of his sudden, brief inner turmoil, Sue compared the biblical account to one of someone disrupting the local Thursday market in town before changing the subject to the plans for the rest of their day. 'Are you wanting to go anywhere today? I had a pretty hard week at work last week and, after us being out so much yesterday, I'd rather we stayed in today to be honest.'

That suited James perfectly. He had lied to Richard the previous weekend, claiming that he was not able to meet with him again for two weeks. He had also lied to Sue that it had been Richard who had been the one to postpone their usual drinking session by skipping a week. So James now feared, even more than he had the day before, the potential embarrassing situation, and subsequent explanations, of running in to Richard in town whilst he was with Sue.

'Staying in sounds just fine to me,' said James. 'I could even peel the spuds this week, just for a change.'

'I'll get changed into my comfy clothes and then I'll get started on the dinner,' said Sue, turning back towards the kitchen door and leaving James alone once again.

After she returned, dressed in her loose-fitting, but still flattering, comfortable clothes, Sue prepared another of her delicious Sunday dinners. This time it was for just the two of them, but she still wanted to put the same amount of effort into it as she had for four, the previous week. James was uninterested in any of the three television choices of a late Sunday morning and early Sunday afternoon, such as political programmes or *Open University* lectures. Instead, he stayed with her in the kitchen and helped her with various peripheral tasks, including the peeling of a few potatoes, all done under her culinary direction and guidance.

They had finished eating their dinner in time for the Sunday afternoon football highlights programme on ITV, *The Big Match*. James was keen to watch it, having missed out on the previous night's equivalent BBC1 programme due to Sue's persuasive bedtime announcement.

'Those pans and trays all need washing up,' Sue remarked. As James knew, she always hated leaving dirty utensils by the sink.

'If we already had that video recorder, I would happily tape it to watch later and do all the washing up now, but we haven't. Can't it wait an hour?'

'I'll do it, then. You can watch your football if you want.'

So Sue, successfully avoiding what she had always

considered to be the mind-numbing spectacle of twenty-two grown men kicking a bag of wind around, accepted the role of washing up the crockery while James watched alone. She made sure that she had completed the task in good time for them to watch the Sunday afternoon film that followed it.

For the rest of the afternoon and into the evening, they sat on the sofa together, watching television and occasionally swapping channels, making cups of tea in the advert breaks. Sue was contented with that, finding the day a welcome relaxation after the several stresses of the week that she had just endured. James was just pleased to be hidden away indoors, with no chance of an unfortunate encounter with Richard.

They were halfway through watching an episode of *Dallas* when, at 9:30pm, Julie burst in through the front door and dropped her small suitcase loudly onto the floor of the hall.

'Hi Jules,' called Sue from the sofa, without needing to confirm the source of the sounds. 'Everything all right?'

'Not exactly,' answered her sister as she appeared in the lounge doorway with her face set in an unmistakable look of annoyance. 'Ian won't be moving in next weekend after all,' she announced. James and Sue realised that, despite her weekend companion, Julie had unexpectedly arrived home without him. Perhaps, thought James selfishly, there had not been such an urgency for his preparations as he had originally thought.

Sue tried to cling to some optimism for her sister. 'So, will it be a later weekend instead?'

'No, it will be never,' said Julie curtly, turning in the doorway and offering no further explanation. 'I'm off to bed.'

'A bit early for that don't you think,' whispered James, in Sue's ear.

'Don't be a fool. She obviously doesn't want to be sitting here with us and having to discuss whatever it is that he's said or done. Sounds like it's probably all over between them, for some reason that's none of our business.' Then, after a pause, she added 'I'll go up in a bit and find out what I can about it.'

'Seems like it will only be the three of us living here soon, then. That is, assuming I'm still invited even with the fourth musketeer now apparently out of the picture.'

'Of course you are,' said Sue, slightly annoyed that he should think otherwise.

'Phew, that's a relief,' said James, reassured.

'You get on to Radio Rentals first thing tomorrow and arrange for that video recorder for us. I'll call Richard too, to ask him to change that socket ready for it,' she said, unnecessarily reminding him of their first joint homemaking decision the previous evening, as if to emphasise their arrangements.

James looked long, and hard, at the single outlet she was pointing at, just above the skirting board in front of them. He was wondering just how lethal such an inanimate object could prove to be.

33

Sue sat at her desk nursing her mid-morning cup of coffee from the office drinks machine, taking small sips. She did not want to have to talk to Richard, still finding it rather embarrassing that things had not worked out for him and Julie after the night that she had first met James. However, he was James's friend, and an electrician with many years of experience, so it was understandable that he should be the one asked to replace the power outlet.

She and James had left the house together earlier that morning, with James heading off to the bus station to make his own way to work. With their parting words, she had reminded him again about arranging their video recorder and the thought of them getting one now quite excited her. As he had been so insistent on Saturday night that it warranted a double socket, she now felt compelled to play her part and at least get her lounge socket replaced in readiness.

With just five minutes remaining of her morning break, not that anyone in authority kept any kind of watch, she finally picked up the handset of her desk phone. After pressing the 'nine' button, she heard the dialling tone change pitch slightly to confirm that she was now connected to an external line rather than the company's internal phone system. Whilst occasionally looking at the business card that James had given to her, she punched in Richard's number.

'Hello, Richard Jennings speaking,' answered a voice after the third ring.

'Hello Richard, this is Sue. James's girlfriend.'

'Hello Sue,' said Richard, his words instantly brighter and more friendly. 'How are you keeping?'

'Doing fine, thanks.'

'And what about that lovely sister of yours?'

Sue did not want to be drawn into a conversation about Julie with this man and purposely ignored the question, getting straight to the point. 'James has asked me to call you to see if you can do a little job for us.'

'What kind of job?' asked Richard, sensing an opportunity to earn some money and making him immediately forget his own question.

'Just a simple one,' Sue said. 'We'd like a single socket swapped for a double one if you can fit us in sometime soon.'

'No problem at all,' said Richard. Sue was sure that she could hear the turning of the pages of his diary in the background. 'How about Thursday afternoon?'

'That'd be great,' confirmed Sue. She was already thinking that she was still owed a paid half-day out of the office in exchange for some unscheduled late working that she had done a few weeks before. She had hoped to have a good reason to claim it before too much more time had passed and her earlier favour to the boss had been conveniently forgotten.

Sue told Richard her full address and assured him that she would be able to get the time off work to be there and let him in. With nothing further to arrange or say, she managed to politely end the call before the end of her official break time and, more importantly, before Richard had the chance to remember and return to his earlier enquiry about her sister.

That evening, James phoned Sue at home, unusually for a Monday, but as always from a call box. She told him of the arrangement that she had made for Richard to replace the socket on Thursday. He assured her that he had also been making daytime calls. Radio Rentals would be delivering a video recorder for them to enjoy within a fortnight. They would be calling her later in the week to agree a specific delivery day.

On Thursday afternoon, Sue was sat in her lounge, having already enjoyed one of those television programmes that had made getting a video recorder sound like such a good idea to her in the first place. The television was still on, but the current programme held no interest for her. It was just a means of filling the room with some sound rather than sitting in silence. She was not in the mood for the alternative of playing some music instead. None of her records were particularly relaxing and she was already feeling tensed by the thought of her visitor potentially questioning her about Julie. Also, she wondered whether she should mention Ian if he did.

Having left work as early as she had been able to, just before her usual lunchtime, she had travelled straight home. Ever since, without making herself any lunch, she had simply been expectantly waiting for Richard to arrive at any moment. She had realised, too late, that he had not specified an exact expected arrival time. She now wished that she had not been in such a hurry to finish the call, leaving the vague arrangement as being for any time after midday. If she had talked to him for just a while longer, or even had the courage to call him a second time, she might have possibly been able to pin him down to a more accurate timeslot. If she had only asked him to be a bit more precise, that might have avoided all the aimless waiting around now.

It seemed that James was calling her every hour throughout the afternoon, constantly asking if Richard had been round and completed the job. However, it was not until just before five o'clock that her afternoon's loneliness was finally disturbed by the ringing of her doorbell. She opened the door to find Richard smiling back at her with a metal toolbox held in his right hand.

'Sorry I'm so late,' he said. 'My previous job took a lot longer than I expected.'

'That's okay,' said Sue, returning his smile and stepping back to allow him into the hallway. 'I've had loads to do around the house this afternoon so I would have taken the time off work anyway. I hadn't even noticed just how late it is,' she lied.

'So I see,' said Richard with a slight hint of sarcasm in his voice as he reached as far as the lounge and faced the television. It was still on.

Sue followed him into the lounge, trying to avoid further mention of his accurate presumption of an afternoon wasted in front of the television. 'I'd just like that plug socket, the one for the television, changed to be a double one please.'

'Easy enough, Sue. You shouldn't miss too much of your programme,' said Richard with a smile and a wink. 'I've brought a double socket with me to put in, if you haven't got one already yourself.'

Sue realised, for the first time, that she had not even thought to buy a replacement socket. 'Thanks. We'll just use your one please,' she said, assuming, and hoping, that she could not be his only customer to have ever overlooked such an obvious purchase.

'Fine,' said Richard, suddenly looking around his surroundings. 'Where's your meter?'

'Why?'

'I need to turn off the electricity,' explained Richard.

'Oh yes, of course. Through here, it's under the stairs,' said Sue, leading him back to the hallway and indicating the small cupboard before leaving him there and returning to the lounge.

Richard opened the cupboard door and looked casually at the components of the electrical supply on the far wall. He flicked up the switch on the fuse box to the off position, to cut the power, and then joined Sue in the lounge where he placed his tool box next to the socket. The television was now off, as he had expected.

As James's former landlord had once told him, many electricians gradually get complacent after doing the job for some time and can unconsciously tend to skip various, essential, safety checks. One of those that he had specifically mentioned during their discussion, years before, was the use of a circuit tester to ensure that there was no current present before touching any electrical wiring. Whether it was the ongoing conversation with Sue that had distracted Richard from using his tester to check on this occasion, or he had developed the bad habit of always trusting the main switch, no-one would ever subsequently know. He just knelt down and pulled the television's plug out of the socket in order to gain free access to its fixing screws.

'We're getting a video recorder soon to go with the television' explained Sue from over his shoulder. 'James said it would look neater with a double socket.'

'I take it that James gave you my number?' said Richard as he rapidly unscrewed both sides with his insulated screwdriver.

'Yes, he thought you'd be the best man to do this for us.'

'Well, well, well,' said Richard as he pulled the single socket away from the metal back box that was imbedded in the wall. He began unscrewing the wires attached to the terminals from the rear of the removed socket plate. 'I was beginning to think that he had no faith in my abilities, actually. A while ago he once talked of me checking out the wiring of his lights, but he hasn't mentioned it since.' Suddenly, Richard registered something else that she had just said. 'Us? We?' he queried. 'Is he living here now, then?'

'No, but he will be soon.'

'I guess he won't be needing me for the lights after all,' he said as he pulled the loose socket away from the three wires and placed it down on the carpet.

'You'd go all that way just to sort out his lights?'

Richard was immediately confused and about to ask Sue to further explain her question. He had always thought that James lived near to the local bus station. That was hardly a large distance to travel and do a job for a friend. However, the sound of the front door opening had caused Sue to quickly exit the room with the briefest of apologies. She had wanted to warn Julie, returning from work herself, that Richard was in the house, knowing that her sister would have no desire to see him.

What made her even more concerned was that, when she got to the hallway, Sue found that Ian was with Julie. The last thing she wanted was a possible embarrassing meeting involving two of Julie's former flames even if, in Richard's case at least, it had only been a very brief encounter.

'I met Ian on the bus home,' explained Julie. 'He's only here to pick up a few things that he left behind in my room, nothing more.'

'Well, maybe the pair of you should go straight up and get them,' said Sue, trying her best to convey the potentially awkward situation to her sister by means of various facial gestures and eye movements. The encoded message failed to register with Julie, even though she had already known that Richard had been due to do some work in their house that afternoon.

'In a minute,' said Julie, walking past Sue into the lounge followed, like a lapdog, by Ian.

Richard was still on his knees and now holding on to the thick grey cable, containing the three separate power wires, which was protruding from the wall. He had been oblivious to the new arrivals in the house. Instead, while he continued working, he was idly replaying his initial conversations with James in his mind, still trying to make sense of Sue's remark about how far away James lived. He wondered which one of them, himself or Sue, James may have lied to about it, or indeed if there was another explanation for the apparent contradiction. As he gripped the bare end of one of the three individual wires to pull it closer to the new double socket that he had just removed from its box, Julie's voice diverted his attention further.

'Oh, hello Richard,' said Julie, suddenly surprised to see him in her house. This was the first time that the two of them had seen each other since the night that they first met. Thinking quickly, she continued. 'This is Ian,' she said, whilst linking Ian's arm to hopefully leave the obsessive Richard in no doubt that she was most definitely out of bounds for him now. Staring up at the two of them, and without looking back down, Richard inattentively continued with his task and gripped another bare end of a wire with his other hand.

In an instant, the surge of lethal current contracted his muscles, involuntarily tightening his grip on the wires. The switch on the fuse box had been rewired from the inside, causing it to be bypassed and totally ineffective for its intended purpose. It allowed electricity to flow regardless of its position, either on or off. Also inside the fuse box, there was a small portion of a guitar string that connected together the two terminals of the individual fuse for the ring main. The current would have probably proven to be fatal long before the original fuse blew but the metal guitar string ensured it. Even if the rated fuse wire had melted in its attempt to break the circuit, it would remain intact and there would be a constant, unbreakable path for the deadly power.

From one of his hands to the other, the invisible current streamed across Richard's chest, freezing his final facial expression and instantly stopping his heart. His lifeless body keeled over forwards, pivoted on his knees, onto the lounge carpet. Julie instinctively screamed at the bizarre sight of the electrocution and rushed forward to try to save Richard. Thankfully, Ian was quick enough to grab her from behind and stop her.

'No!' he shouted authoritatively. 'The electric must be still on. If you touch him, you'll get a belt too.'

Sue quickly appeared in the doorway, sensing that something terrible had just happened, and immediately became hysterical when she saw the aftermath. Richard was lying on her lounge floor, his unseeing eyes wide open, still clutching the two wires which had delivered his fatal blow. Ian attempted, unsuccessfully, to calm both women down while he tried to work out what he should do next.

34

Five minutes later, James was dialling Sue's number once more, from the phone box down the road from his house. He regularly called her on Thursdays but, this week, he also knew that Richard had been expected at some time during the afternoon. He was desperate to find out how that visit had gone.

Once the phone dial rotated back, returning to its resting position after the final digit, James heard the ringing tone until Sue answered at the other end. He briefly heard her voice, sounding very distressed he thought, before the signal cut out. It was replaced by the sound of the familiar high-pitched pips that now demanded his payment in order to continue the call. He pushed hard on the two-pence piece that he had previously positioned in the coin slot. He had to wait a few seconds for the mechanism to stop whirring and for the line to be reopened for his call. When it did, he immediately heard Sue's distraught voice again.

'James? Is that you?' she was saying, in between sobs.

'Of course it is. What's the matter?'

'There's been a terrible accident. It's Richard. Oh, I don't know how to tell you.'

'What kind of accident?' asked James, his thoughts now racing over the possibilities.

'We think he's dead. It looks like he grabbed hold of live wires while he was changing the socket for us.'

James was silent for a few moments as he digested the news and pictured the scene in his mind. A scene that he had imagined, and indeed hoped for, many times since he was a young teenager. He tried to react in a manner that he thought he ought to on hearing that a friend had suffered such a fate. 'Dead? Oh my God. When? Why was he messing around with live wires anyway?'

'I don't know. It all happened so fast. He went to turn off the electric at the meter, so there shouldn't have been any power anywhere. I switched off the television while he was gone.' James immediately realised the significance of the timing before she continued. 'Then he just came back, got his screwdriver out and set to it. Next thing we know, he's electrocuted himself.'

'We?' said James, realising that Sue had already said it twice.

'Julie got home from work just before it happened. It was only a few minutes ago. An ambulance is on its way but we're sure he's dead. He's still holding the wires.'

'Don't touch anything,' demanded James, his thoughts suddenly clear. 'Nothing at all. I'm coming over right now to look at those electrics. There must be something seriously wrong with them and you could get hurt, or worse, yourself.'

It sounded to James as though the entire scenario had played out exactly as he had planned. The electrician who had once wrongly wired those traffic lights that had been such a contributory factor in the 1965 accident had also now died as a result of an electrical wiring error. Some kind of fuse box bypass, keeping the wires permanently live, had always been his intention. The idea had first occurred to him when he had been covertly learning about house electrics from his landlord in Clayborough, when he had also been closing in on Frank. He had finally had the chance to set such a trap during the previous weekend and now it had perfectly been sprung, precisely as he had originally conceived.

However, in exactly the same way as he had always had a total memory block regarding the details of his sabotage of Frank's lorry four years earlier, James curiously found that he now had no recollection at all of tampering with Sue's fuse box either. After the time of him removing the main fuse from the cut-out and staring at the consumer unit, with those many conflicting doubts flooding into his mind, he found that there was simply nothing significant for him to remember. He could only remember having those doubts, trying to summon the courage to act, staring at the unopened fuse box with his screwdriver in his hand and thinking that he should not touch it. There was nothing else that he could remember about the episode, right up until the time that he had returned the main fuse to its rightful place.

He realised that this was now two separate occasions that his subconscious mind had selectively erased all memories of his murderous preparations. He could not begin to understand it, but he confidently blamed his teenage head injury as the underlying reason. After all, he already knew that it had caused him so many other cognitive problems.

Sue's voice interrupted his conclusions. 'Ian said exactly the same thing and is having a look at the electrics right now,' she said, causing him to suddenly inwardly panic.

'Ian? What's he doing there?'

'He turned up with Julie. He came round to collect some of his stuff after they met up on the bus on the way home.'

This was a development that James had not foreseen. His original plan had always included subsequently returning the internal wiring of the fuse box back to its normal state and resetting the switch back to the on position. He needed to be able to quickly, and secretly, make all the necessary readjustments before the lethal configuration was even suspected by anyone else. After doing that, everyone would just assume that Richard had simply not turned the power off.

James had managed to covertly discover, some time ago, that neither Sue nor Julie had any real comprehension of the electricity supply located in their own downstairs cupboard, to the extent that neither of them even realised that it included a switch. He assumed that Ian would know about at least that much. It was very likely that he would soon, or even right now, be trying to understand why the current was still active despite the master switch clearly being off. James had to concede, to himself, that it would now be implausible to get to Sue's house in time to hide the sabotage.

'Can you come over please. I need you,' Sue was saying over his contemplations.

'I'm on my way right now,' he lied. 'I'll be there as soon as I can.' He hung up the phone and, for a moment, rested his head against the handset that he had just replaced on its cradle.

He was now thankful that he had at least had the foresight to account for such a risk in his original planning, but he still regretted how things had now turned out. He had started to really like Sue, despite her original purpose of only being perfect for his upcoming plans. A local householder who could provide him with a place to lure Richard to. He had always refused to be detracted from his primary goal but he had even started to hope that, after the deed was done, that the two of them might be able to continue as a couple. That would only have been possible if he could have removed all the evidence in time. Now, he knew, it would not be long before the entire trap, and his undoubted responsibility for it, was discovered. It was clear to him that it would be much too dangerous for him to ever attempt to return to Sue's house, or her life.

He had told Sue that he did not drive, thus never needing to let her see his car with its distinctive rust patterns. He had purposely been vague about where he lived, even talking of sharing with fictitious flatmates, and in a rough area of Birchstead, rather than on the affluent street where he actually did live. Fortuitously, she still believed that his surname was the pseudonym that he had first used in Clayborough and then, later, to introduce himself to Richard. She did not know where he really worked and she had no phone number for him. He had lied that he was not on the phone, hence his consistent use of the phone box that he now stood in. She would now have no way of contacting, or finding, him again. Therefore, he reasoned, neither would any police that she may now report her lethal fuse box to.

James walked slowly back up the road to his house and, once inside, poured himself a glass of whiskey before sitting down to evaluate the completion of another stage of his adopted lifelong quest. He realised that James Harper would need to be completely disappearing again, leaving only James Pearce. He decided that he should grow his hair long again, just in case any photofit pictures were issued once his obvious involvement in Richard's death became clear. To further alter his appearance from the time he was at the lorry garage in Clayborough, when he had long hair before, he toyed with the notion of also having it permed this time.

He afforded himself a slight smile as he took another sip of the warming liquid and then rose to cross the room towards his record collection in the corner. He soon found the album he was looking for. *The Game*, by Queen. After removing the record from its sleeve, he placed it on his turntable and, once the platter was turning, he gently lowered the needle to play the third track. He sat back down, and smiled more broadly at the familiar bass guitar introduction to the track. The appropriately-titled song *Another One Bites The Dust* filled the room.

He sang along to the title lyric, and felt mixed emotions as he realised that it could equally be applied to his relationship with Sue, as well as to Richard's life.

PART FOUR

1985

35

James looked up from the monotonous list that he had been reading. He had now finally reached the end and neither Mrs. Zyla nor her adult offspring, the final entry on yet another electoral roll, included the person that he had constantly been looking for. It had been his ritual most nights, ever since Richard had met his fate, and it had just proved itself to all be totally pointless. It was late in the evening and, after such another long session of unproductive searching, he felt very tired and despondent.

James slowly looked into the reflection of his reddened eyes in the mirror on the wall next to him. The peripheral sight of his curly mane of long brown hair still surprised him even after so long. In the intervening years since Richard's death, he had let his naturally straight hair grow long again. He had been determined to alter his appearance as much as possible from what may be remembered by Sue, or anyone else involved in that episode. To also keep his look different to what those people he had left behind in Clayborough might also remember, he'd had it regularly permed into loose curls that now rested on his shoulders. It now pleasantly reminded him of how Sue's hair had been, albeit a slightly darker colour, at least throughout the short time that he had known her. Assuming that he would be able to find a way to execute the next stage of his long-term plan, he conceded that he would probably need to adopt yet another persona immediately afterwards.

He had systematically trawled through many lists such as the one he just had, obtained from the local councils, fruitlessly searching for a Beatrice of the correct age. Always initially checking each new list for any entries with Uncle Ray's surname, just in case she had continued to use it since leaving him, James had spent endless hours tediously working his way through the alphabetical registers.

Thankfully, Beatrice was a relatively uncommon name and so he had only ever found a few in each listing. The vast majority of those that he did find were consistently in the wrong age bracket and so could be quickly discarded from further consideration. Simple further investigations of the few remaining potential candidates that he had found had always soon revealed, beyond doubt, that they could not be Auntie Bea, for a multitude of different reasons.

Perversely, and to James's eternal surprise, he now realised that Frank Bird and Richard Jennings had both been much easier for him to find. James sat back in his chair and sipped at his glass of whiskey, wondering what he could possibly do next to secretly trace the woman who was now dominating, and haunting, his thoughts. The document, which now lay open at its last page on his dining table, had been the last of its kind for him to check through. It had been his last hope for this painstaking, time-consuming, and ultimately futile, method. Over the course of the preceding three years, he had read the full names of every single resident of voting age within a thirty-mile radius and come up with nothing.

'I guess the bitch just moved away,' he said quietly to himself, rising stiffly from the hard-backed dining chair and walking over to his comfortable sofa to sit and contemplate. He still held the whiskey glass in his right hand and took another sip before placing it down on the low coffee table at his feet.

James picked up the inquest report, still always kept close, from beside where he had placed the glass. It had been read so often that the corners of the pages were now curled like crested waves. To reinforce his jaded motivation on this unsuccessful evening, he read again the familiar words describing the tragic events of 1965. He read again of Frank Bird's insistent testimony, and mentally ticked his revenge as now complete. He read again of the erroneous traffic light sequence, caused by incorrect wiring, and did similarly. He read the short paragraph on the third page and could only wonder at how he might eventually resolve the confusion that it continued to cause him.

Finally, there was the recorded observation, from the subsequent post-mortem examinations, that his father had been drinking alcohol shortly before the accident, with a clear implication of its relevance. The wrongful suggestion that his father had been to blame, even partly, continued to make his blood boil. He clearly remembered that Bea had encouraged him to drink a few of her red wine spritzers throughout that fateful evening. James had often reasoned that, although relatively weak in alcoholic content, they just may have caused a minimal misjudgement. She could have just as easily given his father lemonade, along with himself and his sister, especially as she knew that he would have to drive home. He looked over at the faded rubber duck toy that always sat on his lounge windowsill, rather than on the shelf in his bathroom, and spoke directly to it.

'I will find her, though. Somehow I will find her.'

The inanimate rubber duck had been his confidante for years. Never judging him, always ready to listen and always faithfully keeping secret everything that it was told. James had found that whenever he earnestly explained his problems to it, speaking out loud so that he could also objectively hear them himself, potential answers usually occurred to him. After a few moments of thinking, he picked up the glass again and turned to fully face the duck. It stared, unseeingly, back at him, but it was ready to hear his dilemma.

'So, this is how it is,' he began. 'Auntie Bea walked out just a few months after I moved in with her and Uncle Ray. I don't know where she went, and I haven't seen her since that day. I was only thirteen and I didn't appreciate anything about forwarding addresses or anything like that, so I don't know of any. I always knew that I would be wanting to track her down someday when I was grown up, though. I suppose that I naively thought it would be straightforward when the time came. I just presumed that she would keep showing up again every so often, still coming back to see Uncle Ray maybe. I would simply be able to choose the right moment to get my revenge. She never did, though. Lifelong smoker Uncle Ray eventually died from lung cancer, so I suppose she would have a bit of difficulty visiting him these days. Rebecca, my sister, was also living there when Auntie Bea left, and she was younger than me at the time. She probably still is.' James briefly paused to smirk at his own weak jokes. 'She wasn't bothered at all that Auntie Bea had disappeared and she never asked where she might have gone either. My cousin, Tom, was eighteen and so was probably a lot more aware of what had happened at the time.'

Suddenly, another possible avenue of enquiry occurred to James and he abruptly stopped talking. He carefully thought more about it in the silence, taking further sips of his drink. After two minutes, he smiled at the duck, raising his glass towards it in a mock toast. 'Thanks my friend. You've done it again.'

36

Early the following evening, having been thinking all day about what, and how much, he would say, James slowly punched the phone number into the numbered buttons of his new telephone. Sat comfortably on his sofa again, with the lead of the phone trailing across the lounge floor to the skirting board, he listened to the ringing tone expectantly. After what felt like an eternity, his call was eventually answered, on the fifth ring.

'Hello,' said the familiar voice from the other end.

'Hello Tom,' said James, cheerily. 'It's James. How you doing?'

'Hello bruv,' said Tom, immediately recognising his cousin's voice and now expecting just another of their frequent phone conversations.

After sharing a house, a twin bedroom, and much of their lives from 1965 until Tom had left home, the pair had always regarded themselves as more like brothers than cousins. It was an acknowledged understanding, and greeting, between them and James was relying on that close bond being strong enough for what he might soon have to reveal and ask for.

'I've been thinking,' said James, to introduce his proposal. 'It's been much too long since we've actually seen each other. I know we still catch up on the phone all the time, but do you realise just how long it's been since we met up and saw each other?' James already knew the answer to his partly rhetorical question.

'I suppose it must be a couple of years by now,' estimated Tom.

'Four,' corrected James. He could clearly recall that he had last seen Tom only two weeks after he had finally bumped into Richard and had started forging that false friendship, nearly four years earlier.

'Four? Shit. Doesn't time fly? I guess we've both just been too wrapped up in other things. I'm right in the middle of trying to organise a school reunion at the moment for one thing.'

'They're surely just a weak justification for a bunch of strangers of the same age to get drunk together,' interrupted James, his tone light. He knew that they were both equally to blame for their total lack of recent meetings, and he took no pleasure from hearing his cousin painfully fumbling around for lame excuses. They had been keeping in touch, and sharing anecdotes, by phone, and that had felt to be sufficient contact at this stage of their lives. However, James now desperately wanted to see Tom again, face to face.

'I guess so, but there's nothing wrong with that,' Tom said, while James was already thinking of his next remark.

'Nothing at all. So, I reckon it's high time that you and me also sank a few together, don't you? We could have our own little reunion.'

'Any time that you suggest my little bruv,' said Tom, rapidly warming to the unexpected idea.

'Friday?' proposed James.

Tom was slightly taken aback by the apparent urgency but would never have dreamt of turning James down if he were available himself. He already knew that he was free that evening, as indeed he was most evenings, so he gladly accepted the invitation. 'Sure thing. How about we meet somewhere half way and find a pub?'

James suddenly felt a wave of unforeseen panic, despite having anticipated the suggestion. If he were to go to the obvious half-way town, Hartview, there was a very real danger of running in to Sue, Julie, or even Ian. 'We could, but that would mean us both driving and not actually drinking. Either that or messing around with public transport. Why don't we have a proper session around here? You could drive it and you're welcome to then stop over until the next morning.'

'That sounds great, James. Thanks. What time?'

'Eight?'

'I'll be there. Eight o'clock Friday.'

'Excellent. Then I can introduce you to one of our watering holes around here.'

After James ended the call, he poured himself a glass of whiskey and started finalising his thoughts of just how much he would, or would not, now divulge to his cousin at the end of the week.

'Well, that's a surprising new look for you,' said Tom, standing on James's doorstep and pointing to the mass of curls that James now had.

James pulled the door open wider to allow his cousin to enter. 'Just felt like a bit of a change,' he said, as Tom walked across his threshold. 'I've had it like this for a while now actually.'

'The last time I saw you, you looked like Freddie Mercury. Now you're more like Brian May. What's next? The really tight perm of John Deacon, or maybe a mullet with your hair dyed blonde, like Roger? Are you working your way through pretending to be each one of them as part of your obsession with the band?'

Tom was referring to the appearances of the four members of Queen during their recent resurgence into the public consciousness with their show-stealing performance at the *Live Aid* charity concert. James had not deliberately based either of his previous looks on members of his favourite group but, with Tom's comment, he now conceded that it may have been subliminally possible.

'If it's good enough for them, it's good enough for me,' replied James, hoping that would finish that line of conversation, which it did.

'It's good to see you bruv,' said Tom, unashamedly giving James a hug in the doorway, which was still open.

'You too,' said James. 'After all, you're my best friend.' James sang, rather than spoke, the familiar line from a Queen song, and he meant it. 'Why don't you just dump that bag down there and we'll go straight out and get some beers?' he continued, acknowledging the small carrier in Tom's hand which presumably contained a change of clothes for the morning.

The two of them walked, and talked, all the way to the pub that James had chosen for the start of their overdue reunion. Even though they had regularly spoken on the phone during the years since their last meeting, it seemed that there were endless things for them to now catch up on. There were no awkward silences and they talked constantly, interchanging rounds of beers, until the pub closed soon after the 11pm curfew.

Back at his house, James poured each of them a glass of whiskey as Tom drunkenly made himself at home and stretched out on his sofa. James had purposely kept their conversation light in the earlier public place, not wanting to risk serious matters being overheard. Now, alone and with their inhibitions and concentration lowered by the effects of the alcohol, he deliberately raised the subject of their joint past.

'It's strange how things turn out, don't you think?' began James.

'How do you mean?'

'Well, you and me probably wouldn't be as close now if it weren't for the accident. Probably wouldn't even be going out for beers, like tonight, for one thing.'

'Maybe not,' said Tom, sipping the spirit, unsure of where the new conversation was leading.

'Like, if Uncle Ray and Auntie Bea hadn't taken in me and Becky afterwards, we would probably have ended up in care, somewhere. I might not have ever seen you again, let alone shared some of my crazy ideas with you.'

'What crazy ideas do you mean?'

'Don't you remember? My ideas of tracing those responsible for the accident and getting some kind of revenge. Making them all suffer according to their involvement. Telling you that everyone must pay.'

'Oh yeah, I remember all that. It was when you were about

fourteen, and obviously still very cut up about it all. You said things like one day, eventually, you'd like to give the electrician such a big electric shock that he would never want to work with electrics again. You also wanted to rig the lorry driver's brakes so that he would have a really bad accident and hopefully lose his licence over it, stopping him from working, and maybe even ending up in hospital for months.'

James had been careful to never divulge the full extent of his plans, even to Tom, always telling him that any revenge would be classed as very serious, but never fatal.

'I also remember almost crashing my Dad's Vauxhall Viva when you and me went for that day out at the seaside,' continued Tom. 'The flask from the packed lunch had rolled under the brake pedal. I said to you, then, that something as simple as that would probably do the trick,' he said, recalling how he had theoretically endorsed James's proposals.

'Yes you did,' said James, now reminded of how the memory of Tom's near accident had later changed his original thinking, and the precise details of his plan. 'Do you remember me also telling you, years later, that I'd actually managed to trace them both?'

'Actually, you found the lorry driver twice, as I recall,' said Tom, somewhat sarcastically.

'I simply made a mistake with the first one,' explained James, remembering the innocent Felix.

'It was only a few years ago that you said you'd tracked down the electrician. Actually, it was around the time I last saw you, wasn't it?'

'That's right,' said James, suddenly adopting a serious tone.

'Tracking them down is one thing bruv, so that you know

who, and where, they are. Actually taking the steps of doing something about it once you have found them all is something else entirely,' said Tom, apparently still not appreciating the full significance of what James was saying to him.

'That's right,' repeated James, eyeing his cousin closely for any adverse reaction to his words.

'Once you get the full set of them in your sights, I suppose you could always arrange your own little reunion. Get them all in a room together and bump them all off in one go,' said Tom, drunkenly laughing now. James was relieved to sense that Tom had never taken his adolescent plans seriously, and that he had even slightly misunderstood the precise sequence of events that he had intended. Tom was clearly under the impression that James was only discreetly tracing the people involved, nothing more. Thankfully, Tom did not question him any further about how he may have used the information that he had already uncovered.

'Well, the next one I'm interested in finding is Auntie Bea,' said James, still carefully watching his cousin for the effect of his statements. 'Any ideas where she is?'

Tom flinched slightly at the unexpected mention of his former stepmother. It had always been a taboo subject of conversation between them before, but he knew why James also blamed her for her part in the accident.

'Oh yes, Bea,' said Tom, slowly and thoughtfully. 'Quite an appropriate name, really. I always thought of her as Dad's plan B.' He sniggered at his own joke.

James also laughed at the comment and how it applied to his memory of the young woman who had suddenly appeared amongst his family after Uncle Ray's first wife, and Tom's mother, had died.

'She couldn't cope after you and Becky moved in with us as well, though. She upped and left within six months,' Tom continued.

'I know that much already,' said James, patiently waiting for an answer to his question.

'We never heard from her at all after that,' Tom said, making James's heart sink for a moment. James now regretted saying as much as he already had about the overall plan and its progress. Even if Tom was wrongly assuming that, to date, it had only gone as far as simply tracing two people, he had said too much. After another slow sip from his whiskey, Tom unexpectedly carried on with what he had begun to say. 'Not until Dad died, that is. Then the cow came sniffing around after she'd heard about it somehow.' James was suddenly sobered and alert, hanging on Tom's every word. 'They were never divorced and so, technically, they were still married. She simply wanted his money and, in the end, she got it too. Thanks to some stupid laws and a dodgy solicitor, she got the lot.' Tom virtually spat the words out, now adopting a serious tone of his own.

'So, you don't like her very much?' said James, fuelling Tom's obvious rising anger.

'I hate her.'

James repeated his original question. 'Do you know where she is?'

'Not exactly. I don't know her address or anything like that, but I do know whereabouts you'd probably find her.'

'Then help me to add her to my little list Tom,' pleaded

James. 'Just in case I ever do want to go through with my plans one day.'

'Of course I will,' agreed Tom, putting down his empty glass and laying his drunken head on the armrest at the end of the sofa. 'Anything for you bruv,' he said with his eyes closed and, with that, he fell asleep.

James left Tom on the sofa, choosing not to disturb him to simply get him to move to the spare bedroom. After a long drink of water from the kitchen tap to, hopefully, help prevent a hangover the following morning, James went to bed himself.

37

The next morning, after they'd shared some breakfast, Tom had left and James was sat alone on his sofa with only his trusted rubber duck for company. He, and the duck, pondered on precisely how much help Tom would ultimately be able to provide. At that moment James was not even sure if Tom could remember any of their last conversation from the previous evening. Both of them had been quite drunk by the end and, although James could vividly remember everything himself, he had no idea if the same was true for Tom. They had spoken over breakfast but neither of them had mentioned anything more of the night's discussion. James, for his part, had been reluctant to raise the subject again so soon afterwards, as he was now starting to have doubts about directly involving Tom in his quest. Despite being unable to think of any alternative method of tracing his aunt, he knew that it was a big risk to involve Tom to such an extent.

With Tom having always been led to believe that James only wanted to superficially ruin the lives of a couple of anonymous people, Tom had always been a willing, albeit inactive, collaborator. James had confided in Tom that he had successfully traced both Frank and Richard at the times that he had. Tom had supportively accepted, and without question, those searches as the forerunners of the abridged version of the plans. James realised the fundamental difference in that he had now effectively asked Tom to feed to him someone that they both knew, personally, from their past. That might yet prove to be a request too far for his loyal cousin. He also worried, now more than ever before, about how Tom might react if he should eventually realise the fuller, darker, murderous version of the story. More importantly, James worried about who else he might tell.

James's first few questions were answered for him almost a week later, when his phone rang one evening.

'Hello,' said James.

'The Railway pub, in Penrow,' said a voice that James instantly recognised.

'Hi Tom. What about it?'

'That's where you'll find her.'

'Bea?'

'Of course. You asked me to find her didn't you?'

'Yeah, but I didn't expect you to be quite that quick,' said James, thinking of the many hours that he had wasted, over years, with the electoral rolls.

'Last I knew she was living in Penrow, so I just took the train there last night to see what I could find.'

'Where's your car?'

'I was going looking for her in local pubs, James. I didn't want to be drinking and driving. You, more than anyone, should understand that,' said Tom, deflecting the irrelevant question. 'Anyway, I got off the train and called in to the first pub, right next to the station. It was just for a quick one before checking around further and there she was, large as life. Literally.'

'Are you sure it was her? Did she see you?'

'It was definitely her and, no, she didn't see me. Not clearly enough to be able to recognise me anyway. Even years ago she had really bad eyesight, but she was always too vain to wear her glasses. Looks like nothing's changed there. Something about the shape of her eyeballs prevents her from wearing contact lenses too. She can only clearly see about ten feet in front of her. I didn't stay in there long and I always made sure that I kept enough distance to be out of her range of focus.'

'I never knew that she had such bad eyesight, but then I suppose there's no reason that I would,' said James, remembering that, unlike Tom, he had only lived with Bea for a few months. 'Penrow, though. That's only about ten miles from where I am here.'

James was now confused about why he had not found Bea's name when he had studied the electoral roll for that area. He could have avoided involving Tom, risking him realising how deadly serious he was about his overall mission. However, having obviously missed her entry, he conceded that there had probably not been any other way.

'According to a guy I quickly managed to speak to in there, she's in there regularly,' Tom was saying.

'What night?'

'Every bloody night. She soaks up the gin like a sponge, apparently. If I had tried to talk to her, I'm sure she would have recognised me. I wouldn't have got anywhere trying to get her address, or anything else, for you. You'll have to go and approach her yourself for that I'm afraid, if you still want it.'

'She'd recognise me too,' said James, panicking at the thought.

'Don't be daft. I was eighteen when she left, and so I probably haven't changed that much. Other than maybe getting even better looking, of course. You were thirteen, and it was over twenty years ago. Your voice is deeper and different now, and you didn't look like Brian May back then either.'

James could see the sense in what Tom was saying and, besides, he did not want Tom to be doing more of his dirty work for him than was absolutely necessary.

'I'll go over there Wednesday night, when I'm next free, but what about me recognising her? Like you say, it's been over twenty years.'

'You'll know her. She'll be the mutton dressed as lamb,' said Tom, certain that would be sufficient guidance for his cousin.

'Thanks Tom. I owe you.'

'Good luck bruv,' said Tom and, with that, hung up the phone.

38

On Wednesday evening James drove his Allegro to Penrow, where he parked in a side road close to the railway station. His Mercedes, complete with its failed MOT, had finally been consigned to the scrap yard, two years earlier. Although the street he had chosen, and all those in the vicinity, had restricted parking regulations, these only applied during the early afternoons of weekdays. They were to prevent the rail commuters from parking in them all day. Not only did that ensure that residents were not constantly annoyed by unfamiliar cars being parked outside their houses, the station car park also became a major source of revenue for the Penrow council. It was already dark so James, as he always had done, left his car under a streetlight and made his way towards the station.

As Tom had said, the unimaginatively named Railway pub was next to the main station entrance. He took a deep breath to try to calm his nerves and walked through the door, passing a chalked board outside on which was scrawled 'Welcome to Platform 5'. James assumed, correctly, that it was a jovial reference to the station's four platforms.

Once inside, he immediately concluded that it was not at all jovial, nor the kind of place that he would normally like to frequent. There were about twenty men drinking in the small, dingy hostelry. Far from being welcoming to any commuters returning after a hard day in the city, James sensed that the room had suddenly fallen silent on his entry and now all eyes were upon him. Cigarette smoke hung motionless in the badly ventilated room. It stung his eyes and made his throat feel dry as he walked to the bar, trying to ignore any stares and exude as much personal confidence in his stride as he could summon.

By the time he reached the bar, he was relieved to feel that the sudden attention he had unwittingly drawn to himself seemed to have dissipated just as quickly. Maybe it had been his long hair that had seemed to be so out of place to the regular drinkers, causing their momentary interest. It was certainly an unusual experience for him in a town pub. It had been akin to walking into a village pub for the first time where everyone else present had known each other for years. As he looked around, waiting for the barman's attention, he realised, mostly due to the abundance of grey hair, that he was also probably a good deal younger than most of them.

'Orange and lemonade please,' James said to the barman, once he had finally attracted his attention.

As the barman mixed the drink for him, James leant his elbows on to the top of the bar and stared down at one of the beer towels that were on it. He was trying to avoid unnecessary eye contact with any of the men in the pub. Suddenly he heard a female voice from behind him.

'That's not the usual kind of drink for winding down with after a busy day in the city,' the woman said. She was obviously assuming that he had just arrived on a train after a day at work and was calling in for a drink before going home.

He turned to face her, at first wondering where she had suddenly appeared from since he had only seen other men during his short walk to the bar. Then he noticed the door directly behind her with 'Ladies' embossed on it and quickly realised where she had probably just been, and why he had failed to notice her before.

'I've not come from the city, actually. I'm just driving through town, and I called in here for a break. I never have any alcohol when I'm driving,' explained James as he took his drink from the barman. 'None at all,' he concluded, quite pointedly. After paying for it, and without another word, he walked as calmly as he could to a vacant table away from the bar to gather his thoughts, with his heart now pounding. He had not expected any such meeting quite so soon and he had been caught off guard. He looked back at the woman who had spoken to him and watched as she accepted a colourless drink from the barman who had just served him, together with a separate, small bottle of similarly clear liquid. Gin and tonic, thought James.

Mutton dressed as lamb, Tom had also said, and this woman certainly fitted with that minimal description. It had to be her, James decided, noting that the previous twenty years had not been at all kind to her appearance. The skin on her face looked wafer-thin after years of excessive drinking and smoking filterless cigarettes, such as the one she was now placing in her mouth as she glanced back at James. Her former beehive of thick blonde hair had been replaced by a wispy bob of unnatural red. The leopard print dress that she was wearing was probably the correct style and size for what a young, slim Auntie Bea would have worn in the 1960s. Now it was at least two dress sizes smaller than required for this woman's expansive frame. Other than the integral shoulder pads, it clung tightly to every bulge, failing to hold in or disguise any amount of the obvious excess weight. Apart from being much too small, it was also much too short for a woman of her apparent age. It barely concealed what she may have been wearing underneath. Whatever her motivation for dressing the way she had, it was not what James would ever describe as a good look.

She was the only woman in the place. Drinking gin and, from the way the barman had supplied her with it, she was a known regular. Tom had also implied her lack of understanding, or caring, of appropriate dress sense. Yes, it surely had to be her. James knew that he would still have to be certain beyond even the slightest doubt before he could take any revenge.

He sat and considered what he should do next, occasionally sipping his sparkling cold drink. He had purposely not made any definitive plans for the encounter as he had felt that there were too many variables to consider. He had simply hoped that he would have been able to improvise and adjust to whatever situation, if any, had presented itself. He had certainly never expected that their first meeting would be so sudden, and so close, with her speaking to him out of the blue.

Since asking Tom for his assistance, James had attempted to increase his disguise by not shaving. The slight beard that he now sported, like his long hair, hopefully altered his appearance even further from the young teenager that Bea may have remembered. Even after being caught unawares and having to speak to her so closely at the bar, she had thankfully not shown any signs of recognising him.

He decided that his first course of action, rather than striking up a conversation with her in front of everyone and risk eventually being recognised, would be to continue drinking his soft drinks as inconspicuously as possible. Later, he would try to follow her when she left. Find out where she lived. Once he knew that, he should be able to confirm her identity by cross-referencing with the Penrow electoral roll that he must have mis-read before. Then, with a final verification that she had once been married to Uncle Ray, he would administer the punishment. James realised that, at the moment, all he had was Tom's word that it was indeed her. She was unrecognisable to him after the apparent ravages of two decades.

While he had been deep in thought, this woman had been occasionally watching him, drinking and sitting alone as he was.

She had plans of her own.

39

The woman in the leopard print dress eventually made her move. Picking up her latest gin and tonic, she walked purposely across the room towards James, who was still nursing his first orange and lemonade in the corner. Although she had briefly acknowledged, and spoken to, a few of the other regulars in The Railway earlier, she had still been largely on her own. She had desperately wanted some company for the night. The entire night, and not just within the walls of the pub. Although she had slept with many of those usual drinkers in the past, none had appeared to want to share her bed that particular evening.

She had first seen the appealing long-haired stranger stood at the bar as she had returned to her barstool after a visit to the toilet. Almost instantly, she had decided that she wanted him, if possible, and if only for one night. Now into her forties, she was acutely aware of her rapidly diminishing attractiveness to the opposite sex and had instantly felt the desire, and need, to appeal to this younger man. She had judged him to be either in his late twenties or early thirties, at least ten years her junior. Even if it meant having to take the conversational lead, as she often had to these days, she would try her best to raise his sexual interest. She approached him and, due to her very poor eyesight, his enticing facial features only now came into focus for her again.

The eyes of more than one man in the pub, many of whom could vividly remember what she looked like beneath the tight dress, discreetly watched her click across the floor atop high heels that were obviously very uncomfortable for her. They each had similar thoughts once they saw the purposefulness of her movements and the determined look in her eyes. Appropriate to her choice of dress, this leopard had clearly targeted her latest prey. She stalked it and was now rapidly closing in on it. The unsuspecting young stranger will be defenceless and simply unable to resist the attack of the predator.

James had not seen her approach and he was taken unawares. His eyes had been fixated on his glass as he was contemplating the situation that he now found himself in. He was stunned to see the gin and tonic get placed on the table next to his own drink, with a sudden background of leopard print filling his vision.

'Hello again,' she said. 'Mind if I join you?'

'Not at all,' said James, managing to keep his composure despite a surge of inward panic. He gestured with his hand, palm upward, toward the vacant seat.

As she sat down opposite him, she pulled a packet of cigarettes from the mismatching handbag that she had placed next to her. 'So, where are you driving to?' she asked.

'Sorry?' said James, confused.

'You said you were driving through and had just called in for a break,' she reminded him. 'Hence the kiddies drink,' she taunted, indicating his choice of refreshment.

'Oh yeah. I am,' said James, frantically trying to think of a plausible line. Before he could, though, she continued, apparently not really interested in the answer to her question.

'I'm Barbara, by the way,' she said, offering him one of her cigarettes after she took one out of the packet for herself.

'No thanks,' said James, in response to the proffered cigarette. 'Barbara?' he questioned, his mind now suddenly racing over how he, and apparently also Tom, could have been totally mistaken about this woman's identity. He was also wondering how he might now escape the situation that seemed to be rapidly developing.

'Yes, Barbara,' she repeated, whilst she lit her cigarette with a slim lighter. She was confused that he would seemingly doubt something as irrefutable as her name. 'Everyone just calls me Bea, though.'

The sudden mention of the familiar shorter name made James's blood run cold, simultaneously swinging his thoughts back towards her being his former aunt after all. 'Why Bea? That's short for Beatrice, surely?'

'It's my initial, isn't it,' she explained, as if it would be immediately obvious. 'I don't particularly like the name, so I just tend to use the first letter.'

Straight away, James realised that he had only ever heard his aunt's name spoken out loud. He had never seen it written down. He could also now see why his method of endlessly searching the electoral rolls had always been doomed to failure. He would not have given a second thought to any Barbara entries, whilst fruitlessly searching for ones for Beatrice. He had not stood a chance of finding her without Tom's help. He wondered if Tom had known of the anomaly all along and had just never thought to ever mention it to him.

It did not matter either way now, though. James was already convinced that he was talking to the woman who had given the alcoholic spritzers to his father before he had driven towards home.

'Well, I'm James,' he reciprocated, truthfully, and with a wide, friendly smile. There was no need for him to use a false name with her. She would always remember her one-time nephew as Paul. His later, preferred, name could not, on its own, spark any recognition.

With James now sure of her identity, he adopted the friendly, but calculating and detached, mode of conversation that he had perfected when he had cultivated Richard's trust. Bea, for her part, was similarly friendly, desperate to prove to herself, and anyone caring to watch, that she was still attractive enough to fire the interest of a younger man.

For the next hour they bought more drinks and talked, with James always mindful of his car parked nearby and avoiding alcohol. As they talked, Bea started to think that there was something familiar about him. She tried to picture him without his stubble and long hair, but their true former connection always eluded her. Thinking along entirely wrong, but understandable, lines, she ran through mental images of past lovers. The process took some considerable time, proportionate to the high number, but she eventually concluded that he was not one of those. An extensive list that she realised, uncomfortably, included many of those that were in the pub at that time. Eventually, she decided that it must simply be because he looked a bit like Brian May of Queen.

With their glasses empty again, Bea offered to get them some more drinks.

'Another orange and lemonade, please,' said James.

'Why don't you have a proper drink this time? I'm sure you're fed up with all that vitamin C.'

'I told you. I never touch a drop when I'm driving.'

'You can have a couple, surely,' she persisted.

'No, nothing thanks. Just the orange. Even a small amount, even if you're technically under the limit, might affect your judgement.' James suddenly felt serious, as if he was lecturing someone who really should have realised such a thing a long time ago.

'Very wise,' said Bea, thoughtfully. 'What about if you didn't drive any further tonight? Why not come home with me? At least, until any effects have totally worn off. You know what I mean?' She spoke slowly and gave him what she hoped would be a suggestive, inviting look.

James looked back at her and tried to look flattered and keen. The thought of what would likely ensue quite revolted him, but he realised that he was being offered the chance to easily get into her home and be alone with her. He had not planned to get so close, so quickly, but he knew that if he turned her down now that he would be very unlikely to receive such an offer, or opportunity, in the future.

'In that case, I'll have a whiskey,' he said, forcing himself to add a smile. 'Thanks.'

40

It was not long before the glasses of spirits were drunk and Bea rested her hand gently on James's.

'Let's go,' she said, quite seductively.

Bea lit herself another cigarette and then they both rose from the table and made for the door, trying to appear inconspicuous. James immediately sensed that a number of the drinkers had turned their heads in their direction and were blatantly watching them leave. It was because so many of the regulars of the pub knew Bea and had no doubt of where she was heading with her new companion, as well as what was likely to be in store for him. They knew that the leopard had sunk her claws firmly into this latest quarry and that, for him, there was now no chance of escape. James noticed that there was more than one who seemed to knowingly smile at them as she passed, and correctly guessed at their reasons.

'Goodnight Bea. See you in here again tomorrow night,' said one with an undisguised wink.

'Goodnight George,' she flatly answered the man, albeit with a smile, and without breaking stride.

After that, James also saw that she was similarly smiling at a few more during their short trek to the exit, including a slight double-take at the man sat at the table closest to the door, as if in only partial recognition. There had probably been too many for her to properly remember, thought James. Then they were outside into the cooler night air and she was quickly leading him away from the station and its associated pub.

On a particularly narrow stretch of pavement, he walked behind her for a short distance while she clicked her way along on those precarious heels of hers. The leopard print mini dress was tightly stretched across every bulge of her body and was starting to ride further upwards. He watched her tottering along in front of him and, as he often did when he found himself in unusual circumstances, he could not help himself from scanning his mind for a suitable Queen song for the moment. Despite his rising panic of the unplanned situation, he grinned as the chorus of *Fat Bottomed Girls* started playing in his head.

His unspoken humorous thought was quickly interrupted when she suddenly left the pavement and led him up a path leading to a two-story block of flats set back from the road. From the layout of the windows, James correctly judged that there would be two flats on the ground floor, either side of the entrance that Bea was now walking towards. Above each of those would be another apartment, on the first floor, making four flats in total.

He estimated that they had only walked a few hundred yards from The Railway. Since they had left it, there had only been enough time for her to smoke the cigarette that she had lit when they were still inside the pub. She dropped the end onto the path and stepped on it as she reached the block. James reasoned that the proximity went some way to explaining why she frequented a pub that he had personally found so unwelcoming, despite the chalkboard greeting supposedly intended for commuters returning home.

Bea typed a four-digit code, that James could not see, into the keypad next to the door. At the sound of the acknowledging buzz, Bea pushed the door open wide to reveal a cold, uncarpeted communal vestibule. There were concrete stairs against the wall to one side underneath which one of the residents, presumably, had left an unoccupied pram. Bea immediately ran up the stairs, leading him towards her front door on the first floor. James followed at the same speed, two steps behind, with her wobbling buttocks at his eye level and inches from his face. He still had the chorus of the Queen song uncontrollably looping in his mind. Such was her hurry that her heels had loudly clacked at least half way up the stairway before they heard the main door, with its spring weakened after years of constant use, closing behind them.

At her door, she hooked her index finger through the horizontal letterbox and looped it around the string hanging inside. She retrieved her door key, attached to the end of the string, and pulled it through and towards the lock. James queried the insecure practice.

'Do you think it's a good idea leaving your key hanging just inside there like that? Surely anyone could just get in if they knew, or even just try looking for it there on the off-chance.'

'They'd have to get in the main door first, wouldn't they,' Bea said, pointing back down the stairs towards the main entrance. 'The other three in this block are all very friendly and we all do it. It saves me endlessly searching around the inside of a handbag, especially on nights when I can hardly even find the zip to undo it.'

James shrugged his shoulders at her lax attitude to household security as she pulled him into the semi-darkness of her hallway behind her. She had left a small night-light plugged into one of the sockets and it was emitting a slight glow. As her door closed, she turned to face him and wrapped her arms around his neck, pulling him towards her and forcing her mouth against his with a passionate kiss. The time for words was over as far as she was concerned, and she just assumed that James, as a young man, would be enjoying the experience. He would surely have been looking forward to the inevitable upcoming intimacy just as much as her, she thought. James responded to the kiss as he might be expected to, kissing her in return, intertwining his tongue with hers, and starting to run his hands over her ample upper body. In reality, he was thinking that her kiss was as revolting as licking a used ashtray.

She pulled away from him again and led him by the hand to her bedroom, the first door on the left. Inside, there was another glowing night-light. It was bright enough for James to be able to clearly see her peel herself out of her exceptionally tight leopard print dress. She discarded it before approaching him for another passionate kiss. As he fumbled with her underwear, she completely, and expertly, undressed him before pulling him down onto the bed on top of her. With her willing assistance, he removed her remaining clothes and tossed them to the floor next to the bed before they locked in a strong embrace of brief foreplay.

James was taking little pleasure from the experience, but he knew that he now had no option other than to go along with it all. He was inside her flat, as he had always planned to be eventually, but things had moved along much too fast, and now in an uncomfortable direction. He just wanted some time to think but to stop now would likely result in him being unceremoniously ejected, never to get as good a chance again. So, he reluctantly had sex with his uncle's widow whilst she screamed her passion in his ears and dug her long fingernails into his back.

She totally dominated their coupling, occasionally demanding varied coital positions and taking the lead in all things. She was insatiable, not allowing him to slow or stop until she was sexually fulfilled, multiple times. Despite all his misgivings, James was able to continue the passion with her for longer than many of his predecessors, coming twice himself. However, through it all he felt emasculated and, for the first time in his life, without any real control over a sexual encounter.

Eventually, she had to reluctantly concede that, even though this younger man certainly had more stamina than most of her recent lovers, he had lost his rigidity and she had taken him close to exhaustion. She released her strong grip around his shoulders and allowed him to roll off her and onto his back beside her, depleted, at least for now.

She decided to let him briefly recover his strength before demanding more. She sat up and shuffled backwards to lean against the wrought iron frame of the bed before reaching to her beside cabinet and pulling a cigarette from the packet that was on the top. As she lit it, she looked over at James, who was looking back up at her from the pillow, bleary eyed, breathing deeply and glowing with sweat.

'So, are you glad you came?' she said.

James involuntarily laughed at the double-entendre. 'Yes I am, and thank you again for the invitation in the first place.' He pulled himself up to also lean back against the head of the bed next to her, properly looking around the dimly lit room for the first time. 'Nice place you've got here,' he said, insincerely but convincingly.

'Insurance and inheritance from my late husband,' she replied.

'Oh, I'm sorry,' said James, again believably, whilst sensing the unexpected chance to discover more of her perspective of past events. 'What happened, if you don't mind me asking?'

'He passed away much too young,' she said. 'We were really happy and had a lovely family together.'

James could not believe the gall of the woman. Surely this bitch was not trying to pretend that everything had been harmonious between her and Ray, right until the end, and that she had somehow been entitled to his money. 'Must have been a big shock,' he managed to say, without any sarcastic inflexion.

'We weren't married long. He already had a teenage son when we met, and then there was this big car accident. His sister was killed, along with half of her own family, so her kids came to live with us. Ray died soon after. He left everything to me so that I could look after them all until they left home.'

James resisted the strong urge to contradict her false account. It would have inevitably given away his own identity before he was ready to. He knew that she had omitted to mention the lost years after she had left Ray and the family. James had grown up without her there and left home long before Ray had died. He knew that she had not cared at all about the children, himself included. He also knew, thanks to Tom, that she had effectively stolen all the money on hearing of Ray's death, much later. However, he now had enough proof, as if further proof were needed, that he was with the right woman. The summarised details of the accident, and its aftermath, were sufficient for him to be in no doubt.

'Life can be so cruel sometimes,' he said, although his words were not intended for Bea as much as for himself.

'Long time ago now,' said Bea, effectively dismissing, and concluding, the topic.

She finished her cigarette and stubbed it out in the bedside ashtray, her breasts undulating with the movement. Then, she moved closer to him and reached down to try to stimulate, and encourage, him into further sexual activity. In spite of his tiredness, and his deep loathing of her, he felt himself rising again at her touch. Bea took full advantage of his reflex, pulling him across the bed and into her once again for her own gratification. He obliged her for as long as necessary until, finally sated after what had seemed like an eternity for James, Bea released him once again. She soon fell asleep beside him.

Although the exertion had exhausted him, James was determined to stay awake. As he listened to Bea's regular, heavy breathing, he felt that he finally had a chance to quietly evaluate the situation that he had unintentionally plunged into. He'd had no such opportunity since he had initially run into her at the bar of The Railway and he desperately needed to think.

His head was now pounding and so his first instinct was

to find himself some kind of pain relief. Surely, she must have some paracetamol somewhere, he thought. He gently rose from the bed, successfully leaving Bea in her slumber, and silently walked out to the hallway. The night lights, still on in the bedroom and the hallway, were enough for him to see his way to the kitchen, where he gingerly closed the door before turning on the overhead fluorescent light. He squinted for a short while as his eyes became accustomed to the harsh bright light and then, suddenly realising that he was standing naked in front of a window overlooking the street, pulled down the blind.

He started to check the cupboards and drawers. As well as the expected tins of food, he found two gin bottles, one unopened and the other a quarter full, in one cupboard. There was an assortment of DIY paraphernalia in a drawer, including a small torch, two screwdrivers and a card of replacement fusewire, all of which reminded him of Richard. Eventually, he discovered a makeshift medical kit in the cupboard that was above the work surface. Thankfully, it contained his desired paracetamol alongside assorted plasters, creams, eye drops and cold remedies. He swallowed two tablets, with the aid of running water from the cold tap directly into his mouth, before sitting down on one of the mismatching chairs at the kitchen table to think.

Although he had not intended to be in this position so soon, it had always been his ultimate goal to be alone with Bea, and with her defenceless. For James, it had not been an evening of pleasure. It had simply all been a means to an end. A way of getting himself into her home and to subsequently have enough time to clinically execute his plan.

He looked down at the gin bottles, still visible in the lower cupboard that he had left open. He wondered how often Bea was drinking those as well as the measures it seemed like she so often had in The Railway. He looked over at the tools and components in the drawer that he had also left open during his frantic search for the tablets. As well as those specific reminders of Richard, there were many other domestic essentials. Two light bulbs, a plastic funnel and some parcel tape formed the first of what appeared to be a number of layers of potentially handy household items. James closed his eyes against the glare of the fluorescent brilliance and, with his elbows on the table, rested his head in his hands to finally think clearly.

He stayed in that position for an indeterminate time, although it was long enough for the paracetamol to start having the beneficial effect of releasing him from the pain in his head. He was intensely aware that, alongside his earlier plots to dispatch both Frank and Richard, he had always dreamt of this moment of opportunity. Setting lethal traps, as in their cases, was one thing, but cold-blooded, face to face, murder was another entirely. He wondered, now that he was on the cusp, if he really did have the necessary steel for it. It would be so much more difficult.

With both Frank and Richard, he'd had to wait a long time to hear them fully admit to, and confirm, their involvement in the accident. He'd had to be absolutely certain that he had found the correct man each time. That also meant that he'd had time to subconsciously consider, and continually reconsider, what he intended to eventually do to them. In Bea's instance, he had found her and heard her confirm her identity within a matter of a few hours, rapidly propelling him to this pivotal decision point.

Just as during those moments when the conflicting thoughts had come and vexed him over Frank and Richard, he deliberated the situation in which he found himself. As then, he knew that he would be unlikely to get a better, or even another, chance in the future if he now chose to walk away. Furthermore, although unlike with Frank and Richard, he realised that if he let Bea live any longer, she might suddenly recognise something about him. She may yet remember who he really was, even after he had left this flat. If that happened, it would probably be impossible to ever orchestrate the same kind of chance to strike. He was now in the most ideal time and place to execute his plan if he was ever going to.

He stared again at the gin bottles, inanimately representing so much of the woman now lying asleep in the next room, and shivered as he made his decision. The shiver made him realise that he was still not wearing any clothes, so he turned off the kitchen light before opening the door and stealthily returning to the bedroom by the soft glow from the night lights.

Having picked them up from the floor, James slowly put on his clothes, successfully managing to remain quiet enough to not disturb, or awaken, Bea. She continued to sleep soundly as, fully dressed again, he walked around the bed towards the bedroom door. With deep hatred, he looked back and down at the maneater who was still oblivious to the effects that he felt she'd had on his life.

He turned and returned to the kitchen.

41

Bea could not be sure how long she had been asleep but sensed that it had probably not been long. As she blinked her eyes open, she saw that morning had still not broken and the bedroom had the level of overnight semi darkness that she preferred. The alternative of blackness was circumvented, as always, by the night light in the socket at the far corner of the room. Naked and lying on her back under the thin covers, she realised that she was resting to one side of the double bed. She immediately remembered the uninhibited sex of earlier and that she was not alone. Her right arm was raised with her forearm resting on the pillow across the top of her head and against the wrought iron end of the bed.

She started to roll onto her left side, intending to move closer to the latest lover that she fully expected to still be there beside her. However, she suddenly felt the tight restraint of a cable tie around her right wrist, binding her to the bedhead. The rush of fear-induced adrenaline made her instantly alert and she instinctively grabbed at the tie with her left hand. Another tie was suddenly, viciously, wrapped around her free wrist and then that was also attached to the bed frame. Her hands were now anchored, six inches apart above her head.

'What the hell do you think you're doing James?' she screamed, as her eyes slowly followed the shadowy outline walking quickly to the end of the bed to switch on the overhead light.

'Wakey wakey,' he said as the bright light, on the ceiling directly over the bed, forced her to close her eyes against the sudden glare.

Understandably misinterpreting his strange actions, she began to protest. 'No. Please don't. Untie me. Please. I'm not one for all this bondage stuff. Never have been. It scares me.'

'Really?' he said sarcastically, moving back up to the side of the bed. 'You do surprise me.' He grabbed at her chin, placing his thumb and index finger either side of her mouth and squeezing them together. 'Open wide now,' he commanded, mimicking a dentist.

Her mouth involuntarily opened under the pressure from his fingers. Still thinking he was indulging in some kind of deviant sex game, and with her eyes still closed against the overhead light, she did not expect it to be plastic that was forced between her lips and into her mouth.

Opening her eyes, slightly more accustomed to the intensity of the light, she could see the inverted cone shape that was now above her mouth. She was confused but realised that it was a funnel. It was probably her own. The one that she always kept in the kitchen for varied uses, including filling the washing machine with powder or transferring the last drops of one gin bottle to the next.

With the obstruction in her mouth, she was unable to speak. She could now only look up at his face, inches above her own, and was immediately shocked by the small amount that she was able to see contrasted against the overriding background light. The attractive smiling man with the kind, alluring eyes was somehow now gone. These intense, staring eyes were like nothing that she had ever seen before.

Bea was still thinking that he had unwelcome, dominant sex on his mind. However, as he leaned back slightly, he started to explain his true intent. With his coat on and its hood up, it made his dark silhouette look like a foreboding angel of death.

'You didn't recognise me in the pub, did you?' he calmly said, looking towards and reaching over to the bedside cabinet. She heard the familiar sound of a gin bottle being unscrewed. All she could do was make a frightened, muffled sound through the funnel as he poured some of the spirit down it and into her mouth. She swallowed, against her better judgement but to prevent herself from choking on the recognisable liquid. 'Why not have another drink while I help you remember?'

Her eyes were wide with fear as she tried to understand what this man was saying, and doing, to her, and why. She was terrified and started to ineffectively pull against the cable ties in a fruitless attempt to slip free of their hold on her wrists.

'Twenty years ago you gave some drinks to James Pearce one night. James Pearce Senior, that is. Your brother-in-law. Remember?'

She certainly did remember, although she could not work out how he would know about it. It had been one of those unforgettable nights, for all the wrong reasons, but she had no way of answering as he poured some more of the gin into the funnel.

'Drinking and driving is always a dangerous mix, wouldn't

you agree?'

She did not know whether she should nod or shake her head in response, and so just kept staring back up at him, her confused mind racing.

'He crashed the car. He died. His wife died. His daughter died. You were the one who gave him the drink that clouded his judgement that night, if only by a bit. You knew that he had to drive a car. You even delayed them all from leaving by pissing around with a stupid bit of pocket money. If he'd driven off when he first intended to, a few minutes earlier, it simply wouldn't have happened. You were as responsible for it all as the bastard who drove the lorry or the one that wired the traffic lights.'

Bea was becoming even more scared of what he was potentially intending for her. Partly as a result of the accurate references to the night of the accident and partly because she now looked at his features very closely for the first time, she finally recognised his face from her history. She had unnervingly thought that there was something very familiar about him when she had first seen him drinking alone in The Railway. She had thought that there might be an intangible link to some point of her former life. Now she realised the connection to her brief marriage to an older man two decades before. The one who had given her an instant full family, for a while. Furthermore, she now understood that she must have always been his target, and the only reason that he had been in the pub at all. There had been nothing accidental about their encounter. She started hopelessly thrashing her weight from side to side, pulling so hard at the restraints that her wrists started to bleed. She was still panicking that she could not free herself from her bonds. The ties still held firm.

'You have to treat alcohol with respect you see,' he said, unscrewing the cap from the second gin bottle. 'Only ever encourage others to drink it when they're not driving, and always being very careful not to drink too much yourself. You can easily die from alcohol poisoning if you're not prudent.' He poured more of the spirit from the new bottle. 'Would you know what too much is?'

She shook her head, already starting to feel the dizzying effects of the gin that she was being forced to drink.

'About a litre,' he told her. 'So, drink a whole bottle and you probably die. You had more than that in your cupboard. That's a shame. For you.'

She incoherently screamed up at him through the funnel that he was holding in place with his left thumb, circumventing all her attempts to squeeze it upwards and out of her mouth. He ignored her muffled pleas, continuing to pour the gin from the bottle in his right hand. She tried her best not to swallow it, to spit it out. However, on her back, it was impossible not to eventually swallow most of what her assailant poured. The potent liquid kept coming.

Keeping the funnel constantly topped up with gin as he monitored the level descending with each involuntary swallow, he did not speak for a while. Bea continually resisted but he was too strong for her, holding her head in place and easily avoiding her attempts to kick him off the bed. As her strength started to noticeably fade, he reminded her of more.

'After the accident, the house was suddenly full to bursting point. We all desperately needed a mother figure, and what did you do? You left us. You destroyed our family and then just walked away, leaving us to get on with it and pick up the pieces. Tonight you pay for that, just like the others have done. Everyone must pay.'

She looked up into his cold, determined eyes one last time before lapsing into unconsciousness. He poured the remaining gin down her throat. After removing the funnel, he stuck a strip of parcel tape over her mouth. He did not want to leave her able to reflexively vomit and dispel some of the alcohol that he had forced into her stomach.

As he stood up to finally leave her to die, he pulled two five-pence coins from his pocket. The modern equivalent of the shillings that were used before the decimalisation of the UK currency in 1971. He dropped one into each empty bottle.

'For your piggy banks,' he said to unhearing ears, referring to that other part of her involvement in 1965.

42

The unforgiving ringing of the alarm clock rudely announced the dawning of the following Monday morning to James. As he groggily reached for the button on its top, he decided that it would definitely be a good idea to get the teasmade repaired, or replaced, as soon as possible. For the past two weeks he'd had to get up and out of bed before drinking his first cup of tea, entrusting his old alarm clock to wake him. He finally concluded that he did not like the enforced change to his established routine.

With his eyes still half-closed, he shuffled towards the kitchen to prepare himself his first hot drink of the day. On his way through his lounge, he turned on the television so that he could at least hear some of the early morning broadcast of what had become known as *Breakfast TV*. Since its inception just two years earlier, pushing aside such things as the niche televised lectures from *The Open University*, James had often liked to watch it. He found that the various articles and news bulletins, both local and national, helped him to gradually wake up at the start of each day. Coupled with drinking tea and eating breakfast, it had become his untaxing norm for about fifteen minutes before his daily shower.

From the kitchen, as he made himself a single mug of tea, he could hear the presenters interviewing a yachtsman who had apparently just broken a sailing speed record. He poured the boiling water onto a solitary tea bag in the mug, as was now his usual method. He had dropped and smashed his teapot long ago and had never bothered to replace it. His habit was now for toast in the mornings, rather than cereal, and, as his two slices popped up from the toaster, he finished squeezing and removing the hot and soggy teabag from his mug.

Carrying the tea in one hand and a plate of toast in the other, he returned to the lounge and sat down in front of the television. He was just in time to hear the final words about the mariner's recent achievement, not that he was particularly interested. The programme presenter then announced that the local news would be next, and a studio newsreader immediately appeared on the screen. This newsreader declared a headline item that caused James to suddenly freeze and sit open-mouthed in shock, his toast hovering inches from his lips.

The studio picture changed to one of a live outside broadcast scene. A news reporter was standing in the foreground, holding a microphone and facing the camera. Behind him there was a small block of flats which had two strips of blue and white tape across its entrance.

'I'm in Penrow,' the reporter said, 'where the body of a woman has been found, over the weekend, in one of the flats of the block that you can see behind me. Police were called to this address in Station Road after a concerned neighbour let herself in and made the grim discovery. The dead woman had been tied to her bed and gagged, with the scene apparently having all the hallmarks of a sex game that had gone wrong. Police are keeping an open mind at the moment, awaiting the results of a post-mortem examination, and are falling short of declaring it a full murder enquiry at this stage. However, they have called it suspicious, and are very keen to talk to a man that the woman was seen with on Wednesday evening in the nearby Railway pub. He is described as an unshaven man of medium height, aged thirty to forty, with long, dark, curly hair. As far as they can deduce, that was the last time that she was seen alive. Police would like that man to come forward and talk to them so that they can eliminate him from their enquiries.'

James felt his heart pounding at the obvious reference to himself and instinctively reached to touch his hair at the mention of it. The reporter continued talking, as a policeman appeared from within the block and stood in the doorway behind him. He looked to be effectively guarding the entrance from anyone who might ignore the tape and attempt to enter.

'The woman, believed to be in her late fifties, was well-known locally and has now been named as Barbara Lester.' Despite the shocking subject matter, James could not help but smile at the wild assessment of Bea's age. It concurred with his own brief opinion of her weathered appearance from the previous week. He thought that the estimate had probably been obtained from a local acquaintance with a similar view. James knew that, in reality, she had only been forty-two. 'She is not believed to have any close family and had to be formally identified by the worried neighbour, a friend, who had found her.'

The news bulletin finished with the reporter proclaiming his own name, repeating his location again to conclude the piece, and then handing back to the studio. James sat in silence, his mouth still open in shock. He did not hear or see the subsequent local news item about flooding in the county caused by the weekend's rain. His thoughts were suddenly in turmoil.

Bea was dead, and now every viewer of early television in the whole region knew about it, together with his accurate description. By the end of the day, the newspapers and subsequent news bulletins will undoubtably have informed most of the rest of the local population. James wondered if Tom had also seen that first broadcast, and how he might now react to it if he had. Tom had said that he hated the woman, but that emotion had different levels of intensity. James doubted that Tom would condone murder, no matter how deep his own loathing was.

James reasoned that his involvement would be plainly obvious to Tom. Not only was there the precise description of his appearance, he had even told Tom the exact day that he had intended to try to find Bea in The Railway. From the televised evidence that he had just seen and heard, James's involvement was obvious to himself too, even though he had absolutely no conscious memory of killing Bea.

As with Frank and Richard years before, he had no recollection of any murderous action. All that James could remember from the end of Wednesday night was getting quietly dressed in the glow of the nightlight in Bea's bedroom before going back into her kitchen. He had pulled the blind back up, looked down at the gin bottles and the DIY drawer, and simply considered what they could potentially be used for. His next recollection was leaving her flat to find his car.

He had sat in the back seat of his Allegro for hours, almost until daybreak, before he was satisfied that all traces of the single whiskey that he had drunk the previous night would have dissipated from his bloodstream. Only then did he get into the driver's seat, start up the car and return home. As far as he could remember, he had completely lost his nerve, panicked and walked away from the perfect chance to kill her.

James turned off the television and then paced around his lounge trying to understand how it was even possible for him to have such fundamental blackouts of his memory. There was a complete blank for every one of the three intense occasions when the opportunity for his desired vengeance had materialised. It had to be a consequence of his head injury in the accident, but why would it only manifest itself at those times? As far as he could tell, there had never been any other lapses.

He suddenly realised that he would not necessarily know if there had been. The only reason that he knew about those three, specific blackouts were because he had been confronted with the indisputable evidence that his intended victims had died each time. There could, potentially, be many memory gaps. There could be other, insignificant, innocuous lost memories concerning irrelevant subjects that would not necessarily be notable enough for him to realise. If so, he would have no way of ever knowing that he had those lesser lapses.

Despite his understandable worries of having developed some kind of *Jekyll and Hyde* personality, James was still delighted to know that Bea had also now been dealt with, whether he could remember doing it or not. He did still remember the appropriate Queen song from Wednesday night, but now, having heard of the manner of her death, another one entered his mind as he found himself standing next to his new hifi system.

With the digital quality and nature of Compact Discs, he liked that he did not have to worry about the clicks and permanent scratches often caused by his lowering of a stylus onto a vinyl record. He also appreciated that he could easily skip over undesired tracks. He now mostly bought, and listened to, any new album releases as CDs, although he still played the earlier vinyl albums of his extensive music collection as well. He had to, if he ever wanted to listen to those older songs.

As he picked up his copy of the 1976 Queen album *A Day At The Races*, he thought, and not for the first time, that the various record companies should seriously consider reissuing older albums as CD equivalents. He would certainly not object to spending out a second time if it meant that those songs were revitalised and he could finally forget about those annoying clicks.

He placed the album on the turntable and left it to automatically play the first track of the first side, without any need to manually lower down the stylus himself. As the introduction of *Tie Your Mother Down* started, he laughed out loud and winked at the duck.

43

After the unanticipated start to his day, James did not bother to shower. With no current job to go to anyway, he dressed in loose, comfortable clothes and sat in his lounge all day, contemplating. He played more music, mostly from CDs, in between the similar news bulletins that came at times throughout the rest of the day. He watched them all, pausing whatever track was playing at the time, but none of them added any details to what he had heard before.

He had anticipated that the phone might ring at some stage, and for it to be an unwelcome call from either Tom or the police, so he had unplugged it. That done, he had then expected there to be a knock at his door instead. Tom might have come round and confronted him directly or, more likely, it would be the police, wanting to question him about the dead woman in Penrow. It would be understandable if it was the police. Tom could have already told them what he knew, and suspected, especially concerning his matching description. However, no knock of any kind came to his door all day. As he turned on his lights so that he could once again see in the lounge that had been descending into the darkness of the evening, he looked over at his reflection in the mirror on the wall.

'First thing to do is to have a shave, don't you think?' he

said to his rubber duck, starting to think pragmatically for the first time that day. 'We don't want some eagle-eyed, bored copper spotting me walking down the street and picking me up on the faint off-chance that I'm the one they're looking for.' The duck seemed to telepathically put a further thought into his mind. 'I know it still won't stop Tom realising. If he hasn't seen the news and worked it out already today, he probably soon will. It'll all be over for me as soon as he goes to the police. That is, if he does. Do you think he might keep quiet? Did he really hate her enough to not say anything? Life in prison for me, without a doubt, if he does tell.'

James tried to suppress his worries about Tom's potential reaction and went to the bathroom to shave off his fledgling beard. Afterwards, as he looked in the bathroom mirror at the resultant image, he tried to make a mental list of all those who might remember him as being unshaven and who might potentially associate him with the vague description that the police had issued.

Eventually, he decided that it was probably only Tom who posed a serious threat. There had not been any photofit image issued by the police, not yet anyway, and everyone that he could think of would only know him as always meticulously clean-shaven. Apart from one occasion to quickly go to the corner shop for some milk, he had only recently left his house one other time without having shaved. That had been the previous Wednesday, when he had driven directly to Penrow and The Railway, and he had not seen anyone else as he left. There were surely many other unshaven men with long, curly hair, and he lived more than ten miles from Penrow. James surmised that none of his friends or neighbours would have any reason to think of him as being the one that the police wanted to speak to. No-one, that is, with the notable exception of Tom.

James could not shake from his mind the worry of the threat that Tom now posed, and he had a sleepless night as a result. By the early morning, he knew that his overall plan would have to be moved forward. He needed to complete it before all of his past actions started catching up with him. He had also decided, without any assistance from his duck, to try to find out how much Tom had deduced and what, if anything, he was going to do about it. James could not bear the thought of living with the constant worry that any minute could bring the dreaded knock and be his last minute of freedom.

After eating his breakfast, and mulling over a few last thoughts, James lifted the handset and punched in Tom's phone number. It was answered on the third ring and, even from the tone of the 'hello', James immediately sensed that Tom had fully expected the early call to be from him.

'Hi Tom, it's James'.

'Hi bruv,' Tom greeted, but noticeably without his usual cheerful inflexion. Then, after a pause. 'I saw the news yesterday. Did you?'

'Yeah, I saw it. I was wondering if you'd done anything about it yet, like maybe talking to anyone in a uniform.'

'I'm not coming forward as one of her family, James. It sounded like they knew nothing about her past and so they're not expecting a long-lost stepson to suddenly appear.'

'That's not quite what I meant,' said James. 'I mean the

description of the guy that they want to talk to about it.'

'Well, I knew that would probably be you, obviously,' said Tom calmly, the attitude surprising James. 'I wouldn't have thought you would be wanting to hold your hands up either, though. They might even start thinking that it was you that did her in.' Tom gave a quick laugh as though amused at the prospect.

Thankfully, then, it appeared that Tom had not come to the seemingly obvious conclusion after all. Not yet, anyway, but James had already decided to try to let Tom know of his unexplained memory lapse. If his cousin should ever realise the full truth, he might not hold him fully responsible if he understood that there was some kind of mental disorder involved.

'There's something I need to explain about it,' James began.

Tom cut him short, apparently unwilling to hear any explanation or possible confession. 'You don't have to explain any of it to me, bruv. I'm just glad she's gone, and I want to leave it at that. Like I told you the other day, I hated her.'

James was silently trying to determine just how much Tom was thinking, or suspecting, but he still could not be sure. Through it all, however, he was getting the impression that Tom would not be going to the police any time soon. Whether or not Tom believed that he was the guilty one, he seemed content to keep it secret, for now. James decided that it would be better for him not to mention the black hole in his memory, after all. Instead, he continued the conversation in a different direction.

'Did you know that her name was actually Barbara, not Beatrice? That she was always just using her initial?' asked James.

'Yeah, sure. Didn't you?'

'No, of course not. Not you, nor anyone, ever said it to me. She had even kept your Dad's surname. Your name. The news called her Barbara Lester.'

'Made sense, I suppose. They never divorced, just separated.'

James found himself wishing that he had somehow known about those few, extra intricate details. She would have been so easy to trace then, using those electoral rolls. He had even specifically checked first for any Lesters in each one before trawling through alphabetically. However, he had always been looking for an explicit Beatrice entry. He must have glossed over her entry at some stage of the lengthy, fruitless process, unknowingly missing its significance.

More importantly, it would have meant that he would not have had to involve Tom to be able to eventually find her. Now that he had, he would always have to live with some fear of the consequences. He could still not be sure of the current extent of Tom's assumptions, but to question him further could fuel otherwise latent suspicions.

Tom interrupted his thoughts. 'Look, James. I know you wanted to teach her a lesson for her part in it, but she's gone now. There's nothing more that you can do to her.' It was still ambiguous, and James was getting frustrated at constantly being unable to read between the lines of Tom's comments. Did he know, did he suspect, or was he just blindly oblivious to the clear facts that James felt were staring him directly in the face? Then Tom said something to make James think that his available time might be limited. 'Just move on to the next one, bruv. Soon as you can.'

With that, James ended the conversation, as politely as he could, and hung up. From some of what Tom had said, James was now confident that he was not immediately going to the police. It meant that James still had some time left to conclude his mission. He might have to hurry, though, as Tom could work it all out at any time, if he hadn't already. James was still unsure of Tom's long-term reaction.

James could run, to another country perhaps, and disappear from the system somehow. He could make it impossible for the police, or Tom, to ever find him. However, there was still one more remaining person left for him to deal with, from his list of those responsible for the accident.

He would not, could not, go anywhere before they, too, had been dispatched.

44

James paused at the foot of the steps leading up to the front door of the unfamiliar house. He checked again the number that was written as part of the address on the scrap of paper from his pocket, confirming that it matched the digits above the knocker. He walked up to the door and rapped on it three times. As his hand returned the paper to the left pocket of his coat, his fingers brushed against the small toy that he had bought, long ago, specifically for this long-awaited reunion. He saw the woman's outline through the frosted glass of the door moments before she opened it.

She looked at James's face, illuminated by the outside lights on the wall either side of her door, and James saw the recognition suddenly fill her eyes as they adjusted to the contrasting light.

'Well, this is a surprise,' she said, flatly. 'What brings my big brother round here after being a total stranger for years?'

'Hello Becky,' said James. 'I was just passing. Thought I'd see how you were.'

'Just passing? That's a good one. You only live five minutes down the road and yet you've not been passing at any time in the past seven years since I moved here?'

James did not know what to say and just shrugged his shoulders. 'I've been busy,' he said, lamely.

Rebecca laughed slightly, although not amused, and pushed the door open wider. 'I suppose you'd better come in.'

James entered his sister's house with its understandable frosty atmosphere. He and Rebecca had rarely seen each other since he had moved out of Ray's, and not at all since she had done so herself a few years later. He had been told of her address but had chosen to never use it until now, not even for a greeting card. They were simply estranged, although there had never been an open argument or falling out to cause the situation. They sat opposite each other on the lounge chairs and it was Rebecca who broke the uncomfortable silence that had descended.

'So, why are you here now? I see Tom more than I've ever seen you.'

This was a complete surprise to James. Although Tom and Rebecca were, like Tom and himself, cousins, Tom had never mentioned to him that he had recently seen his sister.

'You've seen Tom?' asked James, avoiding her question.

'Every few months, I guess. He's godfather to our son.'

'Son? Our?' said James, noticing for the first time the wedding ring on her finger. He was also wondering why Tom had been so secretive about his contact with them all.

'Me and Liam got married five years ago. We sent you an invitation, but you never bothered turning up, or even replying. I guess that's when I finally gave up on trying to keep in touch with you.'

For years, James had been throwing away, unopened, any rare envelope with Rebecca's distinctive handwriting that had dropped through his letterbox. He had purposely kept his distance since their lives had taken different directions. Now he realised that the invitation back into her life must have been unceremoniously consigned to his dustbin, just like everything else that had come from her.

'Liam?'

'We met at work and just hit it off. I gave up working when I was pregnant, but he's still at the same place. He's doing the night shifts this week. That's why he's not here tonight.'

James was thankful that their reunion was not being interrupted by the presence of someone he had never met before. It would have disrupted everything that he had in mind.

'You've got a son too?'

'Fifteen months old. He's in his cot in the other room.'

'Can I see him please?'

Rebecca hesitated, but James could sense her coldness towards him starting to dispel. She got up and briefly left him alone in the room before returning, carrying an infant who was looking intently around the room and at him, showing signs of having just been woken up. She introduced her first born.

'Adam. This is your Uncle Paul. No, sorry, your Uncle James,' she amended.

It was weird for James to hear himself being referred to by his given name for the first time in years. At least Rebecca had quickly remembered his preference for their father's, and his second, name. As he rose to his feet and looked at the nephew that he had not even known he'd had, he started to realise just how much close family he had deprived himself of.

'He's cute,' was all he could think of to say.

'You bet he is,' Rebecca said, smiling genuinely for the first time since James's arrival. 'He takes after his Mum,' she continued, looking lovingly at her son and bouncing him up and down. 'I'd better put him back down, actually, before he wakes up even more and gets restless.'

James sat back down on the lounge chair, while Rebecca returned Adam to his cot, and began to think. By the time she came back into the room, he was close to tears, but he managed to hold them back and coldly hide his emotion.

'What happened to us Becky?' he said.

'I have no idea Paul.'

'James,' he corrected.

'I have no idea James. After the accident you just seemed to be so distant, even though we were both still living together with Uncle Ray, Auntie Bea and Tom.'

James noted that Rebecca had not said anything further about their auntie and her recent fate, which she surely would have done if she had known about it. He concluded that she must have been either blissfully unaware of the latest local news announcements or that she too had not known that the woman's name had been Barbara, rather than Beatrice.

She continued with her assessment of his character. 'You were like it with everyone. Everyone except Tom, that is. It should have brought us closer together, not driven a wedge further between us. After we grew up, you just didn't want to know.'

'I suppose that's the whole point. The accident. It changed everything, and you must know that it wouldn't have happened if it wasn't for you.'

Rebecca was taken aback and was suddenly annoyed.

'Wouldn't have happened? How can you blame me for it?'

'I know it obviously wasn't all down to you,' James admitted, 'but if you hadn't asked Dad to stop at that toyshop for yet another bloody troll to add to your collection that night, we wouldn't have even been in Hartview. Even if we had gone that way home, we would have been through those lights and long gone before that lorry appeared.'

'I don't believe this,' said Rebecca. 'All these years and you've hung on to that thought. That the accident was somehow my fault because I asked Dad to stop at the toyshop. I may have been the one that asked Dad to stop the car, but it was all because of you anyway.'

'Because of me?' he asked, incredulously.

'It wasn't for another troll. It was to choose a silly spaceship model for you. For your birthday. I'd been saving my pocket money for it for weeks. If your birthday hadn't been coming up, neither the detour nor the stop would have happened.'

'A spaceship model,' said James slowly, as the full impact of her words started to sink in and he realised, for the first time, that the slight delay had indirectly been because of himself.

'A rocket, I think it was,' she expanded. 'No-one, especially Dad, could have known what was about to happen. It was an accident. A tragic one that changed my life too, but it was purely an accident. No-one intended to kill the rest of our family.'

James was silent with his thoughts for a moment. If he was entitled to blame anyone for the accident which had consumed so much of his life, then he should also be blaming himself. Blaming himself just as much as those others that he had always held responsible. Rebecca had not been the only one to cause that final delay during the journey home. If it was not for his imminent birthday and his boyhood love of space-oriented toys, their father would not have stopped for those crucial minutes shortly before those traffic lights. If only it had not been so close to his birthday. If only space-oriented science-fiction had not been so interesting for him. If only.

He had always been completely oblivious of her true motive, but the indisputable fact remained that it was Rebecca who had asked their father to stop the car. If she hadn't, none of it would have happened. His vengeful resolve rose in him again and he put his left hand into his coat pocket. His fingers wrapped around the small toy troll that it contained. Rebecca had not invited him to remove his coat and he had not thought to do so. He was now holding the object with which he had always intended to choke her to death.

Despite the inciting feel of it, a wave of compassion and love swept over him and briefly replaced his hate again. Rebecca had a family of her own now. He appreciated that his earlier victims must also have had family or friends to grieve for them, but such secondary people had all been unknown to him and irrelevant to his primary cause. Now, having seen her son, he found that he could envisage exactly where the effects of his planned actions would be so deeply felt in the years to come. Then there was also the husband, unknown to him, that she had referred to. Liam. Could James really deprive these innocent bystanders of a wife and mother. It would make him the one despised in their eyes. This time, more than any of the others, it might be obvious that it was murder, and no accident.

There was also her unexpected involvement with their cousin, and his best friend, Tom. By his own admission, Tom had hated Bea, and that might even mean that he supported James's past actions. The same could not be said of Tom's potential reaction if he should have the slightest suspicion of James's connection to the fate that he had always intended for Rebecca.

James had known nothing of such complications to his original plans when he had arrived at her house. Despite the revelations, she had always been his last intended victim, and that thought started to prevail. He had made no plans or devoted any thoughts to his own life past this point. His mission would have been fully accomplished and any subsequent consequences for him would be immaterial. However, now, as he looked at Rebecca, he was also filled with feelings of potential loss for the first time since laying in that hospital bed, so many years before, with his head pounding and his eyes adjusting.

As he pulled the troll from his pocket, he shook his head slightly to dispel his conflicting thoughts and focus his attention. Rebecca saw the familiar shape from her childhood.

'What have you got there?' she asked, rhetorically.

'Just a little present for you,' said James.

45

As James closed the front door behind him and walked down the steps to the pavement at the front of Rebecca's house, he felt the weight of his lifelong mission lifting from his shoulders. He had been obsessed with his purpose for years, but now it was finally concluded as far as he was concerned. It was a welcome feeling. He was now facing the next chapter of his life with fresh eyes, and more than a hint of optimism.

In the short time that he had been at her house, he had reconciled everything with his sister. As he had always intended, ever since the accident, he had finally told her how he had always blamed her for her part in losing the rest of their close family. He had explained that it was the reason behind their subsequent estrangement, but the revelation of her wanting to buy him a birthday present from the toy shop had entirely changed his perspective of the tragic events of 1965. The crash had been heart-breaking, for him probably more than for anyone, but he now had to concede that it was simply a consequence of an unfortunate sequence of circumstances.

It was very late, and the road was quiet as James walked the two miles back to his own house. There was little traffic at that hour and the pavements were deserted apart from, at one point, a man on the other side, walking in the opposite direction. The man's collar was pulled up against the wind and he was wearing a hat for warmth. It made James realise that he was so deep in thought about the conversations and events of the evening, he was not even aware of the unseasonably low temperature.

Back home, he was surprised to find that he did not have one of his usual tension headaches and that he did not need to take any of his usual paracetamol. He wondered if that could be a result of his new relaxed outlook. He no longer had any of his malicious goals left to fulfil. He slept soundly, remarkably without waking at any time during the night, and did not stir until late the next morning.

After preparing and eating his lunch of sandwiches, he sat on his sofa and replayed all of the previous evening in his mind, as accurately as he could remember it. After a tense start, the ice had gradually melted between the two of them and he and Rebecca had discussed, and resolved, all their past misunderstandings. Although it had been an unexpected blow, he had also learned of the true reason behind that fateful last stop, delaying their father's car. Eventually, he had handed her the troll, that he had originally carried there as a weapon, and had simply given it to her as a peace offering. They had hugged and cried, and he had left, with a promise to return within days to properly meet her husband and become a part of her family once again.

He decided to play himself some appropriate music again and thought of the perfect track for the moment. Coincidentally, the *A Day At The Races* album had remained on his turntable since the previous morning, when he had learned, from the television, of Bea's fate. He turned it over to the second side and cued up the first track.

When *Somebody To Love* was only up to the first chorus, the phone started ringing. It was to be a call which would entirely destroy the memory he had of his reunion with Rebecca.

'Is that James?' the unfamiliar voice at the other end asked.

'Yes, speaking,' confirmed James.

'Hello James. My name is Liam. I know that you don't know me, but I've just been speaking to your cousin, Tom. He suggested that I call you too and he gave me your number.' James thought that the voice sounded strangely unsteady and emotional. He was about to acknowledge the man, saying that he had recently learned that he had a brother-in-law, but Liam continued without hearing James admit to the visit to his home. 'I'm married to your sister, Becky.'

'Yes, I…' began James, but he was interrupted.

'I know that you haven't seen each other, or even spoken, in years. I don't understand the reasons, to be honest, and neither did Becky.'

'Did?' asked James, suddenly confused at Liam's use of the past tense.

Liam continued his prepared speech without answering the question. 'Whatever it was, you're still her brother and so you're entitled to know.'

'Know what?'

'She's dead James. I'm sorry to have to tell you like this, over the phone and out of the blue, but she's dead. I found her on the lounge floor this morning, when I came home after working all night.'

James felt his blood immediately run cold and sank onto the sofa that he had been standing next to since answering the phone. Having just reconnected with his sister, after so many wasted years, she was now suddenly gone. He could not believe it. 'How?' he asked, dryly.

'She choked on a child's toy.'

The words resonated around James's head, stunning him into silence for a few seconds. It was exactly the end that he had originally planned for her. However, according to his memory, he had aborted all such thoughts during the course of the evening.

'A child's toy?' James asked, slowly.

'Yes, we've got a baby so we have loads of toys lying around the house. I really don't know how she could have choked like that though. I suppose she could have been messing around with it in her mouth, maybe entertaining our son, and it somehow got stuck in her throat.'

'A child's toy,' James repeated, although at a much lower volume and speaking more to himself than to Liam. How could he have executed his plan after everything that was said, and after the way he had been feeling, and not even remember any of it?

'Yes, one that I didn't even know that we had. There's so many that I can hardly keep track of them.'

'I don't know what to say, Liam,' said James, truthfully. He immediately realised that it would be extremely unwise for him to mention anything of his visit to their home the previous evening. It would cast a long shadow of suspicion if he did. It sounded as though Liam was blissfully unaware of him ever calling round and seemed to be under the impression that Rebecca's death was purely accidental. Thankfully, the only witness to him being there was a child who was too young to speak or understand.

'Even though you two hadn't seen eye to eye for years,' Tom thought, and so did I, that you were entitled to know. It's up to you if you want to know about the arrangements and everything,' Liam said, effectively concluding the conversation.

'Yes. Yes, of course,' said James. 'Please let me know.'

After he replaced the handset on the cradle, James sat back, stunned and with his head in his hands. The Queen album was still playing, although at a much lower volume than before as he had turned it down to answer the phone. Hearing the track, still playing, now brought a flood of tears to his eyes. Over the course of a few hours, James's emotions had moved from hating Rebecca, to loving her, to mourning her.

He reasoned that, even though he had no memory of it, it must have been him that had killed her. Even though he had found out the truth about the sudden stop during the drive home in 1965. Even though she was now exonerated from the blame that he had always allotted to her. Even though his memory told him that everything had been different, he must have still raised his hand to her and choked her on one of her favourite childhood toys, just as he had originally intended to do. Not only was his memory now blocking out all of the details of a gruesome murder, it was also replacing them with a fictional account.

46

James watched the approaching hearse carrying Rebecca's coffin from the other side of the road to the small chapel before joining the throng of waiting mourners outside. He had not wanted to spend any more time than necessary needlessly interacting with any of the faceless crowd of strangers. He had seen the identical women, wearing a predominance of black, and the indistinguishable suited men with their white shirts and black ties, gathering for the past fifteen minutes.

The cortege pulled up beside the cones that had been placed to keep that portion of the road clear. From the escorting funeral car, which had parked behind the hearse, James saw a man get out carrying a small child. Realising that this would undoubtedly be Liam, with his young nephew, James nodded soberly to the brother-in-law who he had, so far, only spoken to over the phone. He received a cursory nod in return although it was unclear whether or not Liam had realised who he was. Tom, with his distinctive fair hair, got out behind him and, noticing James, whispered something to Liam. Liam turned in James's direction again and, apparently now having been advised of James's identity, nodded again and smiled. Liam took one step towards James but a man from the waiting group suddenly approached him and commandeered his attention.

Although James had been invited, by Liam, to travel in the accompanying car as part of the family group, he had immediately declined the offer. The plausible excuses that he gave included references to the many years of estrangement, successfully screening the guilt and responsibility that he really felt. He had also wanted to avoid speaking to Tom as much as possible, fearing that his cousin may suspect what could have really happened. The pair of them had not spoken since the phone call soon after the news announcements about Bea. James had been fearful of giving away any indication that he had seen Rebecca so soon afterwards, perhaps by unintentionally mentioning that he now knew about Tom being a godfather to young Adam. Strangely, Tom had chosen to not call him either, about any of what had recently happened.

Although James had never known anything of their bond until very shortly before Rebecca's untimely death, Tom and her had apparently been close. James was also painfully aware that Tom had known that Rebecca had always been on his list of people to approach and punish in some way. Tom had even been the one to imply that James should finally confront her as well, during that call after Bea's body had been discovered.

Even though he had never revealed to Tom just how deadly serious his list had always been to him, James expected Tom to soon become more suspicious about the coincidental timings. James may not remember anything about either of the recent murders, but he was aware that the evidence was surely clear for Tom, more than anyone else, to see. It may take until the emotional grief had subsided for Tom's logical mind to realise, but James was certain that he eventually would.

From the seat he chose near the back of the chapel, James could see the back of Liam's head and, next to him, that of Tom. The two men took turns holding the child who could not understand what was going on around him in honour of his mother. Each of them delivered a heartfelt eulogy speech as part of the sombre service. From his front seat, Tom occasionally turned round to look at James, and James wondered about the nature of his cousin's thoughts each time.

As the curtains closed around the coffin at the conclusion, everyone stood up to silently leave. James had already decided that he would not be attending the planned wake afterwards at Rebecca and Liam's house. He had only ever felt compelled to be at the funeral service itself and did not want to have to endure explanations of who he was, and why he hadn't been a fuller part of Becky's life, to a room full of unfamiliar people whilst eating sandwiches. Tom would be the only one there who he would know, and James was becoming obsessed about him and what he may be silently thinking or realising.

Before he could quickly slip away, Liam managed to catch up with him at the chapel entrance.

'Hello James,' said Liam softly, holding out his spare hand for James to shake.

'Hello Liam,' replied James, grasping Liam's extended hand. 'A sad day for us to finally meet.'

'About as sad as it gets,' said Liam. 'Thank you for coming today. I know there seemed to be some issues between you and Becky but I'm sure she would have been pleased you were here. This is our son Adam, by the way. Your nephew.' Liam turned his son, being carried in his left arm, to face James.

James smiled and delivered a believable performance of seeing his nephew for the first time, gently shaking his small hand and stroking his face whilst talking to him as if his words were understood. Adam was far too young to remember James and be able to talk about it to anyone, he thought, thankfully.

'You coming back to the house?' asked Liam.

'I'm afraid I can't. I would have loved to, but there's something that I just can't avoid doing this afternoon,' lied James, provoking a disappointed look from Liam.

Liam was about to say something more when he was usurped by an insistent, but sympathetic, well-wisher and his family. The stranger essentially ignored James's presence and trampled on their conversation, although much to James's relief. Liam was diverted away, only just managing to call back over his shoulder 'I'll be in touch James.'

Tom, who had been stood behind Liam throughout their brief exchange, spoke quietly to James, with a serious tone. 'You and me need to have a little talk bruv, don't you think?'

'What about?'

'I think you know full well. My place. Tomorrow night,' he said, revealing nothing of what was truly on his mind. After James nodded his agreement, Tom turned and followed Liam into the nearby group of mourners.

James left the gathering, largely unnoticed by all except Liam and Tom, and hurried down the road to where he had parked his Allegro. Once back home, he quickly changed out of his suit and tie, and rushed to the bathroom where he promptly vomited because of the tension he was feeling. Just how much had Tom worked out and what was he now intending to do about it?

47

James badly needed a drink. He had finished his last remaining whiskey and cans of beer the previous night, knowing that he had to endure Rebecca's funeral the following afternoon. So, even though he was in no mood for socialising, he pulled on his coat and walked down to the nearest pub instead. It was the same pub where he had taken Tom, when he was underhandedly seeking his help to trace Bea. Now, just a few weeks later, he was a totally different man, emotionally. He now had two recent family deaths weighing heavily on his conscience and a constant fear of Tom's corresponding actions.

He sat alone at a quiet table in the corner with a pint, lost in his own thoughts and indifferently looking out at the other people that were in the pub. There were many tables unoccupied and only a few other drinkers stood at the bar on this weekday evening. So, he was astonished when the blonde woman placed her drink on his table.

'Mind if I join you?' she asked, already sitting down on the seat opposite him without waiting for any answer.

'I guess not,' said James. He was not in any mood for company of any kind but unable to think of a polite way to dissuade her, especially as she was already sat down.

He tried, surprisingly successfully, to banish the dark,

troubling thoughts from his mind and brighten his mood for a while, if only for the sake of his unexpected companion.

'Bit quieter than usual in here tonight,' he said, making a show of looking around the entire room and focusing his eyes on some of the empty tables where he would have expected her to sit if she didn't have any interest in talking.

'I wouldn't know,' she said. 'I've never been in here before.'

He eyed her closely. Her long blonde hair was straight, and pulled back into a ponytail at the back of her head, showing off her pierced ears and strong jawline. She wore a blue coat, the zip fastened to the top against the outside temperature, suggesting that she had only just arrived at the pub and bought herself her first drink. James had not noticed whether she had been there when he had entered the pub himself, and so could not be sure. Maybe she was planning on not buying any more drinks for herself tonight and that was why she had struck up their sudden conversation.

'So why come in here now?' asked James, still trying to decide if he wanted to make something more of their meeting.

'I've been looking around for someone,' she said.

'Someone?' said James, intrigued.

'A man, and now I've finally found him,' she said whilst leaning across the table towards him, instantly rendering James speechless. Never before had he known a woman be quite so forward, so quickly.

She quickly drank what remained of her half-pint of lager and announced that she needed to visit the Ladies. 'You can get me another one while I'm gone if you like.'

Contrary to his original mood, James obeyed, leaving his

coat where he had placed it on the back of his chair to indicate that the table was in use. He left her to initially consult her handbag, as women often do before a trip to the toilet, while he went to the bar to buy more drinks for them both. She had vacated the table and was still not back when he returned with their new glasses, but he noticed that she had removed her own coat and put it on the back of her chair.

While he had been at the bar, ordering, the possibility of it all being a ploy had occurred to him. He now discounted the possibility. Leaving her own coat like that surely indicated that she had not rifled through his coat pockets and disappeared forever with anything that she may have found. Not that he ever left anything of value in his coat pockets, anyway.

A woman with long, flowing blonde hair in a red T-shirt and jeans walked across the floor and suddenly sat down opposite him.

'I'm sorry,' said James, 'but that seat is actually taken.'

'Yes, I know' said the woman, slowly and somewhat confused. 'By me.'

James realised the mistake that he so often made. 'I'm so sorry,' he said. 'You just look different.'

The woman, understandably unconvinced and still very confused, continued to speak slowly. 'A little bit different, I suppose. I've just taken my hair band off as there's no wind in here to blow it in my eyes, and I also took my coat off. It's still obviously me, though. You only saw me two minutes ago.' Then, somewhat sarcastically, 'you surely can't have forgotten me already.'

James shifted uncomfortably in his chair, realising that this woman was probably entitled to his explanation for his sudden, strange behaviour.

'No, it's not that I've forgotten you. Of course not. I've got acute prosopagnosia,' he declared.

'You've got a cute what?' she said, suspiciously.

He was amused at her misunderstanding of what he had said. It had happened before, when he had needed to explain his condition to people. 'Prosopagnosia,' he repeated, much more slowly this time and emphasising each syllable. 'It's a medical condition.'

'A medical condition? What kind of medical condition?'

James had anticipated her reaction, having received similar responses from every one of the few people that he had confided in about his ailment over the years. He also had a well-rehearsed explanation. 'It's generally known as face blindness. It means that I simply can't recognise any faces, even really familiar ones. Sometimes I don't even recognise myself in a mirror.'

'You're winding me up. That can't really be a thing.'

'It's very rare, but it's very real. Very real to me, anyway. It's a condition that I've had ever since I was twelve, when I suffered a very bad head injury. Some people are born with it, or develop it in childhood, and that's known as developmental prosopagnosia. Mine is acquired prosopagnosia, caused by the injury. There's no known cure. I'm just stuck with it.'

'So how do you see people, like everyone who's in here now?'

'I suppose the simplest way that I can explain it is that it's like everyone's face is exactly the same. Just try to imagine living in a world like that. That's what it's like for me, all the time. I just can't register the differences. It's as if everyone is wearing an identical face-mask. The only way I can distinguish between people is to concentrate on things like their hair, maybe its colour or style. Then there's their height, body shape, their clothes, even the way they walk. If I'm talking to someone, there's always their voice that can help, especially with any accent that they may have.'

'Incredible,' she interjected.

'Even then, I sometimes don't recognise people that I know really well if it's out of context. Like seeing them some place where I don't expect them to be and not in their usual surroundings. If I see someone on the street when I'm only used to seeing them in a pub, I probably wouldn't recognise them. My best mate could walk in here right now and, because I'm not expecting him to be here, it's unlikely that I would give him a second look.' James's thoughts briefly turned to his cousin, and best friend, Tom.

'Do all your friends know?'

'Most of them, yes, and I suppose they understand and make allowances for it. They'll always make it obvious who they are when we meet up, anyway. They may just start speaking about something that makes me realise, or at least lets me recognise their voice. It certainly helps if they dress in clothes that I've seen them in before and when they don't change their hairstyle.' He casually indicated her hair, now resting on her shoulders. 'I purposely try not to tell most people about it, though. I just hide it if I think I can successfully bluff my way through. Unfortunately, you totally caught me off-guard by letting your hair down. I didn't have much choice but to tell you about it without looking even more silly.'

'It's not silly, I'm glad you did. It helps me understand so much about you.'

'At least I can see facial expressions. Like I can see that you're still looking pretty confused about it all and, before that, you were nervously smiling about it. Apparently, some sufferers can't even distinguish things like that.'

'Not as bad as it could be, then.'

'No, I guess not,' he said. 'I get frequent headaches too and, very occasionally, I find that I can't remember a thing about some....' he paused, trying to think of a suitable expression to describe it. '....some very intense moments' he eventually said, choosing one.

'That sounds....', it was her turn to pause, '....interesting', she said with a wicked smile.

'Nothing like that,' said James, keen to avoid her misunderstanding his latest admission. 'Just very intense stuff that no-one would want to remember.'

She was now confused but accepted his cryptic explanation without further question of it. 'All this is because you once banged your head?'

'It was a bit more than that but, yes, one simple head injury messed up that bit of my brain for ever.'

'What's it called again?'

'Prosopagnosia,' he reminded her, speaking its name slowly and clearly again.

'Prosopagnosia,' she echoed quietly, trying to commit the unfamiliar term to memory. 'All sounds like a very difficult thing to live with,' she finally offered, feebly, after a pause.

'It can be,' said James with a nonchalant shrug of his

shoulders. He hoped that would effectively conclude the subject so that he could move the talk towards lighter things.

Fortunately, she had nothing more to ask on the painful, awkward subject and so James started to relax and enjoy the rest of their conversation over the drinks that he had just brought them. After three more drinks, all bought by James, and constant talking, she suddenly rose from her chair and pulled on her coat.

'Well, I must be going. I'm so pleased that we met in here tonight James, and it was good to speak to you. Maybe I'll see you in here again and, if I do, I'll try to make sure that I look the same. Either that or I'll just come over and remind you of who I am.'

'I'm in here quite a bit. Probably too much. Come on over to my table any time that you're in here too. It would be lovely to see you again.'

With that, she left, and James let her go without attempting to persuade her back to his home. He was slightly confused at the way the night had abruptly ended, though, especially after some of her initial comments about needing to find a man. The overriding worries about Tom and what the following night might hold had started to return to his thoughts anyway. He acknowledged to himself that it was probably better, for them both, if he was alone for the rest of the night.

48

James did not sleep well. There was something intangible about his evening in the pub that had not felt quite right. He also now regretted revealing so much of himself, and his vulnerability, to a virtual stranger. He wished that he had tried harder to bluff his way out of the initial awkward situation, as he usually did. As unlikely as he was to ever see her again, especially with what he now planned to do, it did not sit comfortably with him that he had said so much to her. The insomnia of the night was mainly caused by more pressing things for him to worry about, however.

For many hours, thoughts of the upcoming evening, with its arranged meeting with Tom, constantly flowed through his mind. Not only was he his cousin, Tom had been his best friend for years. All of that now looked to be irreversibly in the past. After the events of recent weeks, James was now painfully aware of the wedge of suspicion and distrust that had been firmly forced between them. In his mind, James replayed every pertinent conversation and admission he had ever made to Tom. He was unsuccessfully trying to assess just how much, or how little, Tom may have already surmised from all the evidence available to him.

Regardless of the extent of Tom's deductions, James was sure that he could no longer continue to carry the heavy mental burden of the full death toll alone. A toll that had rapidly increased over just the past two weeks and was already unbearably weighing him down. His lifelong mission was completed but he now had the aftermath of it all on his conscience. He was especially saddened about losing Rebecca. Even his unexpected change of heart, that he remembered feeling beforehand, had not, in the end, stopped him from inflicting the vicious revenge that he had intended for too long. What kind of a violent, schizophrenic monster had he become? How could he expect to live a normal life after fulfilling what he had obsessively dedicated the past twenty years to achieving? It was finally time to confess it all, and Tom was the obvious choice. He had decided that he would tell his cousin everything and accept the full, and dire, inevitable consequences of his actions.

At about 4am, in an attempt to feel some justification for himself, James turned on his bedside light and read, once again, the entire inquest report. Frank Bird, in his lorry, should have undoubtedly been driving with a great deal more care, properly obeying the traffic lights. Richard Jennings, although unnamed in the report, should never have attempted to rewire those same traffic lights when he was not competent to do so. Auntie Bea should not have given alcoholic drinks to his father, as detected during the post-mortem, knowing full well that he would soon be driving home. Was any of that really a valid reason to have pursued, and killed, them all?

Something that was never part of the report was that his sister, Rebecca, had asked their father to stop for those few fateful minutes beforehand. He had wrongly believed, for so long, that it had been all about her and her toys. He thought again of her real reasons, that he had only recently learned, and a tear formed in his eye. He now felt that, if anyone, it was him who should have paid the ultimate price for that slight delay, not her.

There was still the unexplained paragraph on the third page which, he decided, would likely confuse him until his last breath.

By the time sleep eventually came to him, just before the rising of the sun, James thought that he had mentally prepared himself for whatever Tom might say and do in response to his revelations. He was confident that he had considered every possible permutation and had prepared for it.

He was wrong.

49

James arrived at Tom's door, just as he had been commanded. He was now fully prepared to deliver his comprehensive confession. Throughout the afternoon, he had rehearsed all that he intended to say, to the silent approval of his rubber duck. Ignoring the door knocker, he rapped on the wooden door with the knuckles of his right hand while his left adjusted the weight of the backpack he carried. An expectant Tom opened the door to him within seconds.

'Hello bruv,' said Tom, although not with the usual open, and friendly, inflexion. 'Come on in.'

As James stepped inside, Tom offered to take his coat. James removed his backpack before handing the coat to Tom who hung it on one of the hooks that was on the inside of his front door. Carrying his backpack in his hand, and without waiting to be invited, James walked into Tom's front room and sat down on his usual visitor's armchair next to the yucca plant that stood in the corner. He placed the bag on the floor beside his feet before briefly adjusting its zip.

Tom had followed him into the room. 'Drink?'

'Thanks, but just a cup of tea, please,' said James. 'I've come in the car and you know how I feel about drinking and driving.'

'Fair enough,' Tom said. 'Did you get parked up all right

in this busy road?'

'There was a space just across the street, so I had no problem at all.'

'Excellent. Tea coming right up,' said Tom as he headed towards his kitchen, past his bright red Gibson ES-335 semi-acoustic guitar. It was stood proudly on its stand in the corner of the lounge.

As James waited, he tried to evaluate the subtle differences that he was sensing in Tom's behaviour and mannerisms. They could be explained by him being slightly embarrassed about keeping secret his involvement with Rebecca and her family, including being godfather to James's nephew. They could equally be the result of Tom's latent, and developing, suspicions. If that were the case, then the nature of James's upcoming revelations would not be particularly surprising to Tom. However, their full extent might shock Tom much further than he could ever have predicted.

Tom brought two cups of steaming tea into the lounge, one in each hand, and placed them down on the low glass table that was between the armchairs. Before he sat down opposite James, he picked up his guitar so that he could lay the body of it across his waist. James knew, from previous visits, that Tom always felt the most comfortable with his precious guitar close.

'I wrote a new song the other day,' Tom said, starting to strum a few basic chords. 'Wanna hear it?'

'What's it about?' asked James, consciously deflecting the conversation while he mentally prepared himself for his planned upcoming speech.

'Oh, nothing much. Just a little ditty about a couple of

guys. They're best buddies at first and then some things suddenly happen which means that they no longer see eye to eye. One realises that he doesn't know the other quite as well as he thought he did.' Tom was staring directly at James as he spoke, still lightly, randomly, strumming chords on the guitar, and trying to gauge James's reaction.

James tried to act normally. He picked up, and just about tasted, his tea, instantly recalling that Tom's tea had always tasted foul to him. He had automatically asked for it, without thinking, before remembering his perpetual dislike of it. He did not know whether it was the brand of tea that Tom used, the hardness of the water in the area or the fact that Tom rarely descaled his kettle. Whatever it was, James found this latest cup tasted even worse than usual. It was only just possible to prevent himself from outwardly showing his revulsion of the drink that he had just been presented with.

'Whose perspective is this new song from?' James managed to ask, putting the cup back down. 'The one who, say, realises that the other had been withholding secrets from him. Things like still being friendly with his sister and her family, maybe? All behind his back?'

'Perhaps,' said Tom, calmly refusing to be drawn into that discussion. 'Or maybe one isn't saying absolutely everything about an old plan that the other thought that the two of them had shared for years.'

So that was it, thought James. Tom must have eventually realised the full gravity and seriousness of his lifelong quest. A quest that had left four people dead in its wake.

'All right, Tom,' said James, decisively. 'I came here tonight to tell you all about it. Everything. What you then do with the information is up to you, but I need to tell you.'

'I'm listening,' said Tom, sitting up and no longer idly tickling the guitar.

James took a deep breath before launching into his rehearsed admissions. 'First, you need to understand that I cannot remember a single thing about any of what I'm going to admit to.'

'You what?' said Tom, in disbelief. 'If you can't remember it, how can you admit to anything.'

'Just listen, please,' said James, trying to reclaim his thread after the unwanted interruption. 'Years ago, you know that I made a small list of people that I blamed for the crash that killed Mum, Dad and Brenda. I told you then that I wanted to find out exactly who they were, and where they are now. Once I had that, I would make sure that I ruined all their lives, just as they had ruined mine.'

'Yeah, I know. I even helped you to trace Bea, didn't I.'

'You did, yes. What I never said, though, was that I actually intended to end their lives, not to simply ruin them to the extent that they would forever regret their involvement.' James paused to let his words register with Tom. 'End their lives, and always in a manner appropriate to their part in it'.

'Like Bea dying from alcohol poisoning?' asked Tom, slowly.

'Exactly,' said James. 'I once told you that I had managed to trace the lorry driver, a Frank Bird in Clayborough. Another time, I also told you I'd traced the electrician, Richard Jennings, who lived in Hartview, where the crash was.'

'You did,' confirmed Tom.

'Well, I didn't just leave it at that, like I said I was going to. I went to both places and I found both of them. I found them both and…' James paused briefly, '….and then I killed them.'

'You killed them?'

'Yes, both of them. As soon as I knew for sure that I'd found the right man in each case. The lorry driver ended up mangled in his own lorry and the electrician paid for his rewiring mistake by having 240 volts sent through him.' Tom was listening intently, in silence. 'You once told me yourself that you couldn't just cut lorry airbrake lines to stop a lorry's brakes from working. It simply wouldn't have that effect. It was while you were teaching me how to bleed the brakes on my old Capri. So, I simply jammed a drinks can under Bird's brake pedal, and he ended up driving straight into a wall. As for the electrician, I rewired the fuse box of a house that he was working in so that he electrocuted himself. It was actually you who originally gave me both those ideas as possible ways of getting back at them. I know the way you meant it was to just give them nasty shocks that they would never forget. I merely took it all a stage further and made sure it was lethal both times.'

Tom was silently looking back at him with a stunned look, knowing that the methods had indeed originally been his suggestions, subliminally planted in James's subconscious.

'Bea gave my Dad alcohol that night,' James continued without allowing Tom any opportunity to interrupt, 'so that's how she had to go. Barbara Lester of Penrow.' James needed his words to be unambiguously precise. Tom was surprised to hear him stressing her identity as well as that of the others. 'I got my chance with her much quicker than I had ever expected, though. It was that first night that I found her, after you suggested where to look. The Railway pub. I got myself into her flat and I must have forced all of her gin into her.'

'You'd always said that you'd get your revenge by just scaring them all,' said Tom in the slight pause that James took to draw breath.

'I know I did. I lied. Sorry,' said James, apologetically. 'Then there's Becky. My own sister, Rebecca. My Dad stopped the car just before the traffic lights that night, and it was because of her wanting to check out a toy shop. If he hadn't, Bird would never have driven into the side of us. I went to see her the same night that Bea was found by the police, for the first time in years. I choked her with one of the toys that I had always thought she was looking at that night. I killed them all, Tom. Bird, Jennings, Bea and Becky. All of them.'

'Quite a tale, bruv,' said Tom, unpredictably calm. 'You did all that? What was all that about not remembering it, though?'

'I can't actually remember anything of killing either Bea or Becky, or even setting the traps for Bird and Jennings. My memory for all those times are total blanks. For each one, I know I planned it thoroughly, and in almost the same way as I told you I would when I was a kid. But, for every one of them, I originally thought that I'd panicked, decided not to go through with it, and walked away when it came to the crunch. But then, afterwards, I learned that they had died and so I worked out that I must be suffering from some kind of selective amnesia. My mind had somehow completely blocked out all memory of what I'd done to them. I swear that I remember nothing of killing any of them, to this day.'

'That all sounds very weird,' said Tom, starting to gently draw his fingers over his guitar strings again. 'Maybe you should ask a doctor about it.'

'Oh yeah, sure. Excuse me doc but I have a bit of a problem. I have a really good memory usually, apart from when I kill people that is,' said James with more than a hint of irony. 'I can remember planning a murder, but never the execution of it.'

James was astounded that Tom had remained completely relaxed throughout it all. He seemed to be deep in thought rather than reacting hysterically, as James had expected. James started to reach for his open backpack on the floor beside him when Tom finally responded, causing him to leave it alone and sit back into the chair instead.

50

'You're quite a character these days aren't you?' said Tom, still maintaining his calm attitude. 'You can kill all these people and yet not remember a single thing about it?'

'I can't explain it, I just know that I have no memory of what I've done.'

Tom smiled at James, although the underlying emotion was cold. 'I must admit that I have been trying to work out what has been going through your head about it all. What conclusions you have been coming to.'

James was confused at Tom's words. 'You've been wondering?'

'Oh yes. I've been wondering a lot about your thoughts. You, the cold-hearted assassin? The 007 of Birchstead? Bullshit.'

As James was about to repeat his insistence of guilt, Tom started playing the melody of a tune on the guitar that he still held in his lap. It was the James Bond theme tune. James initially thought it had been randomly inspired by his cousin's sarcastic reference to the fictional secret agent. At regular intervals, Tom purposely hit a note slightly off-key, perhaps by only a semitone. Each time he did so, he still gave the outward appearance of believing he was playing it perfectly. Furthermore, each time he did, James more clearly recalled the previous time that he had heard exactly the same musical mistakes, played on precisely the same notes.

'The 007 of Birchstead,' Tom repeated after a while. 'I don't think so.'

It was not what Tom said that fired the final recognition in James's memory, it was the way that he said it. With an emphasised Devonshire accent. That, coupled with the tune played in the comedic style of Les Dawson, had gradually reminded James of an afternoon, years before, in a house belonging to his girlfriend at the time, Sue. He looked across at Tom, seeing that he was now grinning broadly. Tom was grinning, but his mouth was within a face that appeared to James to be identical to every other person's face that he saw. One that he could not distinguish from any other because of his condition.

'Ian,' said James eventually, sitting back in the chair as if all strength had suddenly abandoned his lower back.

'Bullseye,' said Tom. 'Well done bruv. I knew that you'd suss it in the end, even if you needed a little prompt.'

'You were Ian,' repeated James, incredulously, and quieter than before. A multitude of thoughts whirred around his head, trying to make sense of what he had just discovered.

'Still am,' said Tom, maintaining the West Country accent. 'Just with a slightly different hairstyle. You're not the only one with a middle name that you can use when you feel like it, Paul.'

It was the second time in as many weeks that James had been referred to by his real first name and it still sounded alien to him.

Thomas Ian Lester sat back in his chair, watching James's

expression changing as he made an incorrect assumption.

'You were there? All the time? You watched me kill Richard Jennings?' said James.

'You still don't get it do you?' replied Tom. 'I could never trust you to keep your nerve and finish him off. I knew that you'd bottle it, despite all your careful planning. You've never kept your nerve over anything, even when you were a kid. My Mum used to tell me about you chickening out all the time, and I saw it myself, many times, as you grew up. The way you had to be carried down from the top diving board after being so bold walking up there. The way you screamed and couldn't go through with it after you looked over the edge of a cliff, having been safely roped up for abseiling. The parachute jump when you got all the way up in the air before refusing it. You had to come back down and land with the plane and give everyone their sponsorship money back. Even when I drove us to the seaside in my Dad's knackered old Viva. You didn't stop talking about going on to the big dipper, all the way there, only to get scared shitless at the last moment. You needed to be helped off by the attendant. Everything that was ever at all scary, dangerous or risky, you couldn't ever go through with. Always been the same. Always getting cold feet in the end. Full of bravado until it came to seeing it through. So, I still had to rig the fuse box for you, even after putting the germ of the idea into your head, years before.'

'You left me to trace him, followed me to him after I told you that I had, and then you rigged the electrics?'

'I think the penny is finally starting to drop.'

'No wonder I couldn't remember a thing about it,' said James, mostly to himself. 'It was you that set the trap. It wasn't me.'

'It was that first night that I stayed over with you at Sue and Julie's. I got up early, before any of you, to get at the fuse box. I had my wire-cutters with me because Julie had asked me to re-string her guitar for her, remember? So, getting the seal off the cut-out was simple. I simply re-wired the fuse box switch so that it wouldn't actually cut the power. Then I added a section of guitar string across the terminals of the fuse to make sure.' Tom paused and plucked the top 'E' string of his guitar. 'I'd only just finished when you came down for breakfast and started looking over it yourself. I wasn't bothered about that as I always knew you would never look too closely and actually go through with it.'

'I very nearly did,' said James, as if trying to excuse himself for not completing the task.

'Every day afterwards, I made sure that I kept running into Julie on her bus home from work. On the day that she finally mentioned they were having an electrical job done, I went the rest of the way to her house with her, saying there was stuff of mine that I needed to collect. So, after Richard fried himself, I was coincidentally there at just the right time to console the girls. As soon as I got the chance, I removed the guitar string and rewired the fuse box properly again. I left the switch turned on so that it looked to everyone there, mainly the police, as if Richard had simply forgotten to turn it off. It just went down in the police files as an accident. Didn't you even think it the slightest bit strange that no-one had discovered the bad wiring and sent the police after you, especially when it was necessary to put that plug socket back? Did you honestly think that you had covered your tracks enough to keep the forces of law and order away?'

'I just thought that I hadn't left a trail back to me.'

'Well, I concede that you had certainly achieved that. Never being seen with your car and using a false name, Mr. Harper. Very clever.'

James winced at the mention of the surname that he had used to mislead Sue, and all the others.

'I have to admit that having a nymphomaniac like Julie as a girlfriend for a while was a very nice bonus for me. I even took her away for the weekend to give you the freedom of the place. It meant that if I hadn't been able to get back in to reverse the changes in the fuse box before someone else checked it over, all suspicion would probably fall on you for tampering with it over that weekend.'

James finally started to understand why he had been a part of Tom's version of the plan to kill Richard. 'Suspicion would fall on me?'

'That's why I always needed you around. If the police ever did get suspicious, they just might have uncovered the ancient connection to you and realised the only possible reason why you might be on the scene so many years afterwards. They would certainly have thought about it being you, long before thinking about me. It means motive and opportunity and all that. You'd have no other excuse for being there. They wouldn't bother to look any further and I'd simply blend into the background, with my connection unnoticed. You might have even cracked under the pressure and confessed, even though you didn't really remember doing anything. We both know that the original intention was still there, though.'

'Always needed me around,' James echoed. 'What do you

mean by always?'

'I'll let you think about that while I get you another cup of tea,' said Tom, leaning his guitar against the outside of the chair as he rose from it. He had noticed that James's cup was empty. When he returned with another tea, James repeated his question, although he was sure that he now already knew the answer.

51

'I couldn't leave you alone to sort out any of them, could I?' said Tom, now adopting a Geordie accent and displaying further his gift for mimicry. Tom always did have a talent for accents and impressions, James reflected, accurately impersonating many famous people and politicians of the time back when they had lived together.

'Robin,' said James after a pause, fully realising at last just how much he had been duped.

'Aye. You're also not the only one who can write a false CV and references bruv,' said Tom, still keeping his voice in character as the lorry mechanic from Newcastle. 'You had traced Frank Bird for us and so I got myself up there to Clayborough, a little bit before you. I even grew a beard while waiting for you to finally show up at the garage.'

'With the same reason for me needing to be there. If the police got suspicious and came sniffing, then they would point the finger at the fraudulent apprentice who just happened to have had his parents killed by the victim,' surmised James.

'Exactly. As Ian, I had my hair cut a bit shorter and combed differently. As Robin, I had a beard. Not what you might call conventional disguises, but easily enough for you and your condition. I left Crossbow a little while after you did, but only after I was absolutely sure that they weren't suspecting anyone of foul play. If it had been looked into more deeply, which it wasn't, your sudden departure would have instantly made you the prime suspect. If they could find you, that is. Only then would they have possibly made the connection and the motive.'

'Pleased I could be of service,' said James, the satirical tone continuing.

'By the way, it took a bit more than just a strategically-placed drinks can. I think I managed to plant the seed of that idea in your mind by using that incident with the flask in the Viva years before. I'd seen the opportunity of that spot, The Cresta Run, when I'd gone to the same fencing place with him myself, a month earlier. So, a drinks can and a jamming of the handbrake lever was all it took to turn the lorry into a runaway. Then, to be sure of crushing him, I also had to remove some of the bolts from the fifth wheel. Think of any newspaper pictures that you've seen of jack-knifed lorries. The trailer is always still attached no matter what. It's normally a very solid and secure fixing. It needed just a little bit of help so that the trailer would sheer off and crush him, even at quite a slow speed. So, left to you, your plan probably wouldn't have been enough. You needed me there that time, and not only because you wimped out at placing the drinks can when you had the golden chance.'

As he spoke, Tom threw his arms wide, knocking his guitar over and onto the floor with the reverberating sound of six open strings. He carefully picked up his prized instrument and checked it for damage before returning his attention to James. When he did, he noticed that James had already finished his second cup of tea, the empty cup replaced on the glass coffee table.

'It's a bit of a shame about Felix, though,' said Tom, using his natural voice now.

'Felix?' queried James.

'Felix Bird. The first lorry driver that you thought had been involved. You originally told me that it had been him that was the driver we were after. It was only after I got rid of him that you realised you'd got the wrong man and found Frank instead. I felt a bit bad about that.'

'You killed him too?'

'We killed him too,' answered Tom, emphasising the first word.

'You can hardly claim this is a joint venture. I knew nothing of you being there for any of them, and it was actually you that killed them, not me' said James. Then he had another thought. 'Bea as well. It was you who killed Bea.'

'Of course. I was sat in The Railway that night, near the door. As the pair of you left, I thought that she may have recognised me, and I'll never be sure if she did at that time or not. I made damn sure she knew who I was later on, though. I followed you into that bleak vestibule of her small block of flats. It was really easy as the door sprung back so slowly. I hid in the space under the stairs, squashed up next to someone's pram. I heard your conversation above me, giving away how she kept her door key hanging on a string on the other side of the letterbox. After that, I just had to wait for you to lose your nerve, yet again, and leave.'

'And I was the one who had been seen with her in the pub earlier in the evening.'

'Precisely. Perfect for me, wasn't it?' Tom grinned again at the thought of his superior planning. 'It wasn't just the drink that she gave your Dad either. She also caused a delay to you all leaving that night by giving you and Becky some extra pocket money. Remember?'

At the mention of his sister's name, James's heart suddenly started pounding so hard that the blood rang in his ears and he finally realised the complete picture. Although he now knew that he had not killed any of them, he wasn't overly sad that the first three of his intended victims had met such untimely ends. However, there was one that he had definitely changed his mind about, rather than simply losing his nerve at the crucial moment.

'Becky,' he said, sadly. Then, accusingly, 'you killed Becky too. Choking her on a toy troll like the one I always thought she'd made Dad stop the car for.'

'After Bea, I thought we should speed up the plan, so I basically said so to you. After dark, out you came, right on cue, and I followed you most of the way to her house. I waited a while until you left and headed home and then I even walked past you on my own way there, on the other side of the road. It wasn't a troll, James. It was a model of a rocket ship, just like the one she had been hoping to buy you for your birthday.'

James realised for the first time that Rebecca's husband, Liam, had not been specific about the toy that she had choked on. James had simply presumed that it had been the troll he had taken to the house that night, and that he had been the one to force it into her throat. James lowered his head so that his chin nearly touched his chest, trying to mentally deal with the torrent of new information. It was completely altering his memories of his life and his perception of himself. He felt a wave of absolution start to wash over him.

'So, all I'm actually guilty of is some evil thoughts,' he said at last. 'Wishing that some people were dead and working out, theoretically, how I might kill them. I meticulously planned murders that I did not actually end up committing.'

'That about sums it up,' said Tom, laughing loudly, 'but, like I said, I needed you there just in case I slipped up. If the police got suspicious and started looking for a murderer, rather than blindly accepting that they were just accidents, I needed them to think it was you.'

'Then why not just encourage me to be stronger while I was growing up? Boost my confidence so that I didn't keep losing my nerve all the time, as you put it. That way, you could have just left me to it.'

'I admit that it would have been far simpler, and safer, for me that way but, for my own sworn revenge, I needed to be the one to pull the trigger each time.'

'Your revenge?' asked James, emphasising the first word. 'Why would you want to kill any of them? It was my parents and my sister that had died, after all. My close family.'

'Yes it was, and I had to listen to you, night after night, talking about what you were compelled to do about it. Hearing about the methods that you would use to ruin the lives of each of those responsible. Always something appropriate to their individual roles in destroying your life. I was constantly supporting you, always coming up with the inventive, appropriate ideas rather than suggesting a simple beating down a dark alley somewhere. All the time holding in my own tears.'

'Your tears?' said James, still not understanding the strength of Tom's emotion reflecting in the rising tone of his voice. 'It was my Dad. My Mum. My sister.'

'Yes, and my unborn child!' Tom snapped back at him, stunning him into silence.

Neither of them said anything for a few moments. Eventually, it was Tom who spoke next, in a much quieter, and calmer, tone than before. 'They took the love of my life from me. The girl I was going to marry and grow old with. And they took away my unborn child.'

James immediately recalled the short section of the inquest report that had been causing him so much consternation for years. It had been amongst the results of the associated post-mortem examinations on the third page. It had simply revealed that the seventeen-year-old girl had been four months pregnant at the time of her demise.

'You? You were the father of Brenda's baby?' said James. Tom silently nodded back to him. 'Listening to records upstairs,' observed James, cynically, his voice now rising in volume as he began to understand the scenario. 'My sister? Your own cousin. She was your cousin, the same as me.'

'No James, she wasn't,' interrupted Tom. 'She was not the same as you. Me and Brenda weren't actually related by blood, were we. Think about it. She was your Dad's daughter, but not your Mum's, and it was your Mum who was my Dad's sister.'

James remained seated despite wanting to jump across the table, from the chair, and physically assault his cousin.

Instead, he tried to concentrate on Tom's counter-confession.

'Why tell me all this now? You could have left me thinking that I was going mad. You could have pretended to accept my version of it all, but now I can go to the police and tell them everything,' said James.

'You'll not be telling anyone anything James. In a few minutes, the crushed sleeping tablets will take effect and you'll pass out,' said Tom, his tone suddenly more serious.

James looked down at the empty teacup on the table in front of him and he realised what Tom must be expecting to happen to him soon.

'Once you conk out, I'll be taking you for a little drive. It'll be in your own car from across the road, using these keys.' Tom held up the car keys that he had removed from James's coat pocket as he had hung it up. 'I've decided that I'm going to leave you at that dark and dangerous level crossing just outside town, on the road to Hartview. When the next train comes around the bend, you're going to die, James. You're going to die in the twisted, tangled metal of a car, just as you should have done exactly twenty years ago.'

James knew the date. It was indeed the anniversary of the fatal crash that had cost him his family.

'Everyone must pay,' Tom continued, 'and they must pay in a manner appropriate to their involvement in the accident. Your own words, James, that you said to me through your tears so many times during those nights when we shared a bedroom. Remember? Even though you never said it, I always knew that you felt even stronger than just ruining their lives. The same as me. They had to know the pain of dying as a consequence of someone else's actions. If Bird had used his brakes properly or if Jennings had wired up the traffic lights correctly. If Bea hadn't given your Dad those spritzers or called you back to give you extra pocket money. If Becky hadn't asked your Dad to stop at the toy shop. Just one difference and then neither of our lives would have been destroyed. They were all responsible in some way, and now there's just you left. Everyone must pay, including you.'

'Me? Why me as well?' asked James, rather feebly, as if he was having difficulty talking.

'I would have thought that was obvious, James. The only reason that Becky asked your Dad to stop at the toy shop was because it was your birthday coming up. If it hadn't been your birthday soon after, then none of it would have happened and I'd now be happily married to your sister with a son, or daughter, nearly twenty years old.'

James's eyes closed and his head slumped forward. Tom got up from his chair and walked slowly around the coffee table towards him, spinning James's keys around his index finger. As he looked down at his nemesis, he wondered whether he should try to move James's Allegro closer to his door before trying to manhandle him out into the street and into the passenger seat.

Suddenly, James's eyes snapped open and he punched up at Tom's throat. The force of the blow to his adam's apple surprised and stunned Tom, leaving him coughing for breath with his eyes watering. In an instant, James had jumped up from the chair and launched himself up onto Tom's back with his arm around his throat. As James had intended, the extra weight and shift to his centre of gravity made Tom's knees buckle and he fell, face first, through the glass coffee table, shattering it into a myriad of sharp pieces.

James quickly jumped off Tom's downward-facing, prone figure, oblivious to the small cut on his elbow and expecting the fight to continue, but it was already over. Tom was out cold and did not move. Without taking his eyes off his unconscious cousin, James reached across into his unzipped backpack. He turned off his portable cassette recorder and hoped that it had clearly recorded all of their conversation.

The tape had originally been intended to serve as both James's explicit confession and his suicide note. He had planned to leave the backpack, still containing the tape, with a bewildered Tom, while he drove straight to the bridge over the river. However, the resultant, fuller recording that he had now obtained could surely be used as irrefutable proof of Tom's guilt instead. In less than half an hour, James's suicidal thoughts of earlier had been totally transformed and abandoned. He had painfully discovered the truth about Tom's parallel, vengeful quest, and the manipulation of his own life for the past two decades. He had also learned the reality of the crimes that he had always wrongly believed he had committed himself.

He rewound the tape for a few seconds before playing a section of it and was pleased to plainly hear a repeated portion of what Tom had recently said. Thankfully, he had left the microphone in a suitable position within the bag. He looked back down at Tom, still unconscious, again.

'A good thing for me that you can't make a decent cup of tea,' he said to the unhearing ears. He looked up for a moment, towards Tom's yucca plant, and wondered how, or if, it would eventually react to the sleeping tablets.

James walked across the lounge to Tom's phone and called the police.

52

James had bought the latest release by Queen when it had first appeared in the shops and he had often played it. He intimately knew all of the songs contained on *The Works*. Today, he wanted to concentrate on just one of them. He placed the CD onto the small open tray and pressed the load button on his stack system to make it retract. Before any music was even played, he was repeatedly pressing another of the buttons to skip forward to the track that he wanted to hear. He stopped when the sixth track was finally indicated on the digital display.

James sat back on his sofa as the familiar keyboard introduction was followed by Freddie Mercury's unique singing voice announcing *I Want To Break Free*, the title of the song, with its first lyric. It had seemed that, at every important moment of his life, he could always find a relevant Queen song title, and today was no exception. Tom was in prison, on remand, accused of five murders and awaiting trial while the police constructed their case. It was expected to be a lengthy process, involving the combined efforts of police forces from Clayborough, Hartview, Penrow, Birchstead and the Midlands, but it was already well under way. There had, apparently, already been good progress with it during the month since his arrest. The recording had been made without

Tom's knowledge or consent and so was probably not admissible as compelling evidence in a court of law. Regardless, it had provided the police with many further avenues for their investigations.

Understandably, James had been forced to provide the police with extensive background details, and answer many awkward questions, when he had first contacted them. He and Tom had then been held in custody while they were both interrogated, separately. James's account and the taped conversation had satisfied them that James was essentially innocent, at least from a legal perspective. They had eventually released him, without charge, after many hours. Following treatment for a few superficial facial cuts, Tom had been formally arrested, pending their further enquiries, and had later been charged with all of the murders.

So, here was another perfect song title. One for Tom to sing out loud from his cell. The title was doubly relevant, as James now realised. It was also time for him to break free himself, from the blinkered, and focused, life that he had led. A life that had, to date, been totally dictated by his desire for revenge. He had sworn to ensure that every one of them would die and, apart from the notable exception of Rebecca, was not at all sorry when they had. For each, he had plotted the manner of their death and with every intention of being the executioner. He had believed that his mission had eventually been completed, and that he alone had been the one to fulfil it, but then there had been nothing left except emptiness and guilt. It had all been so overwhelming that he had very nearly killed himself to end his mental agony. With Tom's confession and revelations, he had realised that he was not the schizophrenic sadist that he had presumed. Intention, on its own, is not a crime. He had simply been a very angry man, but never one who was capable of taking murderous action as a result.

He knew that he now had to finally break free from those constant, vengeful feelings that had dominated his actions for so long. Such dark thoughts had been a normal, and possibly expected, reaction to his trauma. Now he just wanted to start living properly, and fully, like everyone else seemed to do. He would force himself to remember the fatal accident that had killed most of his family as a very unfortunate event in the unchangeable past, and think of it only in those terms. Besides, there was no-one now left alive for him to hate, and blame, for it.

Liam had, understandably, been devastated to learn the truth about Tom, but it had also helped to start a new, strong friendship between him and his brother-in-law, James. James, for his part, was also starting to enjoy his new role as the attentive uncle to Adam. He was getting deeply involved with them both and was looking forward to watching his nephew grow up. James had wrongly believed, for years, that Tom was his one and only friend. Now he welcomed Liam's friendship, just when he needed it most.

As the track ended and the next one started, James finished his whiskey and decided that he wanted to go out and socialise. Today, of all days, he wanted to be with people. He did not have anyone specific to go out with, as Liam was working the late shift with Liam's mother assuming baby-sitting duties for Adam, but he did not let that dissuade him. If the initial search for Richard had taught him anything, it was that he could comfortably strike up friendly conversations with complete strangers, in the right environment. The best environment that he could think of was the pub down the road, so he ejected the CD, turned off the player and pulled on his coat.

Sat at the same table where he had met the mysterious blonde a month earlier, James sat alone with his pint and looked around at the night's customers. It was still early and so there were not yet many people drinking in the pub. Those that were had all sat at other tables, in groups already. So, James just sat quietly, feeling somewhat uncomfortable with the prospect of attempting to join in with an ongoing conversation, uninvited. He started to wonder if going out had been such a good idea after all.

As he absently watched the bubbles rising in the half-full glass on the table in front of him, he did not notice her arrive and immediately approach his table.

'Hello again,' said the blonde from the previous month. She was wearing the same coat as she had done that night, zipped up again, and her hair was similarly tied back. As before, she carried a handbag, but this one was different, and notably larger than the one that she had with her then.

'Hello,' said James, genuinely surprised to see her again, but very pleased to.

'You recognise me then?' she said, obviously referring to his revelations during that previous night. She sat down opposite him, like she had before.

'Of course I do. I've actually been hoping that I would run into you again.'

'Well, you've not been in here since I last saw you. Not any time while I've been here anyway.'

James remembered that, the night they had first met, she had initially said it was her first time in that pub. Had she been coming in regularly ever since, perhaps hoping to see him again?

'Things have been a bit hectic since that night,' explained James, with understated accuracy. 'So, I've not been in here for a few weeks. I really wanted to come out tonight, though. It's my birthday.'

'Well, happy birthday to you,' she said, sincerely.

James started thinking that his new, normal life could well start right there and then. At thirty-three he was arguably a bit long in the tooth to start his life anew. However, the prospect of now getting to know this woman, without the immense pressures that he had been feeling when they had last met, could help him break from his haunting past. She certainly seemed willing to be friendly, sitting down with him again as she had.

'Like a drink?' he asked.

'Yes please,' she said, whilst nodding and placing her handbag on the floor by her feet. 'I'll have half a lager.'

James went to the bar and ordered her beer while he looked back at her taking off her coat and letting her hair down. It was the same changes to her appearance that had caused him to become confused the last time, when he had not seen her making them. He had then felt compelled to explain his debilitating condition and had immediately regretted doing so. Tonight, he was pleased that he had. He now realised that it had probably been a mistake for him to hide it from his only girlfriend, Sue, years before. It had made so many things difficult for him then and, as time had gone on, he had felt even less able to admit to his trouble. At least it was already out in the open with this new woman and she still seemed to be interested in him, despite knowing it.

He returned to their table, with a small beer for her and another pint for himself. 'So, are you looking for a man again tonight?' he asked, placing the glasses down.

She smiled and laughed at his recollection, and misinterpretation, of what she had said on the previous occasion. 'I never stop,' she said, rendering James speechless for a moment.

James sat down opposite her again. They talked, smiled and joked, through three more drinks each. James was now thoroughly enjoying the evening of his birthday and was pleased that he had decided to go out. As the bell was rung to declare that it was time for everyone's last orders, James asked the question that he would have done at their first meeting if only his mind had not been so preoccupied and full of worries, and thoughts, regarding Tom.

'Would you like to come home with me tonight?' he asked, touching her hand and dearly hoping that it would denote that start of a new chapter for him.

'I thought you'd never ask,' she replied, quickly downing what remained of her lager and reaching behind her for her coat from the back of the chair. Once she had put down her empty glass, she bent forward to pick up her oversized, and apparently somewhat heavy, handbag.

James could only manage a few more mouthfuls of his own remaining drink and chose to leave the rest behind on the table. He did not want this firecracker cooling down while he wasted time finishing his beer.

They walked the short distance to his house, with neither of them as sure-footed as when they had arrived, individually, at the pub. They could not be classed as drunk, though, and she readily accepted his offer of a further spirit when they were inside his home. Sat together on his sofa, she sipped the warming liquid and looked invitingly into his eyes. Then she spotted the small rubber duck over his shoulder.

'What's that there for?' she asked.

'He's my little friend. I just tell him all my troubles and he helps me to resolve them.'

'Well, he may be your friend but I'm not up for a threesome. Leave him here and let's just you and me go to bed.' She put down her emptied glass on his coffee table and grasped his hand as she got up. 'You can always confess everything to him in the morning, if you want,' she said with a broad smile, waiting for him to lead her to his bedroom.

53

When he woke, James looked over at her peacefully sleeping. As his eyes traced her outline in the semi-darkness of the early morning, he thought back to how naturally, and instinctively, they had ended up in his bed. It had perfectly concluded their evening at the pub. They had gotten on very well together, as indeed they had a month before, but he had not dared to imagine that she might be so willing to return to his house after the drinks, with everything else that might also imply. That first night, although very friendly, she had seemed to purposely avoid the possibility by leaving so suddenly. Despite his earlier misgivings about going out to the pub alone, it had certainly turned out to be a very enjoyable birthday for him.

With his teasmade still out of action, there was no early bedside cup of tea to offer his guest before getting up. So, he rose from the bed, dressed, and made his way to his kitchen, with all his movements made as silently and gently as he could. He was hopeful that he would not disturb her slumber before making and presenting her with a morning-after breakfast. He squinted against the glare of the light as he turned it on and, as his eyes adjusted to the brightness, he was initially greeted with the daily sight of his saucepans and utensils. They were artfully arranged in size order, hanging from the multitude of small hooks beneath the cupboards adorning one wall. Beside the hob, it was the kettle that first demanded his attention, and it immediately gave him a dilemma. Would she prefer tea or coffee, or maybe something else? Would she want sugar in a hot drink? He realised that he did not really know much about this new woman other than that she had no fear of speaking her mind, drank lager and had a healthy sexual appetite.

He pondered the idea of attempting to form a lasting relationship with her. Perhaps his best approach would be to simply ask to see her again, soon. His overriding, sinister obsession was over and, as part of his new, optimistic outlook on life, it would be good to have someone to share at least some of it with. They had certainly enjoyed each other's company so far, both outdoors and intimately, so it could be worth a try. Right now, though, he was stood in the centre of his kitchen, wondering whether to wake her and ask if she took sugar in her hot drinks.

The quandary was short-lived because she suddenly appeared in the doorway. She was unsurprisingly dressed in the same loose T-Shirt that she had worn the previous evening. She was also carrying her handbag, her hand tightly clasped around the straps. James hoped that it did not mean that she intended to leave already.

'I tried not to wake you,' James said, truthfully. Then, trying to project a tone that suggested fond memories of the pleasure of the night before, 'good morning.'

'Can I put some music on?' she asked him, allaying James's fears of her walking away so soon.

'Sure. I've got plenty of CDs and loads of vinyl in there, or you could just put the radio on if you prefer,' said James, pointing over her shoulder towards his lounge. 'Take your pick.'

He watched her walk over to the corner of the room, where his hifi was, and put her handbag on the floor beside her. As she bent over in front of his record collection to make her choice, the T-Shirt rode up and revealed her skimpy pants underneath. James smiled at his memory of playfully removing them, using only his teeth, just a few hours before. He turned back to the kettle and the mugs that were awaiting some decisive action and he opted for coffee, without involving her in the choice.

In the lounge, she soon found what she had been looking for, and fully expecting to find, among the vinyl albums. It was no surprise to her to find that he had stored his Queen albums chronologically. The early *Sheer Heart Attack* was the third one from the end of that prominent part of the collection. She pulled the record from its sleeve and quickly placed it on James's turntable, turning the player on with her other hand.

Rather than using the small lever to gently lower the stylus, she picked up the arm between her thumb and forefinger and held it above the rotating disc at the point between the first two tracks of the first side. She carelessly dropped it into place from a height of about a centimetre. In the kitchen, James winced as he heard the sickening amplified sound of the needle bouncing into the groove. That would have undoubtedly added yet another click to be heard during every future play of whatever record she had chosen, he thought.

As *Killer Queen* started playing, he decided that, for the sake of their fledgling relationship, it would probably be for the best if he did not say anything about her clumsy, heavy-handedness just yet. He would just have to ensure that he was the one to cue up any future music.

She placed her handbag on the table as she entered the kitchen and then she walked behind him towards the far wall, just past where he stood. 'Good morning James,' she said, unexpectedly flatly, as she passed him.

Suddenly, James realised what it was that had felt so strange and had been subconsciously troubling him ever since that first night. She had also called him by his name then, as she had left the pub, and again now. He still did not know her name, though. He had simply not thought to ask, on either occasion. Furthermore, he now realised that he had never told her his. Yet she knew it. He started to turn to face her, wondering how he ought to phrase his question.

54

James's eyes met hers for an instant but then she quickly, and purposefully, reached for the largest, and heaviest, of the saucepans and removed it from its hook. He looked quizzically at her, assuming that she was now about to offer to make a warm breakfast, such as porridge or scrambled eggs, for them both. Before he could say anything, he felt the force of the unexpected blow on his left temple. To him, the metallic sound from the saucepan matched the sudden ringing inside his head and then, as he dropped, dazed, to his knees, the second blow to the back of his head made him lose consciousness for a short time.

When he opened his eyes again, with his head pounding and lopped to one side, he slowly focused on the familiar sights of his kitchen. Then he saw that his attacker was standing in front of him. He realised that he had been hoisted to a sitting position, on to one of his own kitchen chairs. As he tried to move, he found that his arms were now restrained behind him and attached to the chair. Presumably, from the feel of it, by some thick, unseen string, or perhaps a thin rope.

He could tell that he had not been unconscious for more than a few minutes. *Killer Queen* was still playing from his lounge and he heard the kettle automatically turning itself off, presumably having just finished boiling the water for the coffees that he had been preparing.

'What the fuck is going on?' James shouted in a panic. He felt as vulnerable as he had recently presumed Bea must have felt at Tom's sadistic hands.

He looked into her eyes but, unlike last night when they were so warm and full of invitation, they were now staring back at him as cold and unemotional as the ends of the twin barrels of a loaded shotgun.

'Well James, how are you feeling now?' she asked.

'What is going on?' he repeated, albeit at a quieter, calmer volume. 'How do you know my name, anyway? I don't even know yours.'

'I think you do, lover boy,' she said, cryptically. 'Look deep into my eyes and think back a few years.' She moved her face closer to his. So close that he could feel her breath on his skin. 'I thought I'd play you an appropriate Queen song. Do you like it? I remember how much you always concentrated on song titles, especially Queen's. You always had a song for every occasion, usually superficially singing just the title over and over. You always assumed so much more meaning from that one line than any of the rest of a song's lyrics and what it is really about.'

In his dulled mind he was unsuccessfully trying to make sense of what she was saying. 'You remember?' he asked. 'Where from?'

She continued, all the time speaking louder and more angrily. 'I'm your Queen today. Your *Killer Queen*. Just as I told you a month ago, I have been constantly looking around all of the pubs in this area for a man. One man in particular. You. You bastard.'

'Me? Why?'

She ignored his question and shouted back into his face. 'You were so conceited. You must have thought I was out looking for God's gift to women and thanked my lucky stars when you appeared.'

'Why me?' he asked again.

'You may have grown your hair and had it permed, but I would know you anywhere. Fortunately for me, I'm normal and don't have your little problem with recognising people.'

She leaned back away from him again and sat on the kitchen chair that she had placed opposite his. She reached into the open handbag on the table next to her from where, presumably, she had removed the bindings that were now holding James down.

'You know me? You know me from some time in the past? Where?' James was still desperate to make sense of what was happening to him.

'You really don't recognise me, do you,' she said, pulling a bottle out of her handbag and placing it on the table beside it. 'I lost my job because of you.'

'You lost your job?' echoed James, with an unbelieving pause between each word. 'Because of me?'

'A job I really loved, and then you came along and screwed it up. I was the receptionist at Princeberg Electrics until the day you came in and conned confidential information out of me. Details of past and present employees, remember? When I naively told my boss about what had happened with a so-called tax inspector, he fired me on the spot. He told me that such things simply didn't happen. He said that you must have been some kind of head-hunter trying to poach their experienced staff, and I fell for it. My own fault really. No official inspector would have had such a rust bucket as the car I saw you drive off in.'

'This is all about me getting you the sack?' James asked, amazed at the lengths that she must have gone to for such a relatively trivial thing that had been so long ago. He pulled, fruitlessly, at his restraints.

'Don't be stupid. I got another job soon enough. The same place as where my sister already worked,' she said, calmly again. She removed a tall, narrow box from the handbag and placed it next to the bottle, before opening the cardboard flaps of its top. 'Then I saw you in the Queen's Head, a few weeks later, and so I came over to chew you out about it. I really couldn't understand then why you didn't recognise me, especially after what you'd done to me. I know that I'd had my hair permed in the meantime, but I still thought you would have known who I was. I was amazed when you didn't. I now know why, of course, with your weird condition, but it certainly seemed strange at the time.'

'The Queens Head? You mean the one in Hartview?' said James, realising that was where he would have been drinking regularly, every week, four years before.

'Your eyesight may be defective, but there's nothing wrong with your memory is there?' she said, sarcastically. 'Unfortunately, I was out with my sister that night, and she really liked you, right from the start. So, I had to hold my tongue and be friendly instead. If Sue hadn't fallen for you, I would have happily told you what I thought of you right there and then.'

'Julie?' said James, finally realising who it was that he had spent the night with and who was now hovering over him, holding a teaspoon that she had just extracted from her handbag.

Although she had not intended to be in this position so soon, it had always been her ultimate goal to be alone with James, and with him defenceless. For Julie, it had not been an evening of pleasure. It had simply all been a means to an end. A way of getting herself into his home and to subsequently have enough time to clinically execute her plan.

'That's right,' she shouted back into his face. The rising volume of her voice caused him to wince as she continued. 'You've got a good memory for names too, James. Talking of names, I eventually found out that yours is Pearce, not Harper. That made you very difficult to find, but at least I knew where to start looking. Did you really think that you could completely disappear from destroying someone's life and not pay the price in the end?' She slapped him across the face, unable to control her rising anger.

James turned back to face her again, his cheek stinging from the blow. 'It wasn't me that killed Richard. It was Tom.'

'What are you talking about?' Julie asked, genuinely confused by his response.

'Tom. The man you knew as Ian. His real name was Tom. He was the one who tampered with the wiring in your house and killed Richard, not me. He's on remand for it right now. I would think that the police should be in touch with you and Sue about it very soon, if they haven't already.'

'This isn't about Richard, you idiot,' said Julie, slapping him again, even harder this time. 'I'm not concerned about him and what happened to him.' With that, she dismissed the unexpected information and regained the thoughts of her primary purpose. She plunged the teaspoon into the cardboard box and loaded it with a heap of powder. 'Sue used to lovingly cook for you, remember? Do you? You should. Well, now you can have this little meal on me.'

As James slowly turned back to her once more he managed to see, through glazed eyes, that she was now holding aloft the level teaspoon.

'Here comes the aeroplane' she announced. 'Make sure you're tightly strapped into your seat and ready for the landing.' Then, mockingly, 'Oh, I see you are already.'

As if feeding a reluctant child in a highchair, she forced the spoon into his mouth accompanied by her nasal impression of a combustion engine. Although James instinctively gagged on the foul-tasting contents, Julie persisted her attack by holding his nose with her other hand so that he had to open his mouth to breathe. When he did, she rammed the spoon even deeper.

'This is for Sue. The woman who loved you before you disappeared, leaving her heartbroken, alone and pregnant.'

The revelation stunned James to his core. 'Pregnant?'

'Yes, pregnant. You know how it works, presumably. If neither of you are careful, you end up as three.'

'I had no idea, Julie. I swear. How is she now, and how's my kid?'

Julie ignored the question and started shouting into his face again. 'You abandoned her. You vanished. Only then did she realise that she had no way of finding you. No address, no car registration number. They'd never heard of you where you'd told her that you worked. Just some grotty flat somewhere in Birchstead was all she had to go on, and I'll bet that wasn't even the truth. You were probably living right here at the time.' She was right about that, but James was not about to admit to it.

Julie lost all control and started punching him around the head, screaming incomprehensibly at him. With his hands tightly bound, James could do nothing except bow his head against the painful onslaught. Eventually she stopped the physical attack and concentrated on the words that she had intended to speak, spitting them into his face.

'You'd claimed that you didn't drive, but I'd seen your rusty Mercedes at Princebergs. So, I always knew that you weren't being totally straight with her. I tried to warn her, but she wouldn't listen. I just couldn't work out why you would be hiding who you really were. It was only afterwards that I realised it must have been because you always planned to do a runner someday, or at least be leaving yourself the option.'

'It wasn't like that Julie. I wanted to stay with her, but I just couldn't risk going back to her after what happened to Richard.'

'Why would that have anything to do with it?' shouted Julie, not understanding the relevance. 'You never called her again, and Sue was devastated and scared. You'd gone and totally left her in the lurch. She had to give up the Girl Guides, something that she had always loved, rather than face the disgrace. Those bitches in charge wouldn't condone having an unmarried, pregnant leader. Not a good example to set all those young, impressionable girls, Brown Owl said.'

In spite of everything that was happening, her reference to a bird-oriented nickname coincidentally reminded James of his own lethally motivated search, more than eight years before.

'Well, Brown Owl got what she deserved and is flying around with the angels now. I made sure of that. Now it's your turn,' Julie continued.

James was speechless and frightened by her words. Then he realised that she was scooping the spoon's refill contents directly from a red box of rat poison on the kitchen table, beside her open handbag. Finally, he fully understood the severity of what she was doing. As he opened his mouth to plead for her to stop, she pushed the second spoonful into it, causing him to gag once more.

'Rat poison? What are you trying to do to me?' he spluttered through the remaining dry powder in his mouth.

'Only a rat would treat my sister the way you did, you bastard,' she said with vicious, unhidden sarcasm. 'So, I thought you would like it for breakfast. You wouldn't have heard, or even cared, how Sue fell into depression after the abortion that she paid for herself with what little money she had. Did you even notice the newspaper article about a young woman jumping in front of an Underground Train in London?'

James went silent, while the enormity of it all sank in. Julie refilled the spoon again. Her taunts continued.

'Now here comes the choo-choo train.' This time, with an impression of a loud steam engine assaulting his ears, he was compelled to ingest the third spoonful.

'I'm so sorry Julie. Really, I am. I had no way of knowing. How could I?'

She ignored his feeble protestations. 'Why not have a drink

to wash it down?'

Julie grabbed his hair at the crown with her left hand and forced his head back, causing his mouth to open. Then she tilted the bottle of drain cleaner that she firmly held in her right. Despite all his efforts to the contrary, she managed to successfully pour most of the chemical into his mouth before calmly repacking her handbag.

'You're going to burn in hell,' she said, whilst slowly sitting back down opposite him. 'You can look forward to sharing the eternal flames with a surgeon and a train driver, very soon.'

The smile that James had recently found so alluring was now one of sadistic pleasure. His ears started ringing, his stomach started burning, and his head swirled with dizziness. James heard one final thing before slumping into unconsciousness in advance of his inevitable death.

'Everyone must pay, James,' Julie was saying as she happily watched the life fading from James's eyes. 'Everyone must pay.'

Acknowledgements

The acknowledgements section is where you realise, if you didn't before, that producing a book such as this requires some help and guidance occasionally. For example, I had vital assistance from a very small, but superb, team for copyediting and proofreading after the completion of my initial draft. Even whilst I was first writing that, many other people were often providing ideas and suggestions, as inevitably happens when your friends find out that you are writing a novel. The story itself gradually formed within my mind over the course of many years, and long before the first word was eventually typed onto my laptop, in June 2020. Inevitably, throughout those years, I also absorbed many experiences and influences that are now included, in some form or other, in what you have just read.

Just some of the major contributors are acknowledged here, and they all deserve my heartfelt thanks, regardless of whether their assistance was provided knowingly or not. I am indebted to them all and, whilst the story itself came entirely from my own imagination, it certainly contained elements influenced by them. I feel that these people are worthy of special mention, alongside those who were both inspirational and gave more tangible assistance.

Firstly, I am eternally grateful to that small review team

that I referred to, saving me from the potential embarrassment of so many silly 'typos' and, occasionally, even some dubious phraseology. The superior copyediting skills of my son, Steven Hurrell, together with his invaluable greater knowledge of some legal matters, were essential to the characters and readability of the story. Similarly, the proofreading abilities of my wife, Sandra Hurrell, possibly prevented the need for you, as the reader, to occasionally reach for a dictionary of rather pretentious terms as you read.

I would also like to express my thanks to Paul Roche for his varied inventive suggestions for killing someone off in a way appropriate to their profession. I freely admit that I did end up building on a few of his rather unique ideas.

Donald Booth was once a lorry driver whose experiences and working environment inspired a great deal of the first third of this book. When I was a student, he, and his boss, would occasionally allow me to go out on the road with him to help with loading and so I saw, first-hand, some of how that industry works. As someone who has only ever worked in offices since leaving University, I doubt that I would have gained those kinds of insights in any other way, and so he deserves a specific acknowledgement.

For a few years, when I was working in those various offices, I had the privilege of working with Roy Urquhart and every other member of the DL team (unfortunately too numerous to list here). The teamwork and camaraderie that I had the pleasure to be a part of at that time, showed me that workplace relationships can successfully expand to genuine friendships that last long after the workplace has faded in the memory. This gang was the biggest inspiration for my fictional team of drivers, together with their anonymous nicknames. While my drivers had their 'gallon at the Groom' evening, I will always have the treasured memories of Roy, the team and I, having our own 'poets' days and very many legendary, fun-filled 'gallon and a curry' nights.

My thanks to the producers, the research team and the presenters of ITV's *This Morning* for broadcasting an interview with a genuine sufferer of the little-known cognitive disorder that I included at the heart of this story. Without seeing that unfortunate woman's testimony that day, I would probably have never even heard of the condition that gave me the idea for that particular twist.

I would also like to thank Freddie Mercury, Brian May, Roger Taylor and John Deacon, the songwriters and members of Queen, for their vast catalogue of well-known songs. I used some of those titles, hopefully successfully, as an ongoing theme to illustrate a few thoughts and emotions at various stages throughout the story.

My gratitude extends to my brother, Les Hurrell, and our lifelong friends, Gary Abrams and Paul Clouting. Their tireless assistance with years of painstaking research into the etiquettes and customs of pub environments, in advance of the writing of the numerous pub scenes in the story, has always been appreciated. Latterly, though, I do need to thank these guys for their continual encouragement to finally write some of it down.

Cheers to you all.

A last note from the author

…and finally, a big thank you to you, dear reader, for choosing to purchase and read this book.

It is often said that everyone has a debut novel inside them, and this one has been mine. I sincerely hope that you enjoyed it. If so, I would greatly appreciate it if you would spare just a few minutes to post a favourable online review, on the likes of Amazon, Goodreads or perhaps your own social media pages, to encourage others who may also be considering reading it. Maybe you could even mention it in passing, by word of mouth, to friends and colleagues, in that good, old-fashioned way that we used to do in those days before the internet.

It has been an absolute pleasure to go through the entire process of producing this book, so much so that more from me are now planned for the future. The next one, a murder mystery, is already taking shape. If you would like to be notified when it is released, please connect with me, or just follow me, using Twitter or Facebook.

You can also request, via these avenues, a copy of my suggestions for questions and discussion topics for book clubs, if you run one and would like that addendum. It is not included in these pages because of the potential spoilers that it contains. I will also be offering exclusive, and free, electronic copies of some of my short stories, from time to time, should you be interested in receiving those. Whether it is to ask me for either of those, directly letting me know your opinions, advising of me of a review that you have posted, or anything else concerned with my writing, I'd love to hear from you.

Twitter: @Colin_Hurrell
Facebook: Colin Hurrell - Author